Butch Girls Can Fix Anything

Paula Offutt

Yellow Rose Books

Nederland, Texas

ISBN 978-1-932300-74-1

First Printing 2007

9 8 7 6 5 4 3 2 1

Cover design by Donna Pawlowski

Published by:

Regal Crest Enterprises, LLC
4700 Hwy 365, Ste A
PMB 210
Port Arthur, Texas 77642

Find us on the World Wide Web at
http://www.regalcrest.biz

Printed in the United States of America

Musical Lyric Permissions

Barbara Allen, folk song circa 1666.
Also referred to as *Child Ballad #84* by Francis J. Child, in his five volume work, *The English and Scottish Popular Ballads* **(1882-1898.)**
This song is considered public domain.

I'd like to acknowledge:

Susan Thrower, LCSW, for keeping me relatively sane for umpteen years now and for allowing me to use her "character.";

Robin Smith, for the initial editing, and for educating me;

Jane Vollbrecht, for the final editing, and for educating me yet more, despite my best effort;

Regal Crest Enterprises for thinking I write cool words and actually paying me money to do what I love;

And to Joella for keeping me company, and Lorna for tolerating the light on all night.

To Mom, the reason I am;
To Lorna, the reason I do.

Chapter
One

KELLY WALKER HAD spent the last six hours putting up most of the framework for shelves, and "Ode to Joy" was not a good ring tone for her cell phone — maybe "Ode to Exhaustion." She hefted the toolbox up onto the truck bed and answered the phone. "Walker."

"It's Kaye. We have a problem with one of the rental houses, and I hoped you'd have time to go over there tonight."

She knew if she sat on the tailgate, she'd not have the gumption to get back up; the last thing she wanted to do was another job. But this was Kaye, a good friend who'd helped her get her fix-it business off the ground. "Only for you, Kaye. Which one?"

"The one on Oak Street. Apparently, there's a roof leak."

"Is there damage?" Kelly lifted the tailgate and winced at the pain in her left arm, the one that had been swinging the hammer. Repeatedly. For hours. It reminded her why she had gotten out of the construction field.

"Part of the kitchen ceiling fell in. There's no telling how long it's been leaking. Do you think you can go over there tonight? Please?" Kaye pleaded.

"Yeah, I can at least clean up and put up a tarp or something. I can go back tomorrow when, and if, the rain stops. Send you the bill?" Kelly grinned to herself as she got into the truck.

"Sure, and come for dinner to get paid, though."

"Deal. I'll call you after I see what's going on."

"The tenant is a single mom with a young girl. She's new here, only been there a few months. I'll call and let her know you're coming."

"Thanks, Kaye. I'll be sure to charge you extra." Kelly was too tired to deal with someone's screaming brat.

GRACE OWENS SWIPED the sponge mop across the floor and pushed the last of the standing water into the line of towels. Lucy put another pot under a drip. "I think I got 'em all."

"Good. I am officially mopped out." Grace stretched to ease her back. *When would they invent a mop that didn't mean bending over?* Grace had worked a full shift at the plant, hunched over her table, then came home and had this mess literally land in her lap. Her lower back and the area between the shoulder blades were screaming.

"Want me to get another towel?"

"Yeah, one more. This is going to cost a fortune at the laundromat."

When Lucy returned, Grace took the towel and spread it out under two of the pans to catch the splatter. She squatted down and shuffled the pans back into place. Someone knocked at the front screen door, which caused it to bang out an echo.

"I'll get it." Grace watched as Lucy skipped from the room to the front door. "Hello."

"Hey. Is your mom at home?" The voice was low-pitched enough that Grace didn't know if it was male or female.

"Mom!" Lucy yelled as only a young girl can.

"Yes? May I help you?" Grace wiped her hands on her still-damp jeans and came from the kitchen. The woman at the door, hat pulled low to shade her face, looked tired behind the water dripping off the brim onto her boots.

"Kaye sent me here to check out the roof leak." Kelly held out her business card, so it could be read through the screen door.

"Okay, come on in." Grace unlatched the door. "It's in the kitchen." The woman took off her cap and hung it over the porch's wall sconce.

KELLY WAS RELIEVED to see the kitchen was cleaned up. Along one wall were two metal trash cans full of debris from the ceiling. They were surrounded by several black plastic trash bags. Insulation and ceiling tiles poked out of the untied tops. A sponge mop leaned against the back door, and at least a dozen towels of various sizes either lay under the pans or were rolled up to soak water from around the edges.

"Thanks for cleaning up already. That cuts my time here by two-thirds." Kelly put down the metal toolbox and took her flashlight from its loop on her belt. She grunted a few times as she peered up into the hole and realized this was not going to be an easy fix, perhaps even out of her realm of expertise. "Crap, that must be one heck of a leak up there!" *Nothing like stating the obvious.*

"That part of the ceiling had water stains, but I never noticed them actually being wet. But this afternoon, not too long after dinner, plop." The woman's hands were animated as she talked, and the movement made Kelly dizzy.

"Okay, well, I need to get up on the roof and check it out, but not this late and certainly not in the rain. But I have a temporary fix." As she passed the kid in the wide doorway, she tapped her on the head. She noticed the in-progress chess set on the side table. After a glance, she moved a rook as she went by.

Her truck had a Reading Classic work body. She knew exactly which compartments held her tarp, the cordless drill, and the box of trash bags, each in its designated place. From a five-gallon bucket in the back, she selected two scrap pieces of wood from a rip cut two-by-four and headed back to the house.

Kelly glanced at the chess set as she closed the screen door. An unknown opponent had made a move. She started past it, then took a step back, moved a pawn, and continued into the kitchen, again tapping the girl on the head.

She pulled down several more wet ceiling tiles and stuffed them into the trash bag she had brought with her. She struggled with the tarp as she tried to attach it to the trim along the top of the wall. The tenant used the mop head to push it up and away from her. Kelly used screws and washers to attach the tarp to the wall and the ceiling joists along one edge, secured the scrap two-by-four to a joist near the middle of the hole, and, by attaching the other two sides, effectively pulled it tight to form what looked like an upside-down tent on the ceiling. Kelly nudged the biggest pot on the floor over, cut an 'X' in the tarp at the two-by-four, and the water began draining into the pot.

"Cool." The young girl was grinning up at the rigged solution, obviously impressed.

"I'm glad you like it." Kelly watched it drip for a few seconds. "Do you have another trash can? Plastic would be best—less noise."

"Um, no, all mine are metal, and they're full." Grace nodded toward the line of trash bags and cans.

"No problem. Keep an eye on this for a few minutes while I go get one."

Grace blinked as she watched the confident whirlwind of a woman sprint to the truck and drive away. Kelly looked exhausted, yet she hadn't paused in her work to rest. She had whistled at one point, so faint Grace had barely heard it. Her short, dark hair had been spiked from the wet cap, but her habit of rubbing her hand over her scalp had smoothed it.

Grace reached up and pulled her ponytail tighter. Her hair was a true strawberry-blonde, which Lucy had inherited.

"Mom! The pot is full already," Lucy called out from the kitchen.

"Put another one there, then." Her daughter was intelligent, true, but she was still a nine-year-old with age-appropriate common sense. Grace straightened up the linen closet where Lucy had pulled most of its contents out to find the larger towels. The phone rang, and when she answered it, she heard her landlady's voice on the other end.

"Grace? I sent over someone to check the roof leak. Her name is Kelly Walker, and she'll be driving a big, white pickup."

"She was already here. She left to get a trash can." Grace glanced into the kitchen where Lucy stood, staring up at the tarp, entranced by the sound of the drips on the plastic.

"I'm sorry I didn't call you in time. Kelly is safe. A little odd perhaps, but safe." Kaye chuckled. "She'll get the leak fixed, don't worry about that."

"I have no worries about her skills, that's for sure. Oh, she's back already. Talk to you later, Kaye." Grace hit the off button as she opened the door. Kelly carried a big red thirty-two gallon plastic trash can. "That was fast."

"There's a hardware store just a few blocks down. Didn't you know?" Kelly looked surprised that someone wouldn't.

"No, I didn't. Should I?" Grace watched as Kelly positioned the can and picked up all the containers they had used to catch the water.

"I guess I'm biased. I know where almost every fast-food place and hardware store is near my usual work neighborhoods." She grinned and nodded toward Lucy. "Just like you would know where the nearest toy store is." Kelly used her work boot to scoot the closest towel around the edge of the can. "I'll take these towels and clean them."

"No, I'll take care of them later." Grace bent to pick them up.

"Nonsense. I'd bet you don't have a washer, and it'll cost a fortune to do at the laundromat." Kelly stood, hands on her hips, and stared down the slightly shorter woman. Grace stood up straighter and put her own hands on her own hips to match the pseudo-fierce pose.

"That's what Mom said earlier," Lucy piped up. "What's your name?"

"Kelly. Kelly Walker. What's yours?" She dropped down into a squat to look the kid in the eye.

"Lucille Rebecca Owens. But only my mom uses all three names, and only when I've done something wrong. You can call me Lucy." The young girl held out her hand, inviting it to be engulfed by the larger adult one.

"No kidding? My middle name's Rebecca. My mama would call me by all three names, too. And you may call me Kelly."

"Nope. Gotta call my elders by their proper names."

Kelly gathered the towels and laid them over the edge of the trash can. She turned toward Grace. "Do you have a name other than Mom?"

"Sometimes, I think not. I'm Grace." She put her hand out and was surprised at how gentle the handshake was. Kelly Walker seemed strong enough to crush anything.

"Nice to meet you, Grace. I'll be back to check the roof as soon as it stops raining and has a chance to dry out. Maybe as early as tomorrow afternoon, if the forecast is right. You don't have to be home for me to do it."

"Don't you need someone to hold the ladder?" Grace, always the mother, was quite safety conscious. The idea of someone not only climbing a high ladder, but also walking around on the roof, was crossing the line. After Kelly wrung the towels dry to within an inch of their lives, Grace put them in a plastic bag.

"Nope, but I promise to be careful. I'll either leave a note, or Kaye will call you with news." Kelly again tapped the girl on the head. She earned herself a grin and a poke on the hip in return. Kelly took the towels from Grace and left.

Chapter
Two

"THEY LOOK GOOD, Kelly." Jo, one of the three full-time volunteers at The Pride Center rolled up as Kelly stepped back to eyeball the last shelf placement.

"Thanks." She removed a shelf to resettle its supports.

"Listen, you got a minute? I have another project for you over at my desk."

"Sure, let me finish here, and I'll be right over." Kelly used a towel from one of her boxes and wiped down the shelving. She swept the floor of her sawdust and wood chips and put her tools away. She stored the various boxes on a luggage dolly. The topmost box was wooden and held her most used items, such as her larger notepad and her pencils.

The Western North Carolina Pride Center was located in downtown Asheville. Just inside, beyond the glass doors of the brick building, the main room was hexagonal. The middle was filled with turning racks of brochures, and the edges held the various tables and desks of the volunteers. Kelly's new shelving units, their vertical beams stained a rich walnut and their shelves stained a medium oak, drew the visitors' attention to the three walls they occupied. Most of the shelves were level, while others were at an angle to better display magazines and catalogs. Cabinets were at both lower ends and along the top of the span.

The director and an assistant were already bringing out boxes of magazines, books, brochures, and newspapers to fill the new shelves.

Kelly crossed the room toward Jo Spencer. She was always fascinated with Jo's face, its roundness and a smile that could light up even the blandest of rooms. Kelly knew that Jo's disability kept her in constant pain, much like her friend, Annette's, and Kelly always wanted to scoop Jo up and hold her, to try to make the pain go away and make that smile show more often.

"You did a good job. You should have heard all the comments this morning. All good, of course." Jo sat to the side of her table.

"The Pride Parade is here next summer, did you hear?"

"No, I hadn't. Cool. Y'all will be busy then." Kelly sat down on a metal folding chair.

"Yes, we will. Your shelves'll be seen by several thousand queens and dykes from all over this state. You're welcome to put cards out."

"I'll make sure I have some special ones ready by then." As Kelly spoke, she heard a rustling under the table, then a loud thunk.

"Oh, Masco! You hit your head again? Poor baby." Jo wheeled back and to the side to allow her big service dog to come the rest of the way out from under the table.

"What's she hitting her head on?" Kelly knelt down.

"She hits it there on the support bracket. We've padded it, but I'm sure it still hurts. This is actually the project I mentioned. I need some way to make her more comfortable."

Duct tape held well worn foam pipe insulation onto the bracket. "Why does she stay under the desk?"

"It keeps her out of the way; otherwise, she gets stepped on or attracts too much attention. I'd prefer her to be out from under there, but mostly, it's for her own good. Except for the bumps. On quiet days, she comes out and lies on her blanket behind me."

"So during the weeks around The Pride Parade, she's going to be fairly much living under there." Kelly returned to her stack of tool boxes and retrieved her pencil and sketch pad from the top one. She crossed the room and started to sketch. "How about if she has her own space? A raised platform, on wheels, with two sides, one toward the center of the room and one behind her. That leaves her with space, and she can easily see you." She sat down on the floor next to the dog, who put her chin on Kelly's knee.

Jo rolled over and looked over Kelly's shoulder. "I see what you mean! That looks great!"

"If I make it tall enough for her to stand, I can even put a partial top on, so you can have some storage space for your extra paper and maps." She continued sketching, the idea in her head taking shape on the paper.

"That's actually a good idea. And Masco would be out of the way, out of sight, and yet easily within my reach."

"Exactly. There. How's that?" She handed the sketch pad to Jo as she absentmindedly petted the dog.

"I like it!"

"I can take her measurements and send you the final design, maybe even make a mock-up. That way you can get permission from the board. I'll do it for free, of course, but I'd like it if they approved it being here. I can make the sides out of the same type of wainscoting the wall has, and that'll hide it even more."

"Do you always think this fast?" Jo handed the sketch pad back.

"Yeah, I do. It gets to be annoying sometimes, especially when one idea comes while I'm supposed to be working on another." She unclipped the measuring tape from her tool belt.

Jo gave Masco the command to stand.

"That's a good girl, Masco. Do you ever bite your mama for giving you such a weird name?" Kelly took the measurements of Masco's head height and body length while they talked.

"I've heard there's a rottie near you named Spam."

"Yeah, Nikki Rogers—a tall, thin dyke—has a brother to Annette's Marley."

"Masco is from a different breeder, so she isn't a relative. It's amazing, though, that there are two of us here with Rottweiler service dogs. Oh, and I've seen a big German Shepherd out and about."

"I have, too, but I don't know the handler—got a cool chair, though. Okay, I've got what I need. I'll get back to you on this in a few weeks."

As she put her toolboxes into the truck, Kelly wished that she could relax more around Jo. But the damage from Anna's mess two years ago had left Kelly unwilling to trust. *Besides, she's not the type to like a butch girl like me, with my calloused hands and dirty fingernails. My shoulders are so wide I can only wear men's shirts. Nah, Jo needs a refined woman — something I'll never be.*

GRACE HAD TO force herself to stay awake during lunch. She'd not slept well due to the dripping sounds coming from the kitchen at her home. She downed two caffeinated sodas with her sandwich and returned to her work bench.

She hated this job, but the pay was enough for rent, bills, groceries, and whatever Lucy needed for school. Their bikes, the couch, and Lucy's tiny desk had all been bought from thrift stores. Most of Lucy's clothing came from one just down the street from the house. They often made stories up about where it all had been before.

Just three more months at this job and she'd have insurance. Lucy was eligible for services at the health department, so that helped. She needed to save up for a summer program, so her daughter would have a safe place to be during the day. She'd heard the YWCA had an excellent program.

She realized she had slowed down in her work. She shook her head to clear out the daydreaming and focused on the job at hand.

ON HER WAY to the house on Oak Street, Kelly remembered to stop at the laundry and get the towels.

"Hey, Miss Walker. Did we do a load for you today?" Mrs. Glenn, a little, old woman standing about five feet tall, was an expert on stains and the fine art of folding.

"I dropped off a load of towels early this morning." Kelly nodded in greeting to the other laundry employee who was busy mopping up from a leaking washer.

"Oh, yes, those were easy." She shuffled off to the back table and flipped tags on several plastic bags of washed clothing. "Here. I put some bleach in with them to try and take out the smell and stains. I'll just put this on your tab, dear."

"Thanks, Mrs. Glenn. I'll see you later with my usual load." Kelly patted the old woman on the head, only to get slapped in return. It was their ritual greeting and parting, and, as usual, they were both laughing.

In just a few minutes, she arrived at the rental house. Before she could forget, she carried the towels to the porch. She took them out of the bag to air them out from the perfume-filled soap the laundromat used. Kelly took some of her dirtiest clothes there, especially when she'd gotten some new type of stain. Her other clothes she did herself at the same laundry, usually during a card game with Mrs. Glenn.

Kelly returned to her truck and took the longest ladder from the rack. She set up the ladder at the back of the house, tamped the bottom feet firmly onto the ground, and got up on the roof. Several shingles were gone; others were loose or had corners lifted up. Her boots had trouble keeping a grip on the surface since the grit on the shingles was so loose. The part over the kitchen was the worst, although the rest was not much better. She could see where patches had been put on in two places, neither of which had been done correctly. She looked over the rest of the structure, walking carefully along the ridge.

Almost to the end of the one apex, she looked up in time to see the lady tenant drive up. They waved at each other, and Kelly continued her inspection.

Back on the ground, she pulled out her ever present cell phone. "Got good news and bad news, Kaye. Which you want first?"

"Dammit. Good news first."

"I found the roof leak."

"Oh, good! Wait, bad news?"

"The roof has to be replaced. Those shingles are falling apart. There's also rot in a couple of places." Kelly didn't bother telling her the specific details; Kaye wouldn't understand the jargon anyway.

"I was afraid of that. Okay, well, now what?"

"You call a roofer. I can do patching, but not this. What are you going to do with the tenants? Repairing the roof is going to be dusty and noisy." From where she stood by the ladder Kelly could see out over the backyard where a bird feeder hung from a pole stuck in the middle of what must be a flower bed. Propped against the back of the house were two bicycles, one a miniature version of the other.

"I have no idea. Is she home?"

"Yeah. I'm out back. I just got down from the roof."

"I'll call the house phone and let her know. Oh, if the roofers do their thing, can you fix the inside?"

"Sure, but whoever built this house did a lousy job, so the repair will likely mean redoing the whole ceiling." She unhooked her tool belt, the most used tool of her trade. It carried everything she needed so her hands could be free. She'd even had a leather crafter make a special pocket just for her smaller notepad and a pencil.

GRACE PULLED UP at the house and got out. She panicked at the sight of that handywoman up on the roof. As Grace watched, the brave idiot walked along the highest ridge, then paused to look down and wave at her. Grace waved back, although she wanted to scream for her to stop and get down from up there.

On the front porch was a stack of her towels, washed and folded. Grace shook her head at this woman's many talents and took the towels to the linen closet. She changed clothes in the bedroom before going to the kitchen. She gathered what she needed to make dinner. She cut up the carrots and dumped the scraps into the trash can near the window. She saw Kelly Walker in the backyard, talking to someone on the phone. Grace couldn't hear the conversation, but she enjoyed the view. Kelly had a nice body — wide shoulders and a strong back. She wore jeans and a tucked in t-shirt with the business's name on the back. She stood there, feet apart, one hand on her hip, the other holding the tiny cell phone to her ear. When she unclipped the tool belt with one hand and slung it over her shoulder, it was such a classic butch move, Grace laughed out loud and sighed. She'd always been attracted to the butch girls.

Chapter
Three

KELLY GOT HOME late. She'd spent most of the afternoon at the house on Oak Street and then had worked over at the Fultons' house to replace a gutter and hang their winter bird feeders. Her lunch had been fast food grabbed on her way to the library, where she did research on a project she was doing for Kaye's partner, Annette.

Kelly went into her house, if the old shack could be considered that. It was basically a bungalow with a counter separating the living room-slash-bedroom from the kitchen. The bathroom, a new addition since she had moved in, was to the left, and was nothing more than a shower stall with a toilet in the front corner. There were no photos or art prints on the walls of the house. The only decorations in the place was a calendar from the pharmacy hung on a paneling nail by the bathroom door and on the wall by the back door was a small plaque that read *So I'm not Martha Stewart; get over it*, a gift from her friend, Nikki.

Other than the couch against the counter, the only furniture in the living room was an upturned milk crate holding a small TV, a tall stool by the door, and a green vinyl ottoman with a rip across the top. The rest of the room was littered with fast food bags, two laundry baskets—one with clean, folded clothes; the other overflowed with dirty laundry—and stacks of mostly unread magazines and catalogs. A path free of debris went from the front door to the kitchen, with a side trail along the front of the couch.

The kitchen was no better. Frozen dinner boxes and trays were precariously balanced on the counter, and the trash can was full of others. A small, round table with a single, unpadded chair was against the wall, but the top was covered with junk mail. The inside of the refrigerator was the only clean thing in the house. It contained a tub of butter, a half-empty carton of milk, a box of Reese's Cups, and a jar of strawberry jam. The freezer held an empty ice cube tray and four frozen dinners: lasagna, Salisbury steaks, fried chicken, and fish sticks. The house didn't have an offensive odor, other than from the pile of laundry. The only light came from a glaring ceiling light in the living room.

She emptied her pockets into the bucket on the stool and sat on the arm of the couch to take off her boots. Her briefcase, a canvas one from Duluth Trading Co., balanced on the back of the couch against the counter. In the kitchen, she took out the frozen lasagna to cook for dinner. She used the time to take a shower and change into a pair of holey sweat pants and equally ragged t-shirt. She took a portion from the steaming pan and tossed the leftovers into the 'fridge to be reheated throughout the week. She ate standing at the stove and read the mail that had come in that day. Mail for the house — junk mail and the electric bill — was tossed onto the table with the rest, while mail for her business was put in the briefcase.

Kelly put on a pair of old sneakers, picked up her briefcase, and went out the back door. In front of her, no more than fifty feet away, was the lake with its rippling water reflecting the quarter moon. Stuck out over the water was a twelve-foot dock with a canoe tethered at the end. A startled heron silently flew off to the other side.

She turned and headed toward another building, at least three times as big as the house. This was her shop, built completely new since she'd moved here. The side facing the lake had two garage doors on the end closer to the house and large double doors on the other end. The side facing the road had only a single, windowed door with a light on a timer above it.

She pushed open the nearest half of the double door and hit the light switch with her elbow. The set of lights over the long workbench came on, illuminating the table and the wall above it. The shop was a sharp contrast to the house. In here, everything was in its place. Nothing was left out unless it was integral to an ongoing project. Two tall filing cabinets held the invoices, incoming and outgoing, every manual for every piece of equipment she had, and all of her notes, drawings, and plans that would fit in a simple file folder.

Kelly loved her workshop. She'd fiddled with the plans for it for several years, but didn't get the chance to build it until she moved to High Pond. In here, she was Kelly Walker, owner of Around-To-It Services. She knew what she was doing here; she knew her trades well and had certifications in electrical, plumbing, furniture-making, and carpentry. She had a not-so-small fortune in equipment, enabling her to do almost anything within her trades. She was confident, in control, and ready and willing to push her own limits.

But back at the house, the chaotic, dirty house, she was Kelly Walker, the Fool. That Kelly couldn't care less about herself and her surroundings. She had given herself to Anna, loving her with heart, mind, and soul. She'd even left her family to move to Columbus, Ohio, then to Chicago, because Anna had wanted to. They'd bought a luxurious condo and lived there for nearly two years. Then Anna had died, her lies and deceptions surfaced, and Kelly was left to clean up the mess. Cleaning up after Anna was something Kelly had become good at doing.

She pushed aside those thoughts. She didn't want them in her shop. She filed the paperwork, matched the master calendar on the wall to the jumbled notes on the one from her case, and put the payments she'd received into the safe under the vise end of the table.

Kelly knew she was too tired to work and reluctantly reloaded her briefcase. She pulled the door shut and locked it before heading back to the house. She tossed her shoes to the corner behind the front door and lay down on the couch. Kelly fell asleep, not bothering to turn the kitchen light off.

Only a few hours later, the phone rang, awakening her from a troubled dream. She moved only her arm and answered the phone. "Walker."

"Kelly? It's Harri. I got a problem."

"What kind of problem?" Kelly grabbed the blanket from the back of the couch and pulled it over her head. *Why do my best friends always need me when I don't want to work?*

"I got a flooded basement. As in waist-deep flooded and rising."

"What did you do? Have a pool party down there?"

"Funny. I have no clue. I went down there for something, can't remember what now, and found all this water." She heard Harri light a cigarette.

"Where's the main house valve? And I thought you stopped smoking."

"You mean the one that shuts off all the water? It's down there, in the corner near the hot-water tank. And I did stop for about two weeks this time. Just started back again."

"Where's the breaker box?"

"Out on the back porch."

"Good. Be a butch girl and go flip the main breaker to turn the whole house off. Then go down to that all-night diner near the highway and get me a BLT, no mayo, and a very, very large sweet tea."

"Will do. I take it you're on your way?"

"I need to get decent first. You woke me." Kelly pushed the covers off and sat up. She dug through the hamper.

"You ain't never gonna be decent, girlfriend, so just throw on some clothes and get over here."

"Ha ha. On my way, darlin'."

KELLY ARRIVED TWENTY minutes later and parked her truck as close to the house as she could. She sat on the tailgate to put on her chest-high waders. She stomped her way up the sidewalk, trying to settle them over her boots before she attached the suspenders and clipped the flashlight in place on the bib.

Harri met her at the door with a jogger's arm flashlight strapped on her left bicep. "Want your sandwich now or later?"

"Now. When you flipped the breaker off, were any others already blown?"

"No, I checked. You want it on a plate on in the wrapper?"

"The wrapper will be just fine. It sounds like the hot water tank's not the problem." Kelly took the sandwich and bit into it, chasing it down with a gulp of tea. "If I remember correctly, you have a gravity-fed spring, right? That means the water's still flowing. Let's go see what's down there, shall we? And where's that wild cat of yours?" She rewrapped the sandwich and put it and the drink on the table just inside the front door.

"Lucky's locked in the bedroom. You're safe from the mean old, bad old cat." Harri laughed.

Kelly flipped on her waterproof flashlight as she started down the stairs. A box drifted by as she stepped off the bottom of the stairs. The water was, indeed, waist-deep, and she was glad she'd believed Harri's comment. "There's the tank. You said the valve's over there, too?"

"As far as I can remember, yeah. That's where the water pipe comes in." Harri was good with cars, but lousy with most everything else. She was not as tall as Kelly, but bulkier. The classic dyke: hair in a buzz cut, a tattoo on each arm, and she wore white t-shirts and black jeans. And heaven help them if anyone called her "Harriet" to her face. Kelly, on the other hand, kept her hair an inch or two longer and was almost thirty pounds lighter. She was comfortable around Harri, probably because she was someone she wasn't the least bit interested in sexually.

"Close enough." She waded through the water, pushing aside the various things that floated by — muscle cream, a tube of aloe lotion, a can of spray deodorant, and other such things. When a bottle of sex lube came into reach, Kelly tossed it over to Harri. "You needed to clean up down here, anyway."

"Stay to your right. My weights are near the leg press, that funky thing sticking up out of the water to your left."

"You gonna tell me what the lube is for?" Kelly pushed a half dozen empty water bottles and a basketball out of her way.

"If you don't know by now, I ain't gonna be the one to tell you."

When Kelly got to the corner, she located the water intake pipe for the tank and followed it down below the water. She gasped as the cold water came into her waders and flooded down her chest all the way to her feet. She finally found the valve and turned the water off. "Got it."

Kelly sloshed over to the window and turned the crank to open it. Once the window was open completely, she splashed to where Harri waited for her at the stairs. The flooded waders made her legs and feet weigh much more, and she'd need the help to climb back up the stairs.

Back outside, Kelly sat on the edge of the top step while Harri helped roll the waders off and dumped quite a bit of water out of each leg. "You look kinda like a half-drowned kitten. But I'd enter you in a wet t-shirt contest instantly," Harri walked up the steps past her to retrieve the sandwich and drink.

"Thanks. I love you, too," Kelly muttered.

"Now what?"

"Now I hook up the pumps and get that water out, so I can see what's going on down there." Kelly spoke around the bite of sandwich in her mouth.

After she ate, she carried the gasoline-powered pump to the basement window and tossed in the hose. It took several hours to get all the water out, especially since debris kept blocking the screen at the end of the hose. She and Harri sat in lawn chairs in the back yard. They had to keep getting up to shake the hose free of debris. Kelly changed into the extra set of clothes she kept in the truck, and despite the sound and smell of the pump, she was able to nap sporadically.

"Keep it going, and I'll go on back down to see if it's uncovered anything yet." Slipping the clammy waders back on was not fun, but it was necessary. Harri was respectful and didn't laugh, at least not so Kelly could hear her. The water was now knee deep which made it easy for Kelly to walk through it. She felt around the shut-off valve and found the cracked water line just a few inches above it.

"So what does it need to get fixed?" Once Kelly was back to the steps, Harri handed her another sandwich and a soda.

"Some pipe, a new valve, and maybe a new water heater. How long you had it?" The sandwich was peanut butter and jelly. Kelly was surprised there was actually food in the house.

"It came with the house, so at least ten years."

"You might want to get another." The sandwich had grape jelly. Kelly hated grape jelly.

"Can you do that, too? Put one in, I mean?"

"Yep. I have one in the shop. Still in its box, too." Kelly finished the sandwich and drank the last of the soda.

"How many more sandwiches will this set me back?"

"A lot more if they're this bad."

IT WAS DAYLIGHT before most of the water was gone. They maneuvered the new hot water tank down the steps to the basement. After that, Harri was more trouble helping than she was worth, so Kelly made her leave. With that obstacle out of the way, the rest of the repair went quickly. She was good at plumbing, seeing it as a grown-up's tinker-toy set. With all the pieces dry-fitted and looking tidy, she marked them, took it all apart and reassembled it, gluing them together as she went.

She turned on the water and checked all the joints for any signs of leaking. The new valve turned easily, and she could hear the water going into the tank. It always felt good when a job was finished.

Chapter
Four

"MOM, I NEED help with math homework again." Lucy closed the textbook, trapping the scattered papers inside. She went into the living room where her mother was folding clothes.

"Lucy, when I was in fourth grade, we didn't have to know all this stuff." Grace sighed as she laid a shirt on a stack of others. "Which is a good example of why God invented calculators."

"Fine. But if I become one of the statistics of all the other girls who are worse in math than boys, I'll remind you of this." The girl moved to the edge of the couch and slid to the floor.

"Show me the problem, brat." Fifteen minutes later, Lucy had taught her mother a lot about division but hadn't gotten the answer to her original question.

Frustrated and defeated, Grace went outside to get the two comforters off the line. When she returned, Lucy was sprawled on the floor watching television instead of doing her homework. "Lucille Rebecca Owens, if you don't turn off that TV and get the rest of your homework done..."

"I know, I know. You'll knock my teeth out." Lucy sat up but didn't turn the set off.

"Actually, no. I was thinking more of knocking your head off."

"If you did that, then I couldn't get my homework done." She clicked the mute button on the remote and opened her social studies book, giving up on the math.

"True, but then you also wouldn't want dinner, so I think it'd even out."

"You are, like, so gross, Mom."

"And you are, like, so in trouble if that homework isn't done by five o'clock." She folded the comforters and picked up the stack of folded shirts and jeans. She put hers in her bedroom and Lucy's in hers. "You need to clean up in here, kiddo," Grace called from Lucy's room.

"I did already!" Like most young girls, Lucy's voice was loud enough without her shouting. Grace was glad they didn't live in an apartment or duplex anymore.

"Then you need to do it again." She looked around the small room and wondered just what her daughter had cleaned up. The bed sheets were in a crumpled pile at the headboard, dirty clothing was strewn about the floor, and her stuffed animals and library books looked as if they had been thrown into the air and allowed to land at random on the bed.

"Mom, come check out this new show they're talking about." Grace joined her in the living room but, after a single moment of the commercial touting the program, she knew it wasn't something Lucy would be allowed to watch.

"What time does it come on?" Grace sat on the arm of the couch.

"Nine, I think."

"Darn, too bad, that's past the time when all princesses are thrown into the dungeon without television access."

"Funny, very funny." Lucy went into her bedroom, made her bed, sort of, and put away her clean clothes by stuffing them haphazardly into the drawers. She even picked up the dirty ones and carried them to the bathroom to put in the hamper, but most of the clothes landed around it, not in it. She tossed her stuffed animals in the general direction of their box and stacked the library books neatly on her desk.

"Mom, have you seen my skates?" Lucy went to her mother's bedroom where Grace was sorting socks on the bed.

"Lucy, you don't have skates."

"Exactly."

Mother and daughter stared at each other. "Lucille Rebecca Owens. You are such a—"

"Remember, I'm an impressionable nine-year-old, easily influenced by the environment around me." Lucy slowly backed out of the room.

"I'll leave an impression on you that'll certainly influence you."

Grace dropped the socks and chased after her daughter.

"DINNER WAS GOOD, Mom." Lucy wiped her mouth with her sleeve and ran to her room.

Grace was tired, and Lucy had far too much energy. She wondered, not for the first time, how other single parents dealt with it, especially those with more than one child. Ten years ago, Grace had made a decision that affected her life in ways she never imagined. She'd been dating David for a year, and they'd decided to marry. But the little things she'd been ignoring in him (and in herself) became too heavy to carry further. She'd ended their engagement and moved to California. A month later, she found out she was pregnant. Now, nine years and a row of bad luck later, she was back where her family had lived for most of her early childhood.

"Mom? You okay?"

"Yeah, I'm fine, just tired." Grace sat up and pulled Lucy in for a hug.

"I bet. Being an adult must be a real bummer."

"NOW REMEMBER, YOU'LL be staying for the after-school program. I'll pick you up, and we'll go spend the night at Kaye and Annette's. You remember Kaye, don't you? The woman who was here when we moved in?" Grace zipped the lunch bag closed and put it into Lucy's backpack.

"Yeah. She smiled at me a lot. Okay. How long until we can come back?" Lucy tied her shoes before getting her jacket from the closet.

"Kaye says it'll be two days before the roof's done, maybe three. Once the roof is back on, we'll be back." She kissed her daughter on the head. "I put two dollars in your lunch bag for your milk at lunch and a drink with your snack after school."

"Does that mean the snack drink is non-specific? I can get what I want?"

"It means you can get whatever you want of what they offer, and not what's in the machines down the hall, Miss Smarty. Nice try, though." When she lifted the heavy backpack from the counter and put it on the floor, she made a note to herself to look for one with wheels.

She watched from the window as Lucy and the other kids gathered on the corner to wait for the school bus. She was glad her daughter fit in so well with the other kids.

After the bus had come and gone, she got to work getting the house ready for their absence while the roofers worked. In addition to clothes for three days, she needed to pack up a few of Lucy's books and toys to take along. The chess set was definitely going, as was Mr. Bear who had been a part of Lucy's life from the hour she was born, literally. They were reading the *Chronicles of Narnia* together, so those books went into the box, as well as several others from the library.

Faced with either staying in a hotel or at Kaye's house, Grace easily chose the latter. Having spent two weeks in a hotel-turned-homeless-shelter, she knew she didn't want to expose her daughter to those memories, even by staying in a semi-luxury hotel.

As she picked out their clothing, she heard a horn sounding

out front. She looked out the front window and saw the handy-woman's big white truck. Kelly took a cinder block from the truck bed and used it to prop the gate open. Her pants and shirt were damp, as if she'd walked through lawn sprinklers.

"I heard you might be in need of some assistance, so I thought I'd stop by and give you a hand," Kelly called out as she reached the porch.

"We aren't taking that much." Grace pushed open the door to let her in.

"Some women pack their entire wardrobe just to go shopping for more." Kelly grinned at her.

"Not this woman. Nor her daughter. I have those two boxes of books and these two suitcases." Grace pointed to them on the couch and on the floor of the living room. "And that's all." She resisted sticking her tongue out. "I was going to put these in the car and go to work."

"How about I take them over to Kaye's now? That way they aren't in your car all day. I'm doing a project for Annette, and I need to discuss it with her, so I'm going there anyway."

"I suppose that's a good idea. Lucy's put most of her music CDs in there. They'd warp in the heat."

"Okay. I'll start loading." She stacked the two boxes together and picked them up. "Oof. This is what you get for having a smart kid. If you'd had one who liked dolls, it wouldn't be this heavy." Kelly grinned and headed out to the truck.

Grace shook her head and went to finish gathering their clothes. She wondered if she'd need to cover the couch since the dust from the construction would get everywhere.

Kelly opened the screen door. "Oh, hey, I meant to bring these in. They're all my painting cloths. You can use them to drape over stuff so the dust won't get everywhere."

"Are you a mind reader?"

"Um, not that I know of. Are you thinking what I'm thinking?" Kelly cocked her head to one side and watched her.

Grace laughed, enjoying the sense of humor this strange woman had. "I was thinking I was going to need to cover every-thing, and here you are with the drop cloths."

"See? I'm good for something after all. I also brought hasp locks for the bedroom doors so you'll feel better about leaving everything here. The only room that needs to be emptied is the kitchen, of course. You can put everything into cabinets and tape them shut. This is really the only room that'll need to be draped, since it can't be shut off from the kitchen, unless you want to do the bedrooms just in case dust and stuff falls from the hammering." Kelly tossed the canvas tarps onto the floor in front of the couch.

"Just who are you?" Grace was intrigued. *Whirlwind was still a good description. Maybe hurricane, since she came with the rain.*

"What?" Kelly took a step back.

"I mean, you came here yesterday and the day before and just whip in and out, and then you show up here today with all this and, and, and..."

"Yeah, I've been told I can be overwhelming."

Grace reached out and touched her arm. "At any rate, I appreciate your help. I feel safe knowing you'll be nearby if I have any questions or concerns."

"I don't know about safe, but, yeah, if you have any questions, feel free to ask them. Now, you about ready?" Kelly nodded to the still-open suitcases on the couch.

"I have a question. Where do you get your energy?"

Kelly shrugged and became interested in a speck of lint in the carpet. "I don't know. All the sweet tea I drink, probably. I thought your questions would be limited to the roof repair."

"Most of them, but if you're going to be here a lot, I thought perhaps I should know you better." Grace said the words, but she doubted that was the true reason.

"Okay, well, I'm thirty-six, five foot and thirteen inches tall, about two-hundred-and-twenty pounds, and, yes, I always wear caps. I like to eat, and I eat a lot. I read every chance I can, and I rarely go to the movies unless it's an animated film. I can't cook, I can't sew, and I don't like light beer. Need to know more?"

Grace laughed. "No, I think that's enough for now. And yes, the suitcases are ready."

Chapter
Five

KELLY MERGED WITH the light traffic on the highway. She was still grinning from her conversation with Grace Owens. The woman was cuter than a bug and had a fantastic sense of humor. The fact the woman was not intimidated by Kelly's size was a big plus. Then there was that laugh that was one of the most genuine she had ever heard. She was what Kelly would call a soft butch-tough but feminine at the same time. *Too bad she's straight.*

Her thoughts were interrupted by her cell phone ringing. "Walker."

"Is this Around-To-It?"

"Yes. How can I help you?" Kelly glanced at her watch to judge the time she'd need to do her other jobs.

"Do you do glass, as in window glass?"

"Yes. How soon do you need it?"

"Now. Before the apartment manager sees it."

"Where are you?" Kelly got the address, turned the truck around, and headed back toward Asheville. She needed to stop taking on these "now" jobs and get more "whenever" jobs.

Apartment 693 belonged to a young lesbian couple. They'd apparently had a fight that ended when the window was broken, and one of them had driven away. Kelly knew this because the woman left behind had begun talking about it as soon as Kelly knocked on the door.

"I just need to take measurements and go get the glass."

"Whatever. It's just that we can't agree on anything, you know?" As the woman talked, Kelly tried not to stare, but she just could not get over the three rings piercing the girl's bottom lip.

"Uh huh." She took the tape measure and notepad from her canvas bag.

"Like, why can't she see it my way?" The four rings in the right eyebrow were hard to ignore, too.

Kelly measured the height and made a note.

"And, like, what else can she expect from me?" The hardest to ignore was the thin halter top and the multiple tattoos that obviously continued down onto her breasts.

Kelly measured the width and made another note.

"She says it's all my fault." The short-shorts and leather go-go boots were not lost amid the rest of this girl's early-morning wear.

"Back in a bit." Kelly hurried off to get away from the woman, no, girl. At thirty-six, she felt she had the right to *tsk* the younger generation. She'd never understood the desire to make holes in your body where holes really shouldn't be.

When she returned, she left the sheet of glass in the truck and took in a bucket that held an old metal paint can and several sizes of pliers. She used her kneepads to kneel on the rough concrete patio, then pulled the broken glass out of the window frame, and dropped it into the metal can.

The woman resumed talking exactly where she'd left off.

"We had this fight because she said it was my fault. Like, you know, I had anything to do with it. Just because Tammy looked at me and I, like, looked back, doesn't mean we slept together. You know? We barely know each other. What really set her off was when I said her name. Like, knowing a person's name means we've had sex. Like, I know your name, but we haven't had sex. Have we? No, I'd remember doing someone that old."

Kelly took the risk of looking up but didn't comment.

"Anyway, she said I..."

She blabbered on, but Kelly wasn't really listening. A memory had sprung up in her mind. One of another fight and, ironically, a broken window.

"WHERE WERE YOU last night?" Kelly poured herself her usual cup of coffee, black and strong.

"I stayed late at the office and fell asleep waiting for a fax." Anna sat at the kitchen table, sipping her own coffee — no cream, one teaspoon of sugar — as she read the morning paper.

"You could have called."

"Would you have been awake to answer? No. You didn't even wake up when I came home." Anna didn't look up from the paper.

"I was glad to see you there this morning, though." Kelly bent down to kiss her cheek, but Anna turned at the last minute and kissed her on the lips, pulling Kelly's head down and holding her there.

"I'm sorry I didn't call, babe. I just didn't want to wake you."

Kelly straightened and leaned against the counter. Her head was still spinning from the kiss, as usual. Four years and she can still make my toes curl. "I was up until one."

"Are you accusing me of something, Kelly?" Anna looked up,

finally making eye contact. Somehow, that made Kelly feel better.

"No, I don't think so."

"It sounds like you are. I work hard at the office. I may not have rough hands or smelly clothes to show for it, but I do work hard." A tear had formed in the corner of her eye, balancing there, not falling.

"Hon, I just wonder why you're there so late. Late enough to not come home until three in the morning. How did you sleep at your desk, for Pete's sake?" She didn't mean to, but her voice got louder. She opened her arms wide to punctuate the sentence, forgetting the coffee cup was in her hand. It flew across the small kitchen, over the microwave, and slammed against the window. The glass shattered as the cup continued through and down into the park five stories below. Coffee similarly flew in an arc, dousing the counter, the toaster, and the floor.

"Oops."

"AND THAT'S WHEN she threw the chair at me and it hit the window."

Kelly went to the truck to get the sheet of glass she had bought. She held it up to the window opening to make sure it would fit.

"Oh, good! There she is!"

Kelly did look up then and turned to follow the girl's stare out to the parking lot. Two women were getting out of a little car and coming toward the apartments. Both were carrying Ingles' milk boxes, the kind everyone picks up when they're moving. *This can't be good.*

"That bitch! That's Tammy she's with! I should have known!"

The fight resumed as soon as the two newcomers got close enough. The yelling was loud, especially when Tammy tried to get involved. The fight shifted along this triangulation, and Kelly lost track of who was fighting with whom and why. She finished the job and put away her tools. She wrote up the bill and stood to the side while she waited for someone to pause so that she could speak.

"Here's the bill." Kelly handed it to Miss Piercing.

"Give it to that bitch!" She gestured toward Original Girl-friend.

"No fuckin' way! You called her, you pay her!"

Now, with a fresh subject to fight about, they started all over again. Sighing, Kelly put the bill on the table by the door and left. *That's one I'll never see paid.*

ANNETTE WHEELED OUT onto the deck as Kelly got out of the truck. "You were supposed to be here hours ago. I was about to get worried."

"I got a call. The job was...eccentric. I'll tell you about it in a minute. Where do you want me to put the tenant lady's stuff?"

"The tenant lady? She has a name, you know. Put them in the far back bedroom." Annette shook her head and went back inside. Kelly watched her go, and then picked up the two boxes of books.

Kaye and Annette's place, also known affectionately as "The Goat Farm," consisted of about thirty acres. The west and north border ran along Kelly's property line. Their driveway was almost a mile long, just the way they liked it. Kelly chuckled as she remembered the first time she had topped that last hill and saw the farm. Everything about this place sprawled. The house resembled a mama sow on her side, and all the outbuildings were her piglets. There was a separate shed for everything, from lawn equipment to garden tools to goats and goat supplies.

She carried the boxes down the hallway, and, when she put them on the big bed, all the chess pieces came pouring out of their bag. "Crap." She knelt on the floor to pick them all up, and Marley, Annette's service dog, came in to see what she was doing. "Ah, just what I needed. Marley, see that? Get it for me."

The dog was excited to be able to do something and dove under the bed to retrieve a pawn. When she came back out, she pranced around the room, finally bringing it to Kelly. "You are such a show-off."

"Who are you talking to?" Annette came down the hall, a small pile of bathroom towels on her lap.

"Marley. She got something for me under the bed. She's a handy beast to have around."

"Best reacher I've ever had. Is that all? Just two boxes?"

"No, there's two suitcases still. I'd get them, except you've got that hunk of chrome in my way."

"What? Don't you like it? It's an old one I found in storage. I thought I'd go retro." Annette spun in a circle, the chrome-plated frame flashing in the light.

"Retro? What is that, about ten pounds heavier than your other one? What'd you do, crash again?"

"Oh hush, Miss Fix-it. Kaye dropped it off at the shop today. We knew better than to ask you. You've not let me live down the last time I ran over it."

"You ran over it again? What with this time?"

"No, I didn't run over it. If you must know, I got out of it on the deck, and it rolled away down the steps and flipped several times on the concrete walk. Now, go get their suitcases and meet me in the studio." Annette glared at the laughing Kelly.

Kelly did as she was told and soon joined Annette in the pottery studio up from the house.

"I found this in a book at the library, and I think it's the best option. We dig a pit, kind of like a septic tank, and the clay sludge goes into that. Water overflow then goes into a series of pipes, just like a leach field." She got the drafting sheets from their tube and unrolled the ones that held the drawings for Annette's project. She'd researched several different ideas for the waste system for the pottery.

"Is this to scale?"

"Not really. I didn't know the size of the house. The measurements of the pit are correct, and I guestimated how it compared to the surrounding area. The legend is down here." She used a glaze test mug on each corner to hold it down. "I don't know for sure how long it will last, but I think it will be around five years. By the way, that's an ugly glaze. Why do you keep the test piece?"

"To remind me to always read the label. Now, get back to the plans before you start laughing hysterically again."

For the next several hours, they went over all of them, always coming back to the pit idea.

"I think we'll go with this one. I'll show this to Kaye tonight, and we'll let you know. Do you have a price estimate?"

"I think I did one for that one." Kelly went through her briefcase and pulled out a folder. "Yes, here it is. I tend to over-estimate, but I'd still suggest you add about two to five percent for possible problems."

"Not as bad as I thought." Annette added the sheet to the drawings. "Can you stay for lunch?"

"Afraid not. I've got to go by Harri's and check her plumbing. Then I'll go by the Oak Street house and make sure the roofers have started. Kaye was lucky to find one who could get to it so quick. And I've got two other little jobs to do today." Kelly rolled up the papers and put them back in the tube.

"You might consider turning that damn cell phone off. I'm surprised it hasn't rung yet." Annette tapped the leather case that seemed to be permanently attached to Kelly's waist. The light on the phone was blinking, announcing she'd had at least one call during her time there.

"Well, yeah, I've considered it. Maybe I need an answering service. But I need the money, so I'm not turning anyone away yet."

"What are you saving up for?" They made their way down the path to the truck.

"I want another truck. This one uses way too much gas, and I almost never use the entire bed. If I had a smaller truck, I could get a trailer for those times I need to haul something big."

"Think you'll go new?"

"Most likely. I've never had a new vehicle. I think I'm old enough to get one now." Kelly put her briefcase on the bench seat.

"Oh, how was Grace this morning?"

"She was disgustingly wide awake."

"Kaye tells me she's cute. What do you think?"

"Sure, she's cute enough, I guess. Too bad she's straight."

"Kelly, you need to get out more. She ain't straight."

"But she's got a kid." Kelly put her hands on her hips.

"And? That doesn't change the fact she's also a card-holding lesbian. Hers is just as valid as yours."

Chapter
Six

GRACE WAS TIRED, and her feet hurt all the way up past her knees. She'd gotten up early to start the packing and had gone in to work late, skipping lunch in order to meet her quota. As she stood in the lobby of the school, she looked at the white-washed block walls covered in children's artwork. Since Thanksgiving was just around the corner, the theme this month was the pilgrims. Lucy would bring hers home one day soon, and it would go into the Album of Fame, the scrapbook they kept of all Lucy's artwork.

"Hey, Mom!" Lucy came running from the gymnasium, dragging her book bag.

"How was your day?" Grace took the bag from her and they walked to the car.

"It was good. Mrs. Thomas explained the math to me better-er than before, so now I understand it, and she said to tell you that I can't use a calculator, even if God did invent it."

A half hour later, as they drove up the long driveway, Lucy laughed at the goats that chased them along the fence. When Grace stopped the car, Lucy got out and looked around. Grace stood beside her and breathed in the fresh air.

"Whoa! What's that?" Lucy quickly hid behind Grace's legs when she saw big Marley.

"I think that's Marley, Annette's dog. She's harmless, Lucy."

"I don't believe you."

Annette came toward them and called Marley to her side. "Hi! You must be the Owens women I've heard so much about. I'm Annette."

"Hello, Annette. I'm Grace and the chicken hiding behind me is Lucy. She's a little freaked by your dog." Grace kept her hand on Lucy's back to keep her from running off.

"Ah. Marley, I think Lucy would like a drink. Get a can." Annette spoke to the large Rottweiler by her side. The dog's ears perked up, and she looked excited. She ran back toward the building they'd come from. "Let me give you the quick outside tour.

Over there are the goat barns and other farm-type buildings. Back there is the pottery studio, and this, of course, is the house." She then rattled off the different breeds of goats they had. "The ones with tiny little ears are called LaMancha and the ones with the long ears are either Boer or Nubian. And that one there, the little black and white fella, is called a Tennessee Fainting goat. He has spells like seizures and falls over."

"You have a lot of buildings and goats." Lucy peeked around Grace.

"Yes, we do. Kaye's never happy with any of her sheds, so she keeps building more. And here's Marley again." The dog came up to them, a soda can in her mouth. She dropped it into Annette's lap and sat down at her feet. Annette got a treat from the bag on her chair. "Here's your reward, girl. And here, Lucy, is your soda." Annette gave the treat to the dog and used a towel to wipe off the can.

"Wowzers! That's a neat trick!"

"It is now. When she was young and still learning, we had to use empty cans until she learned not to crush them. Even so, she still gets excited and punctures one now and then. What a mess!"

It wasn't long before Lucy and Marley were best friends. Marley loved having someone with enough energy to keep up with her and to throw the ball for more than a few minutes. And Lucy was thrilled to have such a smart playmate.

"Come on into the house. Kaye is cutting up veggies for dinner."

GRACE WATCHED FROM the living room window as Lucy ran around the yard with Marley. The dog could easily overtake her but didn't. The two of them had been out there for over an hour.

"She's an active child." Annette rolled up beside her.

"Yes, even more now that she's older. When she was younger, she was afraid of everything, but when she started second grade, she began coming out of her shell. She had a wonderful teacher who knew just how to get Lucy to push herself. They wanted her to skip fourth grade, but I didn't want her to." She turned from the window and went to stand in front of the fireplace.

"I can understand that. As long as she has teachers who know to raise the limits to fit her, she'll do just fine."

"Yes, so far it's happened that way. She liked the school here immediately. They have extra classes for kids who need them. She's in the science and math ones. She asks for help with her homework, and I feel like such an idiot." Grace laughed and told Annette about the calculator comments.

Kaye stood in the kitchen doorway. "You know, Kelly's a genius with math. If you ever need the help, give her a call."

"Kelly Walker? The handyman, woman, whatever?"

"Yes, she loves mathematics. She also plays chess. She'd love to have someone to play it with." Annette nodded toward the chess and checkers set on the bookshelf.

"I wouldn't have thought she was that good at math. I guess I just see her as, like, an apartment super."

"Hell, no! She's much more than a simple maintenance man. I tell Kaye all the time that it's a good thing I love her so much, otherwise, I'd leave her for Kelly in a heartbeat."

"I heard that." Kaye yelled from the kitchen.

"You would? Why?" Grace was flabbergasted.

"Why? Cause she's sexy, strong, smart, and can fix almost anything."

"I got three out of four." Kaye yelled again.

"Yes, dear. Bless her heart, Kaye tries to fix things but doesn't always do so well."

"Sexy? I guess I hadn't really looked. Every time I see her, she has on generic work clothes." She paused and realized the conversation felt awkward. "David, Lucy's father, wasn't good at fixing anything. But he was real good at getting into trouble." Grace sat down in the big armchair. *Switching the discussion to David is more comfortable than talking about a certain butch.*

"What happened? Did it just not work out between you two?" Annette had transferred from her chair to the couch.

"It didn't work out at all. I knew David from high school and we met again at our school's tenth reunion. But after we got engaged, I couldn't ignore his bad side any longer. He was always in trouble—he admitted to robbing a convenience store, and he carried a gun. And I couldn't ignore my lesbian side any longer. So I broke it off and moved. I found out later I was pregnant, but by then, he'd finally gotten caught and was in jail. Last I heard, he was in the Ohio state prison system."

"And Lucy doesn't know a thing about that?"

"No. I just told her that he left before she was born, that he'd never even seen her. She's accepted that all these years, but some day, I know she's going to ask questions."

"Dinner's ready, ladies," Kaye called out from the kitchen.Grace stood and went through the doorway of the french doors and out onto the deck. "Lucy! Come eat."

Chapter
Seven

KELLY CLIMBED DOWN the ladder and went to tell Mrs. Maples the bad news. "That tin up there is all loose and rusted. I nailed down what I could, but, frankly, ma'am, you need to have it replaced."

"I was afraid of that." The old woman hobbled with her cane to the kitchen counter. "Do you know of someone who could do it?"

"Actually, yes. You're the second person this week I've had to tell their roof needed replacing. The roofers are at the other place now, and I met with the supervisor today. He was friendly, knowledgeable, and seemed to know what he was doing. He's even going to redo the insulation wherever he finds some that's wet." Kelly sipped the tea Mrs. Maples put in front of her. Sometimes she tended to over sweeten it to the point of almost making Kelly ill. "But I think you need to discuss this with your son. We don't want him coming here and yelling at you for spending money again."

"Well, shit on him. It's my house." She waved her hand as if to dismiss him.

"Such language! Southern belles aren't supposed to talk like that!" Kelly laughed with Mrs. Maples. She liked the woman and often didn't charge her for the odd jobs she did for her. Besides, she always insisted Kelly sit down and eat something. She may be lousy at judging sweetness in tea, but she was a fantastic cook. Kelly bit into the meatloaf sandwich. "But, seriously, you really need to discuss this with him. It's a lot of money. I don't want him saying I pulled one over on you."

"You're right, of course. I'll call him this afternoon. He'll want to get a second opinion, you know. I'll have to make sure he knows he's paying for it, not me." She got her checkbook from a pile of papers in the middle of the table. "How much do I owe you for this?"

"Nothing. I didn't do anything but go up there and look around."

"Nonsense. You were up there for thirty-five minutes, and you banged almost the whole time you were there. Now, how much do I owe you?"

"How about I tack it onto the final bill?"

She slapped Kelly's hand. "Kelly Rebecca Walker, I knew your grandfather and grandmother. And I know you, too. You won't give me a final bill. You never do. Now, I'll ask you again, how much do I owe you? And don't tell me fifty cents again, neither."

Kelly shook her hand where the woman had slapped. "Fine, fine. Just don't hit me again. I normally charge fifty an hour so how about twenty-five dollars?"

"You charge seventy-five an hour, but I'll give you twenty-five anyway just to be orn'ry. You're just like your papaw." She filled out the check, her hand steady.

"I still miss him, but I don't remember Mamaw much at all. He was a big, big man, tall like a tree. We used to hang onto his legs as he walked along." Kelly smiled as she let those memories play through her mind.

"Yes, he was a big man. If you were a real boy, you'd be just like him in looks, too. You have his eyes, that's for sure. I'm so glad someone came to take care of his place." She tore the check slowly from its stub and passed it to Kelly.

"I thank you, ma'am, for the sandwich and the tea. I have one more job for the day then I'm done! I may even turn my phone off this evening." Kelly stood, gave the old woman a quick hug, and left before she started crying.

Kelly loaded her truck, marked her calendar, and drove to the Suttles' house. She needed to finish their gate now that their hard-to-find hardware had arrived. She'd built most of the fence already and poured a new sidewalk. This gate would finish it up nicely. She had the pieces cut already and some of it assembled.

On top a step-ladder on their patio, she found the UPS box with the hardware. It didn't take her long to finish the assembly and to hang it on its posts. Now to finish the last ten or so feet of fence.

As she worked, Kelly tried to keep her mind in the present, but it was difficult after her talk with Mrs. Maples. She missed her grandfather, especially now that she lived on—and owned—his land. Her thoughts of the property led her to remember why she was here in the first place.

Anna.

The woman who stole Kelly's heart six years ago. The same woman who had crushed it four years later. And that was a path she didn't want to go down.

"SHE'S NOT IN, Miss Walker. Would you like to leave a message?" The secretary, a cute little thing, was polite. But something felt odd about the conversation.

"When do you expect her back? Perhaps I'll wait." Kelly shifted her briefcase to the other hand.

"I don't know exactly when that'll be. Here's a message pad. I can leave your note in a sealed envelope."

"No, that's okay. I'll wait for her at home. If she does come in, please have her call." In the elevator on the way down, she went over the bits of the conversation that seemed odd. One, the secretary had called her Miss Walker, which was weird since they'd never met. Second, it had felt as if she were part of a rehearsed play. Third, she'd seen some things as she'd walked through the office.

In the cab ride home, Kelly's mind was filled with subjects she wished hadn't popped up. After paying the driver, she nodded to the doorman and used the stairs to their condominium. In the hallway, one of the maids stopped her and asked about a schedule change.

"I would have asked Miss Lehman, but she..." The woman paused, her head down.

"Yes, I know, she can be a bitch at times. It's fine to come in this Tuesday instead of Wednesday. I'll be around that morning anyway. Don't worry about it."

She and Anna had been through nine maids in their two years there. It wasn't as if they were slobs and the women couldn't stand it. It's because Anna was such a bitch to them, treating them as servants instead of subcontractors.

Kelly stood at the wet-bar in the living room and poured herself a generous shot of whiskey. It burned its way down her throat but she barely noticed. This was the third time in less than two weeks that Anna had not been at work when she said she was. There had been other times, all easily explained away then, but now Kelly wondered just what was going on. Deep down, she knew, but didn't want to touch it.

When Anna came home at one in the morning, she looked shocked to see Kelly, still in her work clothes, sitting on the sofa that faced the window overlooking the city. "Kelly, what are you still doing up?"

"Waiting for you."

"I had to work late at the office. We had meetings all day, and I had to catch up." She took off her high-heels and sat down next to Kelly.

"You've been at the office all day then? You must be brain dead from all that work."

"That would be a good description, yes."

Kelly finished her drink, her fifth of the night, and stood to get another. "*Cute little secretary you have now. Petite.*"

"*Yes, she is. She...*"

Kelly didn't turn around, didn't want to see Anna's face.

"*She's the best so far. She worked for another executive and is good at staving off the phone calls and arranging my schedule.*"

"*Oh? So she also keeps away unscheduled visitors by telling them you aren't there?*"

"*Yes, I suppose. I don't ask her how she does it.*" *She actually laughed.* "*I just tell her I don't want to be disturbed and I'm not. If only she typed faster, she'd be perfect.*"

"*Anna, stop it.*" *Kelly turned around.* "*I was at the office today. I saw your secretary. I saw the open door to your office. You weren't there. Were you in the meeting in a conference room? I could hear someone talking.*"

"*That must have been where I was. I —*"

"*Stop it, I said. I was there at four. There was no meeting in the conference room. I lied. I'm not as good a liar as you are, but I think I can learn by example.*"

Kelly didn't stop the well-manicured hand as it swung through the air and slapped her face. She didn't even flinch. "*You've always had this notion, this fantasy, that I was seeing someone else. You just fill in the blanks as needed.*"

"*Perhaps I once did, perhaps. But lately, especially now, you've started filling them in for me. Who is she, Anna? What does she have that I don't? What can she give you that I can't?*"

They stared at each other, just a few feet apart. "*I'm going to go stay with Brenda and Maggie. If you're sober enough in the morning, come over there and we'll talk.*" *Anna thrust her feet back into her shoes and grabbed her bag and keys as she left.*

KELLY SWUNG THE hammer too hard and hit her hand. Since no one was around, she let the words fly. The acid words quickly went from the pain in her hands to the pain in her soul. Anger she'd held in check for nearly two years started to trickle out, blinding her eyes with hot tears burning a trail down her cheeks. She needed to get a grip on herself, and get back to work. Somehow she finished the job, hit the last nail home, and loaded up the truck again.

KELLY SHUFFLED HER feet, her head down. Her mind, clouded by depression, couldn't focus. As she drifted through the home improvement store, she kept her hat pulled low to cover her face to make it hard for anyone to make eye contact. She willed her

body to breathe and to walk and to maneuver around the other customers. Even her brain's auto-pilot wasn't working and she had to
look up at the signs to find the right aisle in a store that was almost
her second home. Everything was a struggle—mud at her ankles,
mud in her brain. Her face hurt from holding back the tears, just as
it always did when she thought of Anna. Two years and she still
wasn't over it.

The hand that gripped the basket ached, and she switched it to
the other hand. Her gaze flickered over the shelves of parts, as she
realized she had no clue what she was there to get. She frantically
patted her pockets for a list of some sort; her brain told her she had
made one. There, in the front pocket of her t-shirt. No, the check
from Mrs. Maples.

"Kelly?" Someone touched her arm.

"What? Oh, hey, Nikki." She focused on Nikki Rogers, turning
all of her attention to something solid and strong.

"You okay? You look like shit." Nikki gripped her with both
hands.

"I took a trip down memory lane, and I'm still reeling from jet
lag." Her smile was fake, tilted to one side, her eyes still as dark as
before.

"Okay. Hey, I need to get something to eat. Come with me."
Nikki took her arm and pulled. It was easy for Kelly to follow, to
calmly tag along as if she fully intended to enjoy herself.

They got into Nikki's big red truck and went down the road to
a fast food place where Nikki ordered lunch and bought Kelly a
drink. They sat at a table, neither speaking, and just watched the
people around them. When Kelly stole a fry, Nikki slapped her
hand, pleased to see a smile.

"You're looking better."

"Thanks."

"Want to tell me about it?"

Kelly glanced at her friend, the only consistent and true friend
she had. They'd met as kids one summer, a bunch of them at the
lake swimming. Nikki had come over and punched Kelly in the
arm. They'd been friends ever since. She'd come to Ohio when
Anna had died to stand beside her. Looking back, Kelly knew she
wouldn't have survived if Nikki hadn't been there.

"I was thinking of Anna today. As in reliving the day before
she...died. I've not really thought about her and, well, what she did,
in a while."

"That would explain the look. You ever consider seeing a
shrink?"

"Yeah, I have. I saw one a while back when I first moved here.
I got overwhelmed by everything and needed help settling down,

you know?"

"I know exactly. Kelly, it's been two years. I think it's time you moved on. I know I say it like it's the easiest thing in the world, but, girlfriend, it's time." Nikki reached out to clasp Kelly's hand.

"Ha. You who haven't dated much since whatshername left?" Kelly felt better. Not completely herself again, but closer.

"Just ain't found anyone worth the effort of making room for her toothbrush." She let go of her hand and scooted the fries further away.

Kelly grunted, knowing exactly what Nikki meant. "Do you really think that if I just start dating again, I'll get over Anna's death?"

"Date, get a dog or cat, buy a plant, who knows? It'll give you something else to concentrate on. I have Spam and that room that I keep painting. You need something to be responsible for."

"How is that crazy dog of yours? I met Jo Spencer's Masco the other day at The Pride Center—big like Spam, but smart like Marley." Kelly stole another fry.

"I sure hope so! Spam, bless his heart, just ain't right."

"It's the name. You can't expect anything named Spam to be right in the head." She laughed as Nikki smacked her arm.

"He is Spam, as in unsolicited e-mail, you silly goat."

"Not everyone is a computer nerd like you. Some of us go to an actual library with actual books you can hold in your hand." Kelly grinned. This was an old argument of theirs. Stable ground at last.

"Get over it. You are just techno-illiterate and embarrassed about it. So why were you staring at plumbing parts so intently?"

"My brain froze. I couldn't remember why I was there and where my list was. "

"I need some plumbing parts, too, so why don't we go back there and get parted together?" Nikki reached over and touched her hand. "And, Kelly, friend, butch girls are allowed to cry. It's in the manual."

Chapter
Eight

FOR THE FIRST time in several nights, Kelly got a full eight hours of sleep. The last thing she wanted to do was move. She wiggled her toes and felt almost hedonistic with the electric blanket turned on.

She went over her schedule in her mind; there was nothing she could get out of but nothing had an actual scheduled time, either. She could sleep a bit longer. But the telephone rang. "Walker." She wanted to sound whiny but couldn't get herself to do it.

"Kelly, it's Kaye. Where are you? You sound weird."

"Would you believe in bed?" Kelly straightened out on the couch, keeping the blanket wrapped around her feet.

"No! Crap, you sick?"

"Not sick, I just hadn't had the gumption to move yet. What's up?"

"Something trivial. We wanted you to join us for dinner tonight."

She stretched again, her feet pressed against the arm of the sofa. "If I get everything done in time, sure. I'll call Net later to let her know my time frame."

"That'll do. What's your day going to be?"

"Um, following up on the roofers and some other smaller projects that can't be put off. And I need some drafting supplies."

"Sounds like fun. I'll be sitting in the office all day, reading expense reports and applications."

"Gross. With that picture in my head, I think I'll get up now. Tell Net I'll call her." She put the phone down and rolled off the couch. Even after a hot shower and a brisk hunt for matching socks, she was still yawning. It was going to be some day.

THE ROOFERS AT the Oak Street house were already at work when Kelly arrived. The supervisor said they hoped to get done that day, even if it meant working overtime. She thanked him, and after discussing how much damage they had found, she left. She needed drafting paper and went by the office supply place to pick some up. They were out again, but while she was there, she looked over their desks. None of them were quite what she wanted. Nothing fit her body right. One of the staff suggested she try the supply store the architects used. Since the suggested store was located downtown, Kelly had to park two blocks away. The street itself was red brick, and the sidewalk was off-white brick. Several of the stores had horse-hitching posts out front while others had bicycle racks. None had automobile parking, though.

"Clarence! What's an ugly guy like you doing in a high-class place like this?" She shut the door behind her and folded and stuffed the cap in her back pocket as she strolled up to Clarence Thompson, owner of a construction company in High Pond.

"Funny, Walker, very funny. What's an amateur like you doing here with the big boys?" Clarence's bear paw of a hand clasped her shoulder, squeezing hard enough to hurt.

"Looking for a desk. I need a better place to draw up plans." She tried not to wince, knowing if she did he would feel too good about it.

"I use that one, the dark one on the end, at the house. I don't have one at the warehouse, not enough room. Dang mess of an office."

"It's your own fault. File folders have a purpose in this world." She patted him on the back, a good loud thump, and headed over to the desks.

"May I help you?" A young salesman, his face closely shaven, his hair gelled into place, approached her. His white shirt was as crisp as his hair.

"I need a drafting desk, one I can use to do plans as well as sketches."

"Mechanical or architectural?"

"Mostly mechanical, but a good portion of architectural."

"I saw you talking with Mr. Thompson. He has this one." He put his hand on a huge dark mahogany desk. "It's high-end, has all the gadgets for the architect. I think for you it would be overkill. Here, though, these two are for inventors or smaller projects and not houses."

"Wow, big price difference." Her wallet was full, as was her savings account, but she couldn't justify spending that much money on a desk as fancy as Clarence's.

"Exactly. Personally, I like this one." He indicated one made of walnut. "It's adjustable, has plenty of storage, and best of all, it can be set facing out. The other side is just as good looking as the front."

"Good!" Getting a chair, Kelly sat down at the desk, and he led her through its long list of adjustments and capabilities. She felt as if she had a new toy. By the time she left, she had bought a desk, a lamp, a chair, a set of sketch pads in three different sizes, and better still, drafting paper. They would deliver the furniture in two days.

THE REST OF the day was routine, although her knees protested the number of ladders she'd climbed in one day: up one to change lights hanging from a cathedral ceiling; up another to put gutters along the sides of a shed; up a shorter one, numerous times, to hang a ceiling fan; and up yet another to install a new garage door motor.

At four, about to drive to the next project, she called Annette. "Afternoon, woman."

"Kelly, where are you? Still in bed?"

"I wish!" Kelly stuffed the calendar into her briefcase. "I got one more small job to do, then I'll go home and change into someone else."

"Oh good! I was getting tired of the other one. So what time will you or it be here?"

"Six-ish most likely. Will that be all right?"

"That will be fine, little girl."

"Anything I can bring?" She started the truck, cranking the heat up.

"Will you be downtown?"

"Yeah, close enough. Want some Growlers?" They often got the large bottles of beer from the Irish pub on Patton Avenue.

"Yes, um, get three of their IPA and whatever you want. Kaye can drop the bottles off tomorrow on her way to work."

KELLY DROVE UP the long driveway with the truck's window rolled down, so she could smell the crisp air. A group of four goats ran alongside the truck, following the fence line to their barn. Kelly had showered and changed into her best jeans, a grey turtleneck tucked into the jeans, and her nearly new leather loafers. The bottles of beer were in a wooden box in the back since too much trash was on the floor to put them up front. Besides, it kept them cold riding in the back.

When she topped the last hill, she saw a different car parked near the house. She knew it from somewhere, but couldn't place it. She saw Marley and a little girl running back from the hen house, and remembered where she had seen it. Kelly had been looking forward to seeing her friends, having a nice quiet evening with them.

Alone. She had completely forgotten the Owens woman was here.

"Miss Walker!" Lucy ran up to the truck as soon as Kelly put it in park.

"Hey, kid." With the box of beer in her arms, she and Lucy walked toward the house.

"I just saw a hen lay an egg!"

"Yeah? Did you touch it?" She was disappointed she wouldn't be alone with her friends, but she still liked this kid too much to stay that way.

"Uh...."

"It's okay if you did, as long as you didn't leave a dent."

"No, not a dent in it. It was kinda soft," Lucy whispered, as if her mother could hear her confession.

"They are. Weird, huh?" She stood aside as Lucy pulled open the door to the house.

"Kelly! You're early." Kaye took the box from her and put it on the kitchen counter.

"By five minutes, yeah. Want me to go sit outside until then?"

"Nah, 'sall right. I'll let you get away with it just this once. The other two adults are in the living room." Kaye handed her a glass of ice tea.

"I'll stay in here with you for a bit."

"Why? Afraid?"

Kelly glanced over at Lucy who was looking through the glass door of the oven. "I'm not afraid of anything."

"Right. Listen, go on in there. Annette won't hurt you." Kaye winked but tried to keep a smile from forming. It didn't work.

"Thanks, friend," Kelly growled and took her drink to the other room. She wasn't sure why, but she didn't want to go in there where Grace Owens was.

"Kelly! You made it." Annette was in her recliner, tilted half-way back.

"Yeah, all cleaned up, too." Glancing over at Grace sitting on an ottoman in front of the fire, elbows on her knees, facing Annette, Kelly leaned against the wall. "Miss Owens, nice to see you again."

"Nice to see you, too. Thank you for bringing our stuff over yesterday."

"Not a problem." Kelly stood there, near the kitchen doorway, feeling uncomfortable. One hand was stuffed in her pocket, and the other held the ice tea glass.

"Have a seat on the couch, Kelly, and take a load off your feet. How did your day go?" Annette waved her hand toward the long oversized couch.

Kelly bent and kissed Annette's forehead. "It went well. I spent a wad of money today." She sat down, putting one ankle on her knee.

"Yeah? What did you get me?" Annette loved to tease Kelly mercilessly.

"I got *me* a drafting desk. It's huge and exactly what I need." Kelly sipped her tea, feeling a bit more relaxed. "They'll be delivering it in a couple of days. I'll put it in the shop."

"What types of plans do you draw up?" Grace asked from her seat ottoman.

"Different projects I am working on. For instance, the waste system I just finished for Annette. I did those hunched over a work table."

"Is that the miscellaneous fees on the invoice?" Kaye was standing in the doorway.

"Yeah, that and the chips and soda I drank while drawing them." Kelly grinned, finally feeling relaxed enough to know she would have a nice evening after all.

"Make sure she doesn't overcharge you for the trash can she bought the other day to catch the water." Grace liked this ribbing the friends were engaging in.

"Yes, thank you, I'll have to check up on that." Kaye pretended to write a note on her palm. "Dinner is about ready. Are we eating in the kitchen or the dining room, dear?"

"In the kitchen, it's cozier." Annette turned off her heating pad. "Kelly, come push my seat upright, please."

"When are you going to get one of those powered recliners?"

"Someday. But why spend the money as long as I keep you and Kaye around?" She didn't have to ask Kelly to help her into her wheelchair; her friend was already braced to do it. "Grace, do you mind going to help Kaye set the table? I have something to bitch about to Kelly."

Grace laughed and stood. "No problem. Just don't hurt her, Annette. She seems so fragile."

Annette laughed and watched Grace leave the room. "Kelly, are you okay, my friend?"

"Nikki called you?" Kelly took Grace's seat on the ottoman.

"Yes, about something else, but mentioned it then."

"I'm okay, Net. I worked hard to push Anna from my mind, to not think about her and...what she did. But I started remembering things again the other day and just...I...I didn't handle it well."

"Going back to the psychiatrist?"

"Yes, I called today and see her tomorrow. I know it's been two years, but it still seems like yesterday, you know?"

"No, I don't. But I know you. I've learned how you tick. You're tough — but only on the outside." Annette took Kelly's big calloused hands in her smaller smooth ones. "It's time you started to live again. Anna killed herself, not you."

"I know. And I believe you're right. I'm feeling itchy inside, as if I've been sitting still too long, and now I'm ready to go." Kelly stood and patted her friend's shoulder. "Let's go join them in the kitchen before they start putting a glass to the door."

THE KITCHEN WAS large enough to hold a table that easily seated six. The smell of the stew and homemade baked bread lingered in the air despite them eating almost all of it. The table had been partially cleared, leaving the still-warm bread sitting in the middle, each of them nibbling on slices as they talked.

"So these are called what?" Grace poured herself another mug of beer from the glass jar.

"Growlers. Jack of the Wood makes them. They're a pub in downtown Asheville. Great place, wonderful beer and smoke-free. You take the bottles back and either get a refund or get more beer, and it's cheaper since you already own the bottle." Kaye answered her before tipping back her own glass.

"Ah. I've not been downtown much. I go to work then come home to take care of the brat."

"Hey! I'm not a brat! I'm a holy terror." Lucy's defense just made the adults, including Kelly, laugh harder.

"So how's school, Lucy?" Kaye finally managed to say.

"Good. I joined the chess team."

"So that was your chess set by your door?" Kelly asked, putting down her empty glass.

"Yep. You made a risky move. I studied it and figured out what you were doing, though. I'll have to try it someday." Lucy referred to when Kelly had taken two turns on the board when she was over to fix the leak.

"Oh dear, we've lost them, I'm afraid. Let's go to the living room and set up a board. Then they'll be quiet." Annette rolled away from the table.

Chapter
Nine

THE ROOFERS WERE done on the second day, only using two hours of overtime to complete it. Kelly went over early the next morning to check it over from the inside and decide how she was going to do the ceiling. The wallboard around the door, especially above it, was already forming mold and would need to be replaced. The smell of it was in the air, causing Kelly to sneeze.

She had a lot of work to do there. She hadn't planned it and would need to look over her scheduled jobs to see how it was going to be done. Maybe she could come in the afternoons or evenings, and that would mean she'd have to work with someone home.

Why does that concept bother me so much? It's not like it would be the first time.

After taking the tarp down, she used her knife to poke the joists to test them for hardness. She didn't think any of them would need to be replaced; the roofer would have mentioned it. But she never liked to assume.

Is it the mother or the daughter who makes me so nervous? Is nervous even the right word?

Using the claw of her hammer, she removed a section of drywall. The insulation under it would have to be replaced. An inspection of the door frame revealed it was in good shape, although she needed to check how square it still was.

It's the mother. I've been thinking about stepping out of my walled-up self, and right there is a pretty woman. Is there an attraction there? Am I looking at her as the first fish I catch right out of prison?

She'd need to tell Kaye her plans and get her permission before she started. She also needed to not be late for her counseling appointment.

DR. SUSAN TOWER leaned back in her desk chair to read over the session notes for her next client. Soft music came from hidden speakers, adding to the comfortable setting of her office. She wanted her clients to feel relaxed, more like they were talking to a friend than to a psychiatrist. The room was arranged so that there was a possibility of six different seating options, depending on the client's choice.

She had not been surprised to see Kelly Walker's name, although it had been a while since her last visit. Dr. Tower finished reading the notes, already having a good guess why the woman was there. She liked Kelly, liked the way she thought things through, the way she saw problems in front of her. But sometimes Kelly could get stuck on one thing and not get past it.

The waiting room, relaxed like the office, was more of a nice parlor than anything else. Dr. Tower glanced at the clock and knew Kelly should be out there by now, signed in with the secretary shared with two other psychiatrists.

She put her glasses on the desk and went to the door. "Kelly? Come on in."

Dr. Tower recognized the broad-shouldered woman who stood. Kelly put a magazine down on the coffee table. In the other hand was the baseball cap Dr. Tower knew would be there, reminded by the notes. "I haven't seen you in a while. How are you doing?"

"I'm doing good. Well, I was. I thought maybe you could help lead me through some thinking I've got going on in my head." Kelly sat at the end of the couch and moved the throw pillow out of her way.

"Okay, tell me what's going on in that head of yours." She listened as Kelly told her of the episode in the home improvement store and of her time spent with Nikki. Dr. Tower interrupted her several times to get Kelly to admit what she was feeling at that moment, what was running around in her mind then. "And this has led to the thoughts you have now? And just what, exactly, are those thoughts?"

Kelly looked out the window, watching a bird cleaning its beak by beating it back and forth on a branch. "I want to move on, to let Anna go. I want to let my anger go and get on with my life."

"It's been two years since she died, and you two were together for how long?"

"Four years." Another bird came, making the first one leave. This one was holding a sunflower seed in one foot while it banged its head up and down, using its beak as a tool to crack the shell.

"As you know, anger is a valid emotion to have with the death of a spouse. Given the circumstances of her death, anger is even more common."

WHEN KELLY CALLED Brenda's house the next day, they were surprised that Kelly thought Anna was there. "If she was supposed to come here last night, she didn't. Did you two have a fight?"

"Yeah, you could call it that. If you hear from her, call me."

Kelly hung up the phone and stared at the window. She'd been up all night, drinking and pacing. Knowing Anna hadn't gone where she said she was going made her feel like giving up. She stretched out on the sofa and fell asleep.

No one heard from Anna all day, not even her secretary, although she didn't come right out and say it. She said, "Miss Lehman has not checked in yet today." Kelly wasn't worried; Anna was most likely at this other woman's house, whoever she was.

At eleven that night, the police came and knocked on the door.

At midnight, Kelly called her friend Nikki down in North Carolina.

Three days and a lot of disturbing events later, Kelly and Nikki were driving south, hauling a trailer full of Kelly's tools and very few other things from the condo. Anna's will had left everything to her parents, the people who had declared her dead many years before. Choosing not to fight it, Kelly had taken only what was definitely hers and left.

"IT'S NOT ONLY that she's dead, but that we were living a lie. She had two other lovers, not including me. Our alleged friends knew but didn't say anything—some because they didn't see anything wrong with it, some because they didn't think it was their business. And others because, well, if I was stupid enough to not see it happening..." Kelly watched the bird outside singing its little heart out, but she couldn't hear it. There was too much between them.

"That you deserved what you got." Dr. Tower finished Kelly's sentence.

"Exactly." The bird stopped singing and sat there, all fluffed up and looking around.

"That must have felt pretty crappy. Not only was the love of your life dead, but you find out you weren't the love of her life in return. A lot of changes happened all at once, including you packing up and moving. If I remember correctly, you moved in with your parents for a few months then moved here. How's that been?"

"Good. I have several really close friends. My business has taken off—almost too fast." Kelly turned to face the counselor. "I'm uncomfortable with my life, or rather my life outside of my work. I should be arrested for the abuse I put that Kelly through."

"There's no dividing line between you, the crafter, and you, the person. You might want one there, but it doesn't exist."

"Sure it does. I'm sure that when you go home, you cease to be the shrink, and instead, you are the private person. There's a difference."

"There's a difference, yes, but there's no line. Look at it this way, you drive down Patton Avenue, and somewhere along the way, it becomes Smokey Park Highway. And, at one point, it was Highways 19 and 23 at the same time. It's the same road; it just has different names. There's no line. There's no stop sign where we make a choice to go one way or the other."

Kelly stood and began pacing between the couch and the window. "You're saying I am the same person, I just change names. Does it matter? Isn't that the same?"

"Not the way your mind sees it. You see a definite clear-cut line. A gap between you, owner of Around-To-It Services, and Kelly Walker, the one who was made a fool of."

"Okay, I agree with that."

"There's no line between the two yous. When I am home, I don't turn into an inconsiderate bitch who doesn't take other people's feelings into account. Many times, my kids have fussed at me for counseling them when all they wanted was to talk."

"In other words, I can't keep one of me separate from the other." Kelly stopped and took her hands out of her pockets, feeling pain as she released her clenched fists.

"Right. Why can't the at-home Kelly think like the fix-it Kelly? Why can't she look at the situation and take it apart, just like the other Kelly does?" She paused, watching Kelly's face. "Just why are you here in my office?"

"I want...I want to move on, to make Anna go away. I want to remember the good times we had and not just our last few months. I want to have that again, that deep friendship you only get with a partner. I want to get on with my life, you know?"

"Yes, I do know. My husband is my best friend. I don't know what I would do without that level of friendship." Dr. Tower reached under the side table, which was actually a mini-fridge, and pulled out two sodas. "Here, we need a stiff drink."

"Ah, good vintage." Kelly sat back down, her frustration leaking away.

"I thought you'd like it." They paused to open the cans. "Now, why is it you feel you can't get that kind of friend?"

"Who would want me with that ghost over my shoulder, whispering in my ear how foolish I am?"

"No one hears that ghost but you. No one thinks you're a fool. No one sees the fix-it Kelly as a fool, so why should they see the other as one? Hasn't anyone asked you out?"

"Yeah, several women. But they don't know me. They only know Kelly the Fix-it Lady. They don't know Kelly the Fool. Whom, I might add, I know all too well." Kelly raised her hand to stop the doctor from repeating herself. "I know that Kelly doesn't exist except in my mind, but she's still there. I see life through her eyes."

"I think that what happened to you is something a lot of people fear will happen to them. Some, those who knew you then, saw it happening to you and Anna. They didn't want to become involved because it would make it even more real. If it could happen to fine Anna and big strong Kelly, it can happen to them."

Kelly stared at her soda can and heard the carbonation react as she swirled the contents. "It was real. I loved a woman so much that I shut off my own security alarms."

"Exactly. There's no fault in that. To love someone means you have to trust them. I think, Miss Kelly, what you need is to get out of your house and go out somewhere other than a friend's house or your shop or a job. You need to go to a bar or to a softball game, or wherever else you lesbos hang out. You need to flirt, put forth your best charms, and see what happens."

"Wherever you lesbos hang out? Why, Dr. Towers!" Kelly chuckled, watching the psychiatrist's face redden slightly.

"You know what I mean." Dr. Tower watched the grinning Kelly again turn her head to look out the window. "You've said several times now 'get on with my life.'"

"I feel as if I've been on auto-pilot for the past two years, and that I haven't lived, really lived." Kelly rested her cheek on her fist and at last gave Dr. Tower all of her attention. "I'm starting to not want to go home to an empty house. Knowing she was never in it helps, but still, it's empty. I want something to look forward to."

"What was it your friend said? That you needed to be responsible for something alive?"

Kelly grinned. "Yeah, that's about what she said. She said she has a dog that keeps her going. I don't know if a dog is the answer, but it's something to care for outside of myself. The stuff I fix belongs to someone else. I'm removed from that by several layers. Sometimes, even my own house feels as if it belongs to someone else. I want to feel."

"You've not dated since her death?"

"No, not at all. I went to a bar once in Johnson City, but I just sat out in the parking lot. It felt like I was cheating on her—which is really ironic."

"Do you feel that way now? That if you dated someone, you'd feel as if you were cheating? Even considering what a bitch she was?"

"I don't think so. It's more that she is dead. It still feels as if her body hasn't even cooled yet, and I'm on the prowl already."

"It's been two years. She's quite cool by now. If she were alive, do you think you would have held on to being a fool for so long?"

"No. I would have somewhere to direct the anger besides inward on myself."

"Why don't you give dating a try anyway? Why not go out to dinner with someone, see how it feels?"

"When I go, who am I?" Kelly couldn't help but grin.

Dr. Tower put her head back to stare at the ceiling. "Kelly, let's try this again." She looked back down. "Be Kelly the Fool, whoever you think she is or isn't. But look at the world as Kelly the Fix-it Lady. Or, better yet, just go as both of you! One of you will come out the winner of this non-existent wrestling match. You'll make an appointment to see me in two weeks, and I want you to do this before then. Come back and tell me what happened, okay?"

SHE LAY ON the wood floor to use her square and level on the lower corners of the door frame. The door itself was propped against the wall near her feet. Usually it never bothered her to be in a house with the homeowner or renter not there, but this house was different. She felt as if she were trespassing. She never noticed the pictures on the walls in other people's homes. All she saw was the thing to be fixed or put in or taken out. But she saw the artwork on the bathroom door and in the living room; the pictures along the wall of Lucy when she was younger, and even a few of what must have been Grace at about the same age. She remembered there used to be some of Lucy's artwork stuck to the refrigerator before it all had to be put away until the roof was done.

Coming here right after her psychiatrist visit was probably not a good idea. She wanted to be alone, maybe sit and watch some calming cows. But she also knew her schedule and knew how much she needed to do.

Lying there on the floor, eyeballing the level, Kelly began to sing, trying to fill the silence.

> In Scarlet town, where I was born,
> There was a fair maid dwellin',
> Made every youth cry well-a-day;
> Her name was Barb'ry Allen.
>
> 'Twas in the merry month of May,
> The green buds they were swellin',
> Young Jimmy Grove on his death-bed lay,
> For love of Barb'ry Allen.

"I hadn't heard that one in years."

Kelly jumped, hitting her head on the wall hard enough to dislodge a chunk of drywall from the hole she'd made earlier. As the piece came down, she sat up and grabbed it before it hit her or the floor.

"You scared the shit out of me."

Grace wanted to just rip-roar a good laugh. Butch Kelly, all covered in drywall dust and sweat, sprawled there on the floor, the crumbling piece in one hand, rubbing the side of her head with the other.

But it was Kelly who started laughing first. She started with a chuckle, a low rumble that slowly grew to be a full laugh. Grace joined her and had to lean against the counter for support.

"You looked so funny standing there." Kelly wiped her face with a bandanna from her back pocket. "You looked surprised and downright tickled."

"I wanted to laugh, too, you know. But I was afraid I'd hurt those butch girl feelings."

"Those feelings ain't been exposed enough to get hurt in a long time."

Grace saw the flash of sadness in Kelly's eyes. "I see. I'm sorry I scared you. I thought you'd heard me calling out from the living room."

"No, I get involved in my work and lose track of what's going on around me." She stood, dusted off her pants, and tossed the drywall into the trash can.

They were silent for a few seconds, an awkwardness forming between them.

"What needs to be done?" Grace turned away from Kelly, getting a paper cup from the cabinet.

"I'm thinking these fugly ceiling tiles need to come down. I'll put up more drywall to cover up the insulation. The wall around the door needs to be replaced, too."

"When will you be able to do it?" She handed Kelly a cup of water.

"That's the problem. This wasn't on my schedule. I was thinking..." Kelly tipped the cup back and took a big gulp.

Grace waited, finally turning to look at Kelly. "Yes?"

"I was thinking of working in the afternoons and evenings. But that would mean I'd be here, disturbing your life." Kelly looked up, too, meeting Grace's eyes.

"I don't think that would be a problem. Lucy does her homework in the living room or her bedroom." Grace couldn't break the eye contact with Kelly. The pull was too strong.

"Your kitchen would be taken over, you know." Kelly used her

internal safety mechanisms to turn around and rehang the back
door. But that didn't take long enough, so she started cleaning up
the mess she'd made.

"I think I can live with that. How long would it take?"

"A few days, three maybe. I'd start Thursday, giving me the
weekend to finish." Kelly swept the floor, pushing the dust and
chunks into a pile. She jumped when Grace's hand touched her
shoulder.

"I'm sure you need to be elsewhere. I can do that." She tried to
take the broom from her hands.

"I got it." Kelly wouldn't let go.

"Then why don't you hold the dust pan?"

"Okay." Kelly felt strange, almost like when she first started
living the life of a real lesbian, not one hidden away. This being
both Kellys, the good one and the bad one at the same time, was not
going to work. She squatted on the floor and held the pan while
Grace finished sweeping the pile together and onto the pan.

"That's what *Sesame Street* calls 'co-op-er-a-tion.'"

"I guess you saw a lot of that, huh?"

"Yeah, that and that purple dinosaur."

"My condolences."

Grace smiled, looking again into Kelly's eyes.

"I need to get going. I have one other place to be before I can
call it a day. It was good seeing you again." Kelly gathered her
tools, backed out of the room, and almost ran to her truck.

Chapter
Ten

THE NEXT MORNING, Grace buttoned her jacket before she locked the front door and walked to the car. The old Ford's heater hadn't worked in several years. Neither had the radio nor the back window on the driver's side. The door creaked and fell a half inch or more as she swung it open, needing three slams before it remained closed. She twisted the key, the motor turned over a few times, well within the normal routine. She paused, and then turned the key again. The big 351 Windsor engine would need a few rollovers to get warmed up anyway.

After the fourth try, Grace knew something was wrong. The old car had been not running right for several weeks. She suspected the long drive from upstate Illinois to North Carolina had been more than it could handle.

She rested her forehead on the steering wheel and considered her options. She gathered her lunch bag and keys and started to walk the three blocks to the bus stop.

"THANK YOU FOR coming over on such short notice." The woman sat in her wheelchair at the top of a ramp. "Annette just gushed with good words about you. She said you work fast."

"Yep. And I can see what you need. How did it happen?" Kelly took out her pocket knife and used the blade to poke at the wood surface. The last three boards of the switchback ramp had fallen through, the wood rotted.

"I came up with Jake right behind me. It didn't collapse while I was going across, although I did hear a pop or snap. But when he stepped on it, it broke through. I think I may have been mostly on the support beams."

"Is he okay?" Kelly looked up.

"Yes, he's fine. He's quick on his feet." The young woman turned to pat the large black German Shepherd, his head sticking out from the open doorway.

"I think this part just plain rotted through. I suspect the builder didn't clear out underneath it enough for drainage and, over time, the water just did its thing." She straightened up and walked along the side of the ramp. She handed up the section of wood. "I'm Kelly Walker, by the way."

"I'm Rain Moon. My parents were hippies." She grinned down at Kelly and examined the spongy wood. "So what are we to do?"

"I was thinking about that on the way here. You know there's that composite wood, plastic and wood really, that never rots? They're using it on beach ramps and in other wet locations. I was thinking it would also make good wheelchair ramp material. It's more expensive than regular decking, though. But I could use it to replace the last few feet. Then we'd know the basic price, and you could save up. I can finish the rest of the ramp if you like it enough."

"I've heard of that. Is it slick?" Rain leaned her arms on the railing, her chin on her wrists.

"No, it's not. Wood gets fuzzy with mold and that makes it slick, but this stuff won't mold, so as long as it's put in right, it should be just fine. I'll check the remaining parts of the ramp to make sure there aren't other bad places. Usually the bottom end is the part to rot first." Kelly, looking up at the woman, realized Rain was cute, sexy even. She wondered how old she was.

"When it rains, the water stands there. It drains away after the rain stops, though."

"I'll need to take a look at that as well." Kelly looked at the roof and the ground leading up to the foundation of the double-wide trailer.

"Then let's go ahead and use this new stuff. Can't hurt, right? I may need to borrow money from my sister later in the month, but it's not like I am blowing it on on-line poker, right?"

Kelly laughed with her. "I've got to go to my toy store to get the lumber. You need to come down from there, or are you okay for the time it'll take me to finish this?"

"I think I'll be okay locked in my tower. Jake may need to go out before you're done, though. I can let him out the front if you can take him around back to the fence."

"No problem. I'll be back in a bit."

GRACE GOT THE tub of electronic component boards and took them to her station. Her job was to solder on the larger parts that the assembly line couldn't handle. She had two hundred boards in this run, the tub held the first fifty.

The boards—she had no idea what they were for—first went

through the assembly line, the folks put the electronic components on by hand, bending the ends to hold them in place with a bizarre tool called a banger. From there, the boards went through a machine that soldered those parts in place. This left sharp points on the underneath of the board and kept Grace's fingertips tender.

For her, the work was a no-brainer; she found a routine and sank into it. As each board was done, she checked it over before putting it into another tub. When she had twenty-five done, she took them to the washer. Jerry, the older man who ran that machine, was busy elsewhere, so she laid the boards on the conveyor grids, getting the twelfth down just as the first reached the other end.

"You taking over my job?" Jerry grinned, took the first board from the wash and stood it in another tub. He had to shout over the noise of the washer.

"No way, man. I do enough washing at home."

"I'll finish running them through. Thanks for starting them."

She laughed when he winked at her as she returned to her own workspace.

"Is this station in use?" A woman spoke behind her.

Grace turned to find a woman with a smaller set of boards. "Not on the day shift."

"I use it in the third shift." She sat down and immediately went to work. They sat side by side, each doing their own work until the first lunch buzzer sounded off.

"They said I had second lunch. You?" The new woman stretched, flexing impressive bicep muscles.

"Second as well." Grace stretched her fingers, tired from holding the heavy boards, and the parts she was putting on it. One of her fingertips was bleeding from one stab too many from the sharp points. The new woman passed her an adhesive bandage from her tool box.

"My name's Deb. What's yours?"

"Grace. Thanks." She put the strip bandage on her finger, wrapping it with a new piece of green gauze tape.

When the lunch buzzer rang again, they turned off their solder irons and went to eat. Deb joined her at the table to eat heated soup from the machines.

"Want some of my soup? I bought more than enough."

"No thanks, I got my PB and J right here." Grace lifted the wax paper covered square.

"Ah, the old standby." They sat in silence, each focused on her meal. Deb drank some of her soda. "You don't talk much, do you?"

"Nope." But Grace did smile a little bit.

"There now, that's more like it." Deb ate more of her soup. "By the way, some folks don't like to sit or work with me because I'm gay. You don't mind, do you?"

"Nope." The smile was bigger.

"I thought so."

KELLY'S LEFT KNEE hurt from the stones under the ramp. Her right hand ached from a whack of the hammer and from when the drill slipped off a screw. The skin wasn't torn, but the double bruising would be interesting later.

Jake lay a safe four feet away. She'd made him back up when he'd come over one time too many to stick his wet tongue in her ear; he was used to such commands and had obeyed beautifully. He would get up, wander the yard, and return to the same spot and lie back down.

Kelly drove the last of the screws through the composite plank into the joist. She stomped around on it to test if for bounce, and then began putting her tools away.

"I heard the tool boxes closing. You're done!" Rain came out onto the top landing.

"Yep. Come on down and give it a try. I'll catch you." Kelly stepped up and braced herself at the bottom of the ramp. Rain maneuvered into place and came down. The switchback slowed her speed some as she leveled off and turned to continue down, coming to the concrete pad at the bottom and stopping.

"It didn't feel much different from the rest. I'm surprised."

"Good! It's the first time I've used it on a ramp, so I was assuming it would work. I've used it on decks and steps, but not a sloped surface. Here's the invoice. I stapled a business card to the top. When you're ready, just give me a buzz, and I'll replace it for you. I checked the rest of the ramp, and it's all fine. The end must've gone first because of the water. Next time it rains, I'll try to remember to swing by, but it depends on where I am."

"No problem. Hold on a bit while I write the check."

"SO, WANT TO go out for coffee or...something?" Deb walked with Grace toward the time clock.

"No, I can't, I have to get home before my daughter."

They clocked out, the loud thunk of the stamp signaled the end of another long day. It had a steady rhythm as the line of workers placed their time cards in the horizontal slot.

Deb started toward the parking lot, but Grace turned toward the street to go to the bus stop. "Hey, you take the bus?"

"Yeah, my car wouldn't start this morning." Grace walked

backwards down the sidewalk.

"Want a ride home? I'm a safe driver." Deb jangled her keys.

"Well..."

"Ah, come on. I'll be nice."

"Okay, thanks, why not?" Grace followed Deb up the walk to the parking lot. Deb's car was a relatively new car, a Mercedes something, and the inside of the car screamed luxury. Not that Grace didn't like it, but it made her nervous, afraid she would break or stain something.

As they drove away, Deb turned the audio on. It was a CD of soft music, the kind one listens to while drinking wine with candles lit nearby. Grace found the music annoying. On her way home, she usually listened to rock music from her boom box on the passenger seat, letting out all the frustrations of the day.

After rattling on about how great the car was, Deb finally got around to involving Grace in the conversation. "Where do you live?"

"Oak Street in the Montford area, between Acorn and Pecan. Take the Haywood Road exit." She shifted in the seat and made squeaking noises on the leather.

"What odd street names. I guess they ran out after a while." Deb shifted the car like a pro, smooth and even.

"Seems like it, doesn't it?"

"So it's just you and your daughter? Where's her dad?"

Grace took a deep breath. She hated that type of questions. "He left before she was born."

"Bummer for you. What's the kid's name?"

"Lucy. She's real smart, gets straight A's and loves to—"

"How about I take you out to dinner one night?" Deb sped up on the highway.

"Um, we'll see." Grace thought back to the last time someone had taken her out for dinner.

"I'd be honored. Do you know someone who can watch the kid?"

"We'll see."

Chapter
Eleven

AS KELLY DROVE from Rain Moon's house toward the house on Oak Street, she thought about asking Miss Moon out for dinner. She was cute, seemed nice and polite enough. Why not?

She put the truck behind Grace's car. She took her briefcase in with her as well as her multi-purpose tool box. Lucy opened the front door as soon as Kelly reached the porch.

"Hey, Lucy. How was school today?"

"Good. I tried your chess move and beat Joe!"

"Way cool! Congratulations. That must've felt good." Kelly knelt on the floor and clasped Lucy's shoulder.

"Yeah, it did. I said it was the Walker Maneuver, and they bought it."

"Heh. That's a good one. I gotta get to work, kid. I'm going to be making a mess in the kitchen, so you might want to stay in here, okay?"

"Yep. I have to finish homework anyway."

Kelly looked up to see Grace folding laundry on the couch. "Oh, hey. I didn't see you sitting there." She stood and paused by the end of the couch at the kitchen doorway. "Is it all right if I get started?"

"Of course, go right ahead. Let me know if you need help." Grace went back to her task at hand.

Kelly had to return to the truck to get the ladder, but she returned through the back door, so she wouldn't disturb Lucy. She went up the ladder and peered into the hole in the ceiling. She took a good look at how the dropped ceiling framework would best be taken down. She came down the ladder and turned to see Grace in the kitchen, leaning against the counter.

"What will you need to do?"

"The dropped ceiling comes down first, then its framework. That'll take up most of the afternoon. I'm saving the wall around the door until last since it'll be the messiest. That, and it will stay clean."

"Sounds like you almost know what you're doing." Grace grinned and enjoyed the smile on Kelly's face, too.

"Almost." She used an old broom handle to poke the light-weight ceiling tiles up, causing them to come down so that she could arrange them in a neat stack against the wall. With each tile was a layer of dust, dead bugs, and bits of debris from the roof repair. Kelly took the bandanna from her pocket and wrapped it around her nose and mouth. She had a real mask out in the truck; she just didn't want to go get it for something this small. Grace used one of the painting tarps to cover the stove and table, and she put a fan in the window.

When she had all the tiles down, Kelly started on the frame-work, but soon became frustrated since most of the screw heads were stripped. She wanted to use words someone as young as Lucy shouldn't hear.

"What will you do with these?" Grace was near the stack of ceiling panels.

"I'll take them to my shop then on to the dump on my next run."

"I can take them to your truck."

"I can get them. Are they in your way?"

"No, I just thought I'd do something to help."

"Um, well, if you just have to do it, use the duct tape in my box there. Wrap five at a time into bundles. It makes them easier to handle. And they have insulation on them, so be careful."

GRACE OPENED THE brushed metal tool box and was immediately impressed. The contents were neatly arranged, each item having its own place. The duct tape was against the edge, a thin piece of wood between it and the rolls of electrical tape. Next were pliers and snips, each with a different colored handle. Then there were several baby food jars containing nuts, bolts, and screws. Attached to the inside of the lid was a box cutter, a small dentist's mirror, and a small flashlight with an extension that allowed the light to be pinpointed.

Grace used the box cutter to cut the duct tape and wrapped the tiles into bundles. When she was done, she made sure she put the two items back in the toolbox in their correct positions. Wearing a long-sleeved shirt she had worn the day before, she carried the first two bundles out to Kelly's vehicle. Once again, she was impressed. The truck bed, narrower because of the outside boxes, was well organized, too. The tools were standing upright, held in place by either PVC pipe or black rubber bungee cords. There were two different kinds of brooms, two different shovels, a hoe, and a rake.

There were several five-gallon buckets containing odds and ends, most of which she couldn't identify.

She was tempted to open one of the side boxes to see if they were as organized. On her final trip, she peeked inside the cab and was shocked. As neat as the rest of Kelly's truck and tools were, the cab was equally chaotic. The floorboard of the passenger side was so full of trash it was level with the bench seat. The dash was stuffed with napkins and french fry boxes. Grace was at first stunned but realized it was just another twist to the complexity that was Kelly.

INSIDE THE HOUSE, Kelly got the last of the framework down and began bundling the pieces together. When Grace came back from her last load, Kelly asked if she could go back out and bring in one of the buckets. It was rare for her to ask a customer for help, but she was on the floor, surrounded by piles of metal pieces. Asking for help was well within reason.

It took Grace just a few seconds to return with the bucket. "Wow. The ceiling looks huge now. Even larger with that big gaping hole up into the attic."

"Yeah. It'll still look big when I get the drywall up. I'll put it right on the edge of the beams. It'll be about two foot higher than the dropped ceiling." She used the measuring tape to point it out. "I guess you don't want to know those details."

"Actually, I like to know. I like learning these things. That way, I can do my own repairs and not have to pay someone like you to do it for me."

"You'd call me to come fix whatever you broke in the process. You ever do drywall before?"

"No. I've punched a fist through it, though; does that count?" Grace looked at her left fist, flexing it as she remembered the event.

"Ha. I've got one up on you. Never try to punch through drywall where the two-by-four is."

"Ouch! Is that how you got your bruise?" Grace pointed to Kelly's hand where the drill had hit it earlier.

"Oh, I forgot about that. No, I had a fight with a drill." The knot from earlier was gone, but the bruising was spectacular.

"Hazard of the job. You ought to take your boss to OSHA."

"I should. She's a real bitch, though." She started putting her tools away, uncomfortable with the ease of the conversation.

"By the way, nice vehicle."

"Think so? It's showing its age, poor thing." Kelly got the last of the scrap pieces together and put the smaller pieces, the screws, and other bits into the bucket. Once the floor was clear, she began taking the dismantled framework out to the truck. The framework pieces were heavy enough to hold themselves in place, but she used two cinder blocks to weigh the ceiling tiles down.

"I've got to bring the drywall tomorrow, and I'd like to stack it in here, in that corner. It'll be twelve or thirteen four-by-eight sheets." Kelly stood in the kitchen, looking big and imposing to Grace.

"No problem." She handed her a paper cup of water. "About the same time?"

"Maybe a little earlier. What time are you home?"

"Normally, around two-thirty, but if I have to take the bus again, it won't be until almost three-thirty."

"Bus? What's wrong with your car?" Kelly tipped the cup back, drinking all the water in just a few gulps. The dust and mold from the ceiling always made her throat dry.

"It's been having trouble starting, and this morning, it didn't start at all. It' getting old, so I'm not surprised. I think I'm its fifth owner." Grace shrugged it off, not overly concerned whenever the old thing acted up.

"Good luck with it. It sounds like the starter's dying. Anyway, I still have Kaye's key. If I get here before you, I'll let myself in, if that is all right?"

"Sure, just keep your hands off the silver." Grace took Kelly's cup and refilled it.

"Yeah, I'll do that." She downed the second cup of water just as quickly as she had the first and picked up her toolbox to leave.

"Miss Walker? My desk is all wobbly, and I'm afraid my 'scope will slide off." Lucy stood in the doorway.

"I'll take a look at it. Most of the time it's just that one leg needs a support underneath."

"Kelly, you don't have to do that. I'm sure you have somewhere else to be." Grace flashed her daughter "the look."

"No problem, it'll just take a minute." Kelly put her toolbox down on the floor near the doorway to the living room and followed Lucy to her room. Against the wall near the window was the smallest desk Kelly had ever seen. Its height was normal, but its depth and length were almost comical.

"See?" Lucy pushed on one corner and the desk did indeed have a wobble.

"I see. Why don't you clear off the top while I look underneath?" As she peered up from the floor, Kelly immediately saw the problem: one of the front legs was barely on, causing the desk to tilt with just the slightest pressure. "Be right back."

Kelly went to her truck and returned with a hammer, three small blocks of wood, and a handful of nails. She turned the desk upside down and pried off what little was holding the table leg on.

"This nail ain't never going to be straight again." She held up the twisted nail for Lucy to see.

"It looks like it has arthritis."

"It's probably old enough." First she nailed the three wooden blocks to the table, and then started attaching the leg inside the triangle they formed, holding it in place. "I only had three this size, but I'm sure it's more than enough to hold it there. Just don't move the desk around too often. Or, if you do, pick this end up."

She had the leg balanced in place as she drove in the first nail. The wood was so old it was rock hard. As the leg jumped, her hand slid down and slammed against the three braces. Two of her knuckles were scraped and bleeding. She didn't pay it any attention, though, and used her knee to hold the table and leg in place. The nails went in with effort but finally all were in place.

"There, that'll do it." She flipped the table back over and gave it a nudge. "See? Not a wobble."

"Miss Walker! You're bleeding!"

"What? Oh, yeah, I guess I am."

"Lemme see." Lucy took Kelly's hand. "Ouch. I'll get a boo-boo patch. Stay right there." A second or two later, the young girl returned with a box of Band-Aids. "Mom gets the ones with cartoons and glow in the dark stuff. She says kid Band-Aids stick better than grown-up ones."

"Yeah? I didn't know that." Kelly grimaced as Lucy put two of the strips on the scraped knuckles. "Golly, that smarts." She spoke through her teeth.

"There. Now, go ask Mom to kiss it."

"What?" Kelly's head snapped up, her eyes wide as she stared at the girl.

"Ask Mom to kiss it. I don't know how she does it, but somehow it works. The pain goes away." Then, in a low whisper, "I think it's magic."

Lucy stood and waited for Kelly to stand, too. She took her by the hand to lead Kelly to Grace in the kitchen. "Mom, Kelly hurt her hand."

"How? You okay?" Grace was stirring a pitcher of lemonade. She laid the long wooden spoon down on the counter and came over.

"I banged my knuckles." Kelly's hand was lifted up and presented to Grace. "I do it all the time. It's not a big deal."

"Ouch."

"You've got to kiss her boo-boo."

Kelly and Grace looked at each other. As adults, they knew that the magic of kissing boo-boos only worked when on children. However, with Lucy looking up at them, neither could argue with that fact.

Grace took Kelly's hand and leaned toward it, placing her lips gently on the bandages. She lowered the hand and told Lucy to go put everything back on her desk. "Here, she put them all on crooked." She peeled off the strips and winced at the wrinkled and raw skin underneath. "Sit. I'm getting some ointment."

Kelly sat down, realizing she was being ordered around by both Owens women. And she didn't mind it one bit. Odd, that.

"Are you allergic to the calendula plant?"

"The what?"

"This flower." She showed her the box with the orange flower on the front.

"Nope."

"Good. This is a petroleum-free cream with calendula in it, which is good for wounds like this. It'll also keep it from sticking to the bandage."

"I hate it when that happens."

"What do you normally use?"

Kelly looked at her, blinking. "Um, nothing. I wash it and cuss a lot. I have a supply of butterfly bandages in the truck to use for cuts. If it's bad enough, I go over to Annette and make her fix it. She likes to do that. Gives her a chance to fuss and feed."

Grace put a single bandage on the one bleeding knuckle and left the other one open. "There. I think you'll live." She picked up Kelly's hand and kissed it again. "Now it's sure to heal."

Kelly sat in silence, staring at the multi-colored bandage on her hand. It had been a long time since anyone had put one—unsolicited—onto her wounds.

"KELLY? WHAT'S WITH the blood all over the carpet? Oh, gross, what did you do?" Anna put down her briefcase and took a few slow steps forward.

"I cut my hand on a knife when I was cleaning out the truck."

"You got blood everywhere."

"Well, babe, that happens in situations like this. Can you help me with it?"

"I'll clean it up later. You'll only make it worse."

"No, Anna, I meant my hand."

"Oh yeah, sure. Um, what?"

Kelly sighed and shut her eyes. She felt a little queasy from the deep slice at the tip of her finger. Keeping her eyes shut, she gave Anna directions.

But first Anna had to change; she didn't want blood on her clothes. She put on some of Kelly's instead. Then she didn't want blood on the good towels and got clean rags from the laundry room. She wouldn't touch the finger, not even the hand. Instead she handed everything to Kelly. Only after the bleeding had stopped and the tiny butterfly strips had closed the wound did Anna get close enough to see.

"It's such a small cut! You'd think you'd cut your finger off. Here's some more rags for you to use to clean the floor."

"MISS WALKER, I put your hammer and nails on top of your toolbox." Lucy patted Kelly's cheek. "Don't worry, it'll get better."

"I'll take this out to the truck for you, so you can rest that hand for a few minutes." Grace picked up the box, grunting with the weight of it. "My gosh, woman, what do you have in here? Bricks?"

"No, those I keep in the red one. I have stones in the silver one." Frowning, she stood and took the toolbox away from Grace. "I can carry it. It's not like my hand's broke or anything."

KELLY DROVE HER truck up the driveway, then backed up to the shop. She put all the ceiling tiles and the scraps of metal onto a set of pallets already holding several other boxes and bags of waste from other jobs. She covered it all with a tarp and, after getting her briefcase out of the truck, went into the house.

For some reason, her usual routine seemed bland, almost painful. As she dumped everything from her pockets into the bucket, she looked around the living room. Two hampers, one of unfolded non-work clothes and the other of neatly folded work clothes, sat on the floor at the end of the couch. She saw all the other trash, magazines, and catalogs lined against the wall and behind the door. She took her boots off, but instead of just dropping them there, dirt and all, she took them out front, clapping the big soles together. A cloud of dust formed, disappearing in the brisk wind. She stood there a moment, the only light from the living room behind her, and looked out over the mountains.

Back in the house, she put the boots by the stool at the door. She went into the kitchen, but her appetite began to falter. *How, when, did it get this bad?*

She couldn't take another minute of this. She ran out to the truck, knowing exactly where her heavy-duty trash bags were. Back inside the house, she hopped around as she took off her wet socks. She held a large trash bag open with one hand and used the other hand to clear the counters in the kitchen.

Two hours later, wearing her old sneakers, she took the last of five bags of trash out to the pallets. She'd only managed to clear out the kitchen and barely touched the living room. She was tired but she felt good, as if she had just finished a very difficult project. *No, I've just started a difficult project – me.*

Chapter
Twelve

"SO, DID YOU give any thought to going out to dinner with me?" Deb asked as her foot stroked Grace's lower leg.

"No, actually, I haven't. The landlady is having some work done at the house, and I was busy with that."

"You can always come and stay at my place. I got a comfortable couch."

"Funny." Grace didn't say anything more, choosing instead to finish her lunch.

Three hours later when the end of shift buzzer sounded, Deb stood outside waiting for her. "So, get your car fixed?"

"No, it's still being stubborn."

"Come on, then; I'll give you a ride home."

Grace hesitated. Other than being assertive, Deb had stayed within limits. "Sure, it's not out of your way?"

When they pulled up in front of the house, the big white truck with four sheets of drywall still in the back was backed up to the gate. "Rude sons of bitches to block your gate." Deb left the car idling, the big engine smooth as a kitten's purr.

"I guess they have to do what they can to get it done. Thanks for the ride home. I appreciate it. I'll see you Monday at work." Grace had her hand on the door about to open it when Deb hit the master lock.

"You know, you can see me sooner than that if you want. Here's my number. Call." As the woman handed Grace her card, she pulled her over for a kiss. At first, it seemed as if it was going to be a simple little kiss, so Grace didn't really resist. Deb took her compliance as permission and tried to stick her tongue inside Grace's mouth.

Grace pushed Deb off and stared at her, unsure what to say and still be civil. She decided it wasn't possible and opted not to say anything at all. She manually unlocked the door, got out of the car, and walked toward the side gate.

KELLY HAD MOST of the sheets of drywall carried in. She stood just inside the living room as she tipped back her water bottle. She wanted to pour it over her head, but since she was indoors, she didn't think it would be a good idea. As she heard the rumble of a car pull up near her truck, she looked to see if she had anyone blocked.

The vehicle, one of those high-end sport models built for the Autobahn and not the mountain roads of North Carolina, sat idling just behind her truck. The windows were tinted but she still recognized Grace's profile. She didn't mean to be spying, but that's what it was. She was watching as Grace and the other person kissed.

The emotion and turmoil from Anna and her affairs welled up inside her. She felt the fool again, taken advantage of by someone she...*Someone I what? Just what is Grace to me?*

She heard the back door open and shut, loud enough to be considered a slam. Grace came into the living room and tossed her lunch bag onto the couch with enough force to make it bounce onto the floor.

"Some women! Locking me in the damn car! Don't they think a person wants to be asked before they kiss them? And gross! Tongue dancing?" Grace screamed and kicked her shoes off. "I'm going to take a shower."

As Kelly watched the tantrum, her own anger and depression popped like a bubble. *What the hell?*

UNDRESSED AND STANDING in the shower, the warm water flowing from her hair and down her back, Grace started to relax. But she soon realized who had been standing in her living room during her tirade. "Crap."

Kelly Walker must think I'm a psycho off my meds.

As she was drying off, she realized her robe was in the bedroom. Usually she got it or a change of clothing before starting her shower. "Crap. This is not a good day."

Grace peeked out the door and saw Kelly go into the kitchen carrying a sheet of drywall. She could wait until Kelly went back out to the truck for the next one, then dart into her bedroom. She waited. And waited.

"Um, Kelly?"

"What?" Kelly's voice came from the kitchen, muffled by the distance.

"Um, what are you doing?"

"At this very second?"

"Yes, dammit."

"Don't throw another tantrum now!" She came around the corner and into Grace's view. "I was in the kitchen measuring the distance to the light fixture, so I could either cut a hole in the drywall or cut notches on the edge of two of them. That's exactly what I was doing the second you called. I was also up a ladder, both hands up like this." She put the pencil in her mouth and raised her arms up, the measuring tape in one hand and the end of the tape in the other.

"Smart ass. Go into the kitchen, and stay there until I say so."

"Why?"

"Because."

"You forgot your clothes, didn't you, Mama Bear?" Kelly grinned as she leaned against the wall.

"What? Listen, just do it. Please?"

"Well, I reckon. You sure you can make it by yourself without getting mad at someone along the way?"

"Shut up and go!" Grace tried not to laugh, she really did. But when Kelly put her hand over her eyes and felt her way back into the kitchen, Grace chuckled. And as she darted for the bedroom, she heard a wolf whistle.

GRACE CAME OUT of her bedroom, bringing the basket of laundry, and started doing this mundane, perfectly normal activity in hopes of alleviating her embarrassment. Folding laundry was usually relaxing. She could sit and not really think about what she was doing.

"They're so little, the shirts." Kelly reached out to touch a t-shirt, white with some yellow, square cartoon character on the front. She'd remained in the kitchen until now.

"I know. She's growing tall while I grow wide."

Kelly looked down at Grace's body. She wasn't fat, just pleasantly plump. Round in just the right places.

"And I hate it when people say I'm not fat, but that I'm pleasantly plump. It really pisses me off." Grace picked up the empty clothes basket. "Listen, about earlier—"

"Nah, nothing to explain or apologize for. It happens to everybody once in a while." Kelly drained her water bottle. "When does the kiddo get home?"

"Any minute now. You'll hear the kids long before you hear the bus." Grace continued folding clothes while sitting on the couch.

"You need to talk about it? Need me and my butch girlfriends to go beat up whoever was in that fancy car?"

"No, no, nothing as drastic as that. I just let myself get into a situation I never should have gotten into."

Kelly waited a bit before speaking again. "Know for sure

what's wrong with your car?"

"Other than age and time? I haven't a clue."

"That's a Ford Crown Vic, right? Eighty-six?"

"No, eighty-four."

"That's a tank, not an automobile."

"I know. I wanted a safe vehicle for Lucy, and that's the one I found." Grace finished folding Lucy's shirts and stood to fold the jeans. "I'd like to trade it in for something else, but I haven't got the money."

"What are you looking for?"

"I was thinking of a mini-van or truck. Whatever it is, it won't be another Ford."

Kelly laughed then. "Ford versus Chevy is a debate that's been around a long time. Like John Deere and Massey Ferguson. Listen, um, you want to go out to dinner with me? I need to eat soon, and I'm sure Lucy and you do, too. Your kitchen is still a mess."

"Go out to dinner with you?" Grace watched as the other woman's face reddened. "I don't know. Where were you thinking of going?"

"No idea. I usually just drive 'til I get to something that interests me."

"I'd like to go somewhere that you can hold a menu in your hand." Grace sighed. They'd not been able to go out for dinner in a long time.

"Yeah, I know what you mean. Looking down at the menu instead of reading a board over the register. I'm buying, by the way."

"No, I got paid today. I'll—"

"It was my idea. Don't argue with me, woman." Kelly tried to look fierce, but she could tell Grace wasn't falling for it. "I'll be in the kitchen, working."

"I LIKE THE *Magic School Bus*. I watch it on Saturdays on the PBS station." Kelly surprised herself by admitting that in public.

"You do? Wowzers." Lucy shoved three fries into her mouth at once.

"Yeah, I like Lily Tomlin."

"Who?" It was hard to say much with her mouth so full.

"She's the voice of Ms. Frizzle." Grace pushed back her plate. "Dang, that was good."

"I agree. I haven't eaten this good in a while." Kelly used her napkin to wipe her mouth and hands.

"You look to be in good shape for someone who eats heart-attack-in-a-wrapper all the time."

"Thanks, I think." Kelly blushed, something she wished wouldn't happen as often as it did. "But I work hard. Physical labor beats a wrapper hands down."

"Do you only do rental properties?"

"No, I do just about anything. Mostly little things and emergencies." She leaned forward, putting her elbows on the table, watching the young girl continue to eat. "She got a hollow leg?"

"I believe so. She can really put it away. Yet she stays scrawny."

"I got high metblism."

"High what?" Kelly had no clue what she just said.

"She said high metabolism. And she said it with her mouth full of food." Grace whapped her daughter with the napkin. "What else do you work on besides windows, doors, and flooded basements?"

"Paint, gutters, decks, stuff like that. I based my business on doing those things that no one ever gets around to doing or are too small to call a professional to do. It would cost a small fortune to have a construction company come and repair the railing on a deck. And most folks take forever to get around to doing it themselves. Explains the name of my business, Around-To-It Services." Kelly tapped the front of her shirt where the logo and business name were printed.

Grace laughed, but her daughter looked confused. "Never mind, honey, I'll explain it when you're older." Lucy just rolled her eyes and shook her head. "Since Wimpy is still stuffing her face, are you interested in a dessert and coffee?"

"Coffee, yes. Dessert, no. Well, maybe." Kelly looked around for their waitress and motioned her over. The waitress, anticipating their needs, brought over the dessert menu.

"I highly recommend the chocolate mousse or the strawberry parfait after such a heavy meal."

"I'll take the strawberry parfait and a cup of decaf coffee, if it's brewed." Grace didn't even bother to look at the menu.

Kelly stared at the dessert list, knowing which one she would get, something she hadn't had in a long time. "I'll take the chocolate mousse and a black coffee, please."

"Yes, the decaf is brewed, and I'll return with your desserts in a moment."

"WHAT'S THIS?" KELLY looked down at the small plate Anna had just put in front of her.

"It's a mousse."

"Ugh! A what?"

"A mousse, you twit. It's a dessert. Fluffy chocolate pudding, to put it in redneck terms." Anna bopped Kelly in the back of the head.

"Pudding? Why didn't you say so to begin with?" Kelly took her spoon and scooped a bit of the dessert out. *"Mmm. Not bad for an elk."*

"Sometimes, I wonder why I bother making you the finer foods. You downgrade them and me." Anna stomped over to the other end of the kitchen and slumped against the counter.

"No, I don't downgrade you. I just don't know what to do with fancy stuff. I'm rough and barbaric. When it comes to stuff like chocolate moose, I don't know what to do with it. I feel like an idiot sometimes."

"You aren't an idiot, sweetheart, you're a philistine."

"MISS WALKER? YOU home in there?" Lucy tugged on Kelly's sleeve.

"What? Did I miss something?"

"I asked you if you liked chocolate."

"Yes. I do. Very much. Everything is good with chocolate."

"Tommy says his uncle once had chocolate-covered ants."

"Uh, well, almost everything."

BACK AT HER own house, Kelly began working on the living room. This was going to take longer than she thought. She went to the shop to get some boxes. She emptied the big trash can that held wood scraps, putting an old boom box and another roll of trash bags inside before heading back to the house.

The music blasted as she sat on the floor and began sorting. She tried not to get caught up in the magazines as she found them, but, three hours later, she still had a lot to do.

Chapter
Thirteen

THE NEXT MORNING, Kelly stopped for breakfast at the diner, enjoying the ribbing one patron was getting for turning fifty the day before. Clarence Thompson came in not long after she did.

"Walker, I heard you got a desk." Clarence sat down across from her.

"Yeah, they were supposed to deliver it the other day, but something came up. It should be at the house Monday." She used the edge of the toast to hold her eggs in place for the fork.

"Let those monkeys bring it in for you. The damn thing weighs a ton, at least mine did. I guess you saw the price tag on my model?"

"Yep. You forked over a lot of money for a desk with an off plumb top."

"I did, and don't you dare breathe a word of it to my wife. She'd kill me if she knew." He wagged his big finger at her.

"Your secret's safe with me, old man. How's the business?"

"Going good, almost too good. I heard about you from a roofer I work with. He said he liked you, despite you being a girl and all." Clarence added several packets of sugar to his coffee.

"I liked him, too, despite the fact he had testicles. He and his crew did a good job. I gave their card to another customer of mine."

"So your business is going well?"

"Yeah, it started slow, but it's picking up. I'm getting my cards out and around." Kelly pulled one out and handed it to Clarence.

"I'm thinking of expanding mine in the spring. But I need to get that alleged office straightened up first. If you know of someone, a woman who can hold her own with me and the boys, send her out." The waitress brought his meal over, and they ate in silence until Kelly stood to leave.

"I'll see you later, Clarence." She put on her cap as she went to the register. The waitress running the register had never liked her and was taking her sweet time coming up front from the kitchen. Kelly opened the door and shook it, making sure the bell at the top rang loud and long. Thinking Kelly was leaving without paying, and knowing that meant she would get into trouble for not watching the register, the waitress came running to take the money. As Kelly left, she heard Clarence laughing.

"LUCY, I STILL don't get it. I'll never understand math. I didn't when I was your age, and I still don't." Grace threw the pencil down on the book. They were sitting on the floor, the math book and two pads of paper spread out in front of them.

"Maybe I should stay after school with a tutor." Lucy tossed her pencil down, too, blowing out a loud dramatic sigh.

"It depends on if we can afford it, baby girl."

"Hey! Miss Walker's here!" Lucy opened the door and was running down the sidewalk before Grace could tell her to put her coat on.

"Hey, Lucy, you look chipper." She could hear Kelly's deep voice and Lucy's higher-pitched one.

"I got up early, so I could get my homework done, so I could maybe watch you work, but Mom doesn't know that's why I did it, but it doesn't matter anyway 'cause we still don't got my math done, and—"

"Slow down, slow down. If you want to watch me work, you have to ask Mama Bear first. And second, what kind of math?"

Grace looked up as the two of them came through the doorway.

"Hi, Kelly."

"Hey, Grace."

"It's math homework, and Mom is a math idiot and can't help me, so I have to do it myself, and I sometimes just don't like it, and—"

"Slow down again. What kind of math? One word!"

"Division."

"Easy. Show me."

Grace scooted back and up and sat on the couch, intrigued as the big fix-it woman sat on the floor with Lucy. She wasn't really listening much to what the two of them were saying; she was transfixed by the expression on both of their faces as Lucy learned and Kelly taught.

"Work backward? Are you bonkers?"

"Yeah, but not about this. What is the opposite of division?"

"Multiple-cation."

"Right. So, work a problem backward if you don't come up with the right answer, or if you want to check your answer." Kelly led her through the problem until Lucy found where she went wrong.

"Oh! Now I get it!"

"Yep. See, I use math all the time. I gotta go backward, forward, and sometimes slide sideways. I have to look at it from all directions. Even non-math stuff is that way. Let's say a door won't close. First thing you look at is where the door and the door jamb meet."

"Ew! Jam on the door?"

"No, j-a-m-b—jamb, the frame around a door."

"Oh, good, 'cause that was kinda gross."

"I imagine it would be."

"So you check the jelly, then what?" Lucy grinned but otherwise looked innocent.

"Then you just follow the parts of the door until you find it."

"Kinda like when a computer won't turn on the first thing you check is to see if it's plugged in."

"Exactly!" It was Kelly's turn to laugh. She looked over at Grace, as if remembering where she was and what she was supposed to be doing. "Okay, I need to get to work if this is to get done today." She stood, nodded to Grace, and went to the kitchen.

Grace watched her leave and turned to see Lucy already hard at work on the rest of the math homework. She was still amazed at how well Kelly could help and how good Lucy was at listening.

IN THE KITCHEN, Kelly got to work setting the room up for her job. She put her toolbox by the door then covered the floor with the tarps left there from earlier in the week. That done, she went out the back door to her truck to bring in the drywall jack.

She wrestled the contraption up the sidewalk, and Grace met her to hold the storm door open.

"Thanks." Kelly paused to take a breather.

"What in the world is that?"

"It's a doohickey thingy. Aintcha never seen one before?" She picked up the jack again.

"Yes, but never in that color." Grace stepped back into the house and let the door shut, keeping Kelly outside.

"What the...?" She grunted, almost dropping the jack.

"Doohickey thingy?"

"If I told you what it's called, would you believe me? No. It's called a drywall jack. It holds and lifts the drywall up to the ceiling."

"No, I don't believe you. Surely it has a more sophisticated name."

"Nope. Drywall jack. Some call it a drywall lifter. Now open the damn door, woman."

"What's the magic word?" Grace crossed her arms and tapped her foot.

"Please, dammit?"

"Close enough!" She couldn't help but laugh at Kelly's face.

"Thank you." Grace watched as Kelly brought it in and finished setting it up.

When she put the first piece on and had the jack lift it to the ceiling, Grace was impressed. "Cool toy you got there, Miss Walker."

"Why else do you think I'm in this business? I get to play with all sorts of cool toys."

With the four-by-eight drywall panel held up by the jack, she was able to move it into place, right where she needed it.

"I still need to get the mud and stuff in here. Do you mind watching this and not let Lucy in here while I get the rest of it in?"

"Sure. Just be sure to take some off Kaye's bill since you're getting free help."

"Or I could charge her extra for the same reason." Kelly went out to the truck and brought in the rest of the things she had loaded at the house or picked up that morning from the home improvement store: buckets of drywall compound, her trowel, wide joint knife and hawk, the drywall tape, and the tool box she kept just for this type of work.

"You need all that to put up drywall?"

"Yep. I don't do the work that requires stilts. I draw the line at those and build an indoor scaffold instead." Part of Kelly wanted to get to work and stop talking. But another part, the one just peeking out for the first time in a long time, wanted Grace to stay.

"Anything I can do to help?"

"Um, no, not really. I'm used to doing this by myself. But feel free to stay and watch." *Please stay.* Kelly got the ladder into place, briefly wishing there was more floor room for a scaffold. With the sheet of drywall in place, all she had to do now was drive in all the screws.

"Lotsa noise in here!" Lucy stood at the door, hands on her hips, a perfect mimic of her mother.

"It happens. Done with your homework?"

"Yep. Can I sit here and watch?" She looked from her mother to Kelly. Grace looked at Kelly, and Kelly looked at Grace. "One of you say something."

"It's fine with me." Kelly shrugged and got back to work, trying to be indifferent. She knew usurping Mama Bear was not a good idea.

"Sit right there and do whatever Miss Walker tells you to do, okay?"

"Yes, ma'am."

By the third panel, Grace was moving the ladder out of the way while Kelly set up the next sheet. Once the drywall was situated, Grace set the ladder back into place. When the screw bag on Kelly's belt grew empty, Grace dumped another half-box in. They worked like this throughout the morning, Lucy making comments, Grace making comments, and Kelly patiently taking it in stride, much better than she thought she would.

"That's twelve, by the way." Lucy called out from her seat on the floor.

"Twelve what?" Grace asked but Kelly knew.

"Twelve screws Miss Walker's dropped."

"Do you know where they all are?" Kelly loaded another screw onto the bit.

"Yep."

"Then will you please pick them up for me? But stay out from under the ladder, and be careful around the jack."

Lucy was up like a rocket and able to collect ten of them.

"Now, did you see which way they were facing when you picked them up?"

"Huh?"

"See, if they were on the floor facing that wall, then they're north screws and can only be used for north walls."

"Oh! No! I didn't notice! Have I messed them up?" Lucy stared at the screws in her hand.

"No, it'll be okay. I got a jar I put the unknowns in. See that wood box? There's a jar in there of screws just like those. When one falls and it's safe for you to get, you can go get it. Just remember which direction it faced."

"I will, Miss Walker." Lucy got the jar from the box to put in her now mis-directed screws.

Grace reached up and smacked Kelly's thigh but didn't correct her.

AT ONE IN the afternoon, Lucy called a halt to the work. "Look, grown-ups, I'm a kid and need to eat soon."

"You have to feed her every day?" Kelly took the bandanna from her pocket and wiped her face.

"Sometimes more than once." Grace took a big swig from her cup of water.

"I guess. There's a deli down the street. We can walk there, get something, and bring it back here."

"Yeah, yeah!" Lucy jumped up and down in place.

"I think a walk would be a good idea." Grace stepped back so

Kelly could come down from the ladder.

"We got more done that I thought I would." Kelly looked up at the panels on the ceiling. "I'll tape and mud them today, then tomorrow sand and paint. Cool beans."

"Cool what?" Lucy stopped jumping.

"Never mind."

Chapter
Fourteen

KELLY ARRIVED HOME, the place dark until she approached the house, triggering the porch light. Emptying her pockets into the bucket by the door, Kelly tried to figure out something: even when walking to and from the deli at lunch, there had been something in the back of Kelly's mind, something she should remember.

She stood by the door, hands in her pockets, her feet rocking back and forth in their boots. The living room was looking good, although the big box of magazines and catalogs still stood in the middle. She needed to take the trash out and put the big trash can back in the shop.

The wind had picked up, and the temperature had dropped once the sun went down. At the pallet, she wrestled the bags out of the can, covered it all back up again and dragged the can into the shop. When she put it near the workbench, Kelly automatically glanced at her large wall calendar. *Monday, I have a job over at...*

She broke out in a cold sweat, staring at the three-inch square that was today's date. She felt ill, appalled she hadn't remembered. Her soul numb, she walked out of the shop and stood motionless on the rise above the lake, the bitter wind hitting her in the face, the tears nearly freezing on their way down. Her mind was going at a high speed, jumping from memory to memory. She and Anna at someone's birthday party, sitting close and holding hands. She and Anna at home, sitting on opposite ends of the couch, each reading her own book, their toes often touching, stroking the shin of the other. Anna's face, head tilted back and laughing at something Kelly had done or said. Such beauty and freedom!

"Keeeeellllllyyyyy."

"Hmm?"

"Keeeeellllllyyyyyy."

"What?" Kelly looked up. Anna stood in the bedroom doorway, wearing nothing but one of Kelly's over-sized t-shirts. Her arm was raised, poised for effect. The hem of the shirt pulled up, revealing a

top of the thigh and the beginnings of dark hairs.

"I have something to show you."

"I think you're showing me a lot right now." Kelly set aside the book she'd been reading. Lee Lynch would have to wait.

"Walk this way." Anna curled her finger, calling Kelly to her.

Kelly complied eagerly by standing up on the couch and walking toward her partner, finally stepping off the arm. By the time she got to the doorway, Anna was lying on the bed, posed and ready. The closer Kelly got, the higher Anna hiked up the shirt. By the time Kelly made it to the bed, the t-shirt was just sliding over Anna's breasts.

Kelly knelt on the side of the bed, reaching out with a shaking hand to touch Anna's abdomen softly, gently. She circled the belly button with a fingertip, slowly making her way upward. She flattened her hand, spreading the fingers until her palm touched flesh. The hand continued upward, cupping the breast.

NIKKI PUT AWAY her dinner dishes. The only sound in her big house was Spam drinking, slopping water onto the floor to form a two-foot-square puddle. She went into the living room and turned on her television, a big monster of a screen that took up half of the wall. She flipped to the weather, settling back to hear about the possible snow. She noticed the date at the bottom of the screen. "Shit."

ACROSS HIGH POND, Kaye took the plate from Annette and put it up in the cabinet. "Good dinner, babe." Annette filled their mugs with coffee. Kaye got out the milk while she read the television schedule. "Oh, shit."

Before Annette could ask, their phone rang. It was Nikki, telling them what day it was. "Yeah, I just saw that, too. I'll meet you at her place."

KELLY TURNED FROM the lake and headed back to the house. In the kitchen, she put water in the kettle for hot chocolate. She was still crying, not yet done with her trip down memory lane.

Now her memories were bitter.

The look on her friends' faces when the older woman arrived at the memorial. Then the other one, the dark-skinned student from Israel.

Back at the house, the two of them came up to Kelly and introduced themselves. They even said it together. We were Anna's other lovers.

Other lovers. As if that was all Kelly was. But perhaps it was not far from the truth. The two women took turns telling Kelly about their relationships with Anna. Behind them, Kelly saw her friends staring at the floor, several getting their jackets and leaving.

The next several days had been a blur of confusion, anger, and hurt.

Brave Nikki shielded Kelly as much as possible. They moved all of her personal things out of the apartment. They went through to remove any items of Anna's that Kelly didn't want anyone to find or to have — things that were just between them. She knew Nikki had done something to the computers, but she didn't know what. Then she just walked away, loaded up the moving trailer and got into the truck with Nikki.

KELLY STARED AT the steam that was starting to rise from the kettle. Anger was slowly overtaking the deep depression she'd been wallowing in for the past two years. Anger at Anna for dying. Anger at Anna for dying and leaving her with a mess.

This emotion, denied for two years, had risen too close to the surface to be pushed down this time. It exploded inside her, volcanic fury causing her heart to pound in her chest. It continued to come to the surface and pour out from the inner pressure. She turned around, her ears roaring with the hot blood that raced through her. As the tea kettle began its whistle, she punched her fist straight into the paneled wall. Again. And again.

NIKKI ARRIVED FIRST, Kaye and Annette not far behind. When Nikki reached the porch, she could hear the thumping and screaming from inside the house. She didn't bother to knock, just opened the door and charged inside. Kelly stood in the kitchen; she was using her fist as a battering ram against the wall by the door. The paneling had already splintered in several places, but efficient Kelly had just moved further left. The table was overturned and the glass in the back door was shattered.

"Shit, Kelly, stop!" Nikki jumped up onto the couch to climb over the counter. Grabbing Kelly's arms, she stood between her friend and the wall. Kaye ran over to take Kelly from behind, holding her with both arms around her chest. "Kelly! Stop it!"

Annette, rolling through the doorway, saw what the others had not: Kelly's bloody hand. She saw the wall and the glass and the blood smears, the splatter marks on Kelly's face and shirt, the white of bare bone. "Nikki, her hand. Get her to sit down."

Last year, on this date, the four of them had met at the Goat

Farm where they'd all gotten rip-roaring drunk, crying insanely together. This was different. This was madness that had been held in for too long. Annette was glad to see this release happen at last. But there were safer, healthier ways to do it.

Nikki and Kaye were grunting from trying to hold Kelly in place. The woman was stronger than both of them. Once Kelly stopped struggling, Kaye was able to hold her in a firmer grip, and Nikki was able to support her mangled arm.

Annette grabbed towels from the hamper in the living room and wet them in the shower. When she came back, they had Kelly bent over the counter, her rage slowing. Annette transferred from her chair to the arm of the couch, putting herself level with Kelly's hand, held in place by Nikki. After just a look, Annette knew they wouldn't be staying there long.

"Kaye, hand me your cell phone." Annette left it on the counter while she wrapped the bloody hand in the wet towel. Kelly cried out but didn't fight them anymore. "Nikki, hold the towel. Should I call nine-one-one, or do you think you can handle her?"

"We can handle her in the van." Kaye rubbed Kelly's back.

"The damage is done, so let's give her a minute to pull herself together. Kaye, can you reach that damn tea kettle?"

Chapter
Fifteen

THE NIGHT BEFORE, Grace and Lucy had joked they would call Kelly at six A.M. She'd threatened them with bodily harm, but mother and daughter decided it was worth the risk. At six on the dot, Grace dialed the number on the business card while Lucy giggled.

They were disappointed when Kelly's voice mail answered, and Grace left a message, mostly of them giggling.

"Bummer. Betcha she knew we were going to do it, so she turned it off." Lucy picked up her bowl to drink the leftover milk from her cereal.

"Betcha she did." Grace turned to get the toast just before the phone rang. "Should we answer?"

"I don't know, Mom. She can't hurt us through the phone line, right?"

"I hope not." Grace mussed Lucy's hair as she picked up the receiver. "Hello?"

"Grace? I'm sorry to wake you. This is Kaye."

"You didn't wake us. We've been up for a few minutes already."

"Good, good. Listen, I have a favor to ask. Kelly Walker hurt herself last night, and we're here at the hospital. Annette is coming back to get me, but we need someone to stay here in case she's out of surgery before we get back."

"Surgery? Yes, I'll be right there."

"We were thinking that Lucy could come to the house with me and Annette"

"I'm sure Lucy would love that. I'll get a book to read, and we'll be right there. Which hospital?"

"St. Joe's ER. Nikki—a friend of Kelly's—will stay with you for a while."

AFTER A SHORT cab ride, Grace and Lucy walked into the lobby of the emergency room and quickly spotted Kaye. "What happened?"

Kaye glanced over at Lucy who was staring up at the tall Nikki. "She broke her arm and has some cuts, among other things. Nikki can fill you in later. Oh, Grace, Lucy, this is Nikki Rogers. Nikki, this is Grace and Lucy Owens. They rent the house on Oak Street."

"Nice to meet you, ladies." She knelt on the floor to be closer to Lucy's height.

"You know Miss Walker?"

"Yes, I do. I'm her best friend." Nikki said quietly.

"Is she okay?"

"Not really, but she will be soon. Adults sometimes do some stupid things that get them hurt."

Lucy nodded. "I tell Mom all the time that being an adult must be a bummer."

"Lucy, tell Miss Rogers about Kelly's screws. You know, the directional ones." Grace patted her daughter's head.

"Yeah! I messed up some of Miss Walker's screws by accident. She dropped them from up on the ladder and let me pick them up, but I didn't keep them in the direction they fell, so they had to go into a special jar, but all the others I kept facing right."

"Oh? You mean the ones for north walls and south walls?"

"Yeah, you know them?" By the tone of Lucy's voice, Grace knew Nikki had just risen up a notch in hero worship. "Do you think she can still use the ones in the jar?"

"Oh, you know Kelly; she'll find a way to use them." She was very serious, but Kaye couldn't hold back for very long.

"Come on, guys, you're not going to let her keep believing that, are you?"

"I don't know, Kaye, if Kelly says that's the way it is, maybe we shouldn't contradict her, you know?"

ANNETTE HAD ARRIVED and taken Kaye and Lucy back to the Goat Farm. Grace and Nikki settled back into their seats to await news.

"How long you known Kelly?" Nikki asked.

"Not long actually. She's doing repairs to my kitchen ceiling."

"Why did Kaye call you to come sit here?"

"Good question. We've been at their house and had dinner with them and Kelly. She's been helping Lucy with her math homework. They play chess together, too."

"That explains it, then. Anyone who's had dinner at their house is part of the family." Nikki turned, so she could see Grace better. "Kelly doesn't have much of a temper. Whenever she does get mad, she cools off real fast. It's one of her better traits. I've seen her take a stick and whomp it against a tree. I've seen her take a hammer and bust up a rock until it's nearly sand. But that's when she was really mad and upset, and it's only been those two times." She paused. "Last night, Kelly got mad at something and used her hands instead of a stick or hammer."

"Oh shit."

"Exactly. When we got there, she'd busted up the wall, the glass back door, the table, and some other stuff. We've not gotten the final account, but we know she's got a broken arm, and a bunch of deep cuts on her hands, especially her left. They're not going to set the arm yet, but they had to take her into surgery to take care of the arteries and stuff in her hands. They said it would take a while."

"Isn't she left-handed? Did they say anything about...long-term damage?"

"Yes, she's a lefty, and no, but they hinted at some possibilities. There's some important nerves in the back of the hand, and they weren't sure what condition they were in."

"What happened? What set her off?"

"It was an important date in her life, one with bad memories attached."

"She never said anything about it yesterday. She was at our place all day."

FORTY-FIVE MINUTES later, a nurse came to get them. "Miss Walker will be going up to a room soon, fourth floor. There's a waiting room just outside the ward. They'll get you from there as soon as she's settled."

Another half hour later, another nurse came to get them from the waiting room. "We need help with her. She's very strong, and she's fighting us. We can't give her any more medication without risks. If she'd just relax, the meds in her would knock her out. We're hoping that seeing or hearing a friend will calm her down." She took Grace and Nikki down the hall and around a corner.

Grace entered the room, stunned to see two large male orderlies holding Kelly down. The I.V. setup—its ignored beep adding to the cacophony of sounds—lay on its side partway under the bed. Kelly's left hand was already in restraints from the shoulder down but her free right hand gripped the front of one of the men's shirt. The tray table was wedged between the guest chair and the wall, its top covered in scattered papers and equipment. If the orderlies had more room, they wouldn't be having so much difficulty.

After that brief second of shock, Grace knew what to do. "Kelly Rebecca Walker, you stop that this instant." She used the Mom Voice. And it worked. "Just what do you think you're doing? Let go of his shirt right now!"

Kelly let go. Immediately, they put a restraint on her right arm and straps across her legs.

"Now, close your eyes. Do it. There you go. Just relax, Kelly, let it take you to sleep." Grace had come closer as soon as the two men moved. She rubbed Kelly's right shoulder where the gown had slid down, exposing skin. "There, see? No one's going to hurt you. They're here to help."

"Don't go." Kelly's voice cracked.

"I won't. Now close your eyes. There now. Shhh, I got you. Just relax."

Within a minute, she was asleep, deeply enough for the orderlies and the nurses to relax and slump against the wall.

"Out." The nurse in charge shooed them all, Grace included, out the door.

"Thank you, ma'am. I'll have to remember that in the future. How old is your kid?" One of the men smiled at her.

Grace grinned back. "Nine. I don't know why it occurred to me to do that."

"It doesn't matter. It worked." The two orderlies left, rubbing their arms.

The head nurse came out of the room, shutting the door behind her. "Surprisingly, her tox screen showed that she wasn't on any drugs. Any idea what made her so enraged?"

"Whatever it is, it must be big because she doesn't get mad easily." Nikki shrugged but didn't say anything more.

Chapter
Sixteen

KELLY'S EYES FELT as if they were glued shut and weighed five pounds each. She tried to move but couldn't. Then the pain hit. Her head pounded in sync with her pulse. Her left hand hurt all the way to her ribs. Her legs ached and hummed.

Sounds came to her next. She heard a click and something began squeezing her legs, then slowly let go. Clattering noises, plastic and...marbles? Not very far away. Then a voice over a loud speaker, "Dr. Sullivan, call six-six-zero-four. Dr. Sullivan, call six-six-zero-four."

She put more effort into opening her eyes. The room was dark, but she could see sunlight peeking in under the curtain. She tried to sit up and realized she was tied to the bed. "What the hell?"

As she spoke, the door opened, and a concerned-looking Grace and Nikki entered the room. "Hey Kelly." Nikki grinned at her but kept her voice down.

"Where am I?" Her mouth was dry and the words felt as if they were ripped from her throat.

"Here, they said you could have ice chips." Grace used a spoon to put ice in Kelly's mouth.

"Don't you remember? Yesterday at your house? The wild sex party that went wrong?" Nikki sat on the edge of the bed, so Kelly didn't have to look up so high.

"I'd remember seeing you naked."

"Ha. I told Grace already, but it won't hurt her none to hear it again. Yesterday was October twenty-seventh." She paused as Kelly's eyes widened. "Kaye, Annette, and I went to your house to find you beating your kitchen senseless. You've not seen your hands yet?"

She looked down at her throbbing left hand. It was heavily wrapped, all the way up to just past the elbow. The arm was attached to a board to keep it still. Her right hand was not as immobilized, but there was blood showing on the gauze over her knuckles.

"What did I do?"

"Damage-wise? You won't be picking your nose with your left hand for quite a while." Nikki waited while Grace fed Kelly more ice chips. "I'll let the doctor or nurse tell you the specifics. I don't want to tell you wrong. But the other problem, girlfriend, is that you went nuts on the staff here." Nikki touched the strap on Kelly's thighs.

"I what?"

"Exactly. Grace here was the one to get you to stop."

Kelly closed her eyes for a moment. She opened them again and looked at her best friend. "Am I dreaming?"

"Afraid not." Nikki's voice was gentle, just the right tone to convince her. "I'll go tell the nurse you're awake. Maybe they'll untie you now."

As Nikki left, Kelly closed her eyes again and sucked in a ragged breath. She knew Grace stood there. *But what can I say?*

"Kelly, don't run away now. Look at me."

She turned her head, opening her eyes.

"You don't scare me. You don't look stupid. And I see you no worse than I already did." She smiled, a kind of smile Kelly that made her feel warm, safe. That smile was just for her.

"Lucy?" Her dry voice croaked the word out.

"No, she wasn't here, if that's what you're asking. She's with Annette and Kaye."

The nurse came in, a hulking orderly close behind. "Miss Walker?"

"Yeah?" Kelly's voice caught. Her eyes were growing heavy again.

"Why don't you just go back to sleep, honey? We'll talk about these restraints later when you're more aware." She had that no-nonsense kind of look and voice and no one argued with her. "This is Paul. He'll stay here while you're awake."

"No."

"I'm sorry, Miss Walker, but you don't have a choice in the matter."

Kaye had come in and heard most of the conversation. "But I do. May I speak with you out in the hall?"

Grace remained with Kelly while the nurse and Nikki went out in the hallway to talk. Kelly felt herself drifting off again. She tried to stay awake, to find out what was going on, but she couldn't.

"MA'AM, I'M KAYE Gillespie. I have medical power of attorney." She handed the nurse a brown envelope sealed with wax.

"Are you willing to take the risk of her exploding again? We don't know what damage she did to her arm earlier."

"Ma'am, I know my friend, as does Nikki." Kaye spoke to her tall friend. "You spoke with her?"

"Yeah, she's groggy and really out of it. She doesn't remember a thing, not even at her house. At least not yet."

"That's probably the medication. It'll come back to her later." The nurse looked at the two of them. "They've required a psychiatric eval be done when she is more coherent."

"She has a psychiatrist. Would she be able to help?"

"Actually, yes. If you'll give me her name and contact information, I'll take care of it. As for the orderly..." She shrugged, took the information card from Kaye and returned to the nurse's station.

"KELLY WALKER, WHAT have you done? I told you to branch out, not break out." Dr. Susan Tower came into the hospital room at precisely 5:30 P.M. "Hello, I'm Dr. Tower. You are—?"

"I'm Nikki Rogers, and this is Kaye Gillespie and Grace Owens. It's good to see you." Nikki stood, towering over the doctor.

Dr. Tower looked up at Nikki's face. "Ah, I should have known. She said you were tall." She turned to the others. "Kaye, it's good to meet you, too. Grace, it's nice to meet you, as well. Now, I need time alone with the big brute for a while. Take that goon by the door with you."

After the door shut, Dr. Tower sat on the edge of the bed and undid the buckles around Kelly's right wrist. "So, tell me what happened?"

"I forgot. I mean, I forgot what yesterday was. And, for some reason, the more I remembered what day it was, the madder I got. The rest is still a blur."

"Are you mad now?"

"No, actually I don't feel much of anything except pain. I feel like I wrestled a bull." She chuckled. "More like about four Nubian goats."

"Tell me about that anger. How did it feel?" She reached over and undid the hook-and-loop fastening around the bandages on the left arm.

"It wasn't anger. It was rage. I will forever know the difference. Being angry is yelling, or chopping wood for a few hours, or being mad enough to cry. Rage is quite different. It's out of control fury. It's literally seeing red. I remember the sound of the ocean in my head, violent waves hitting the rocks. I was a berserker in one of those fantasy books."

"Have you ever felt that before?"

Kelly adamantly shook her head. "No, never. Oh, I've been mad enough to throw things. And I've punched walls before, but more from frustration than anger. But I didn't feel the pain this time. I felt nothing but this, this rage."

Dr. Tower stood to undo the straps on her legs. "What were you doing yesterday? Prior to coming home?"

"I put up a ceiling at a rental house."

"What else?"

"That's about it."

Dr. Tower leaned against the wall at the foot of the bed. She crossed her arms over her chest and gave Kelly "The Look." "So all day, you did nothing but put up a ceiling?"

"I put up a ceiling in a rental house. Grace Owens and her daughter Lucy are the tenants of that house." Kelly began flexing her legs. The Sequential Compression Devices on her legs prevented her from moving much, but her cramped thigh and calf muscles still protested.

"Ah, so, it must have been pretty annoying, having a kid and an incompetent woman watching you work on their house."

"No, actually, it was rather nice. Lucy did her homework then sat against the wall. She asked a lot of questions but stayed put. And Grace, well, she just jumped right in to help. It made the work much easier."

"She's ugly to look at, too, huh?" Dr. Tower winked at Kelly, noting slight red tint coming to Kelly's pale face.

"Yeah, there is that."

"What else did you three do?"

"We walked down the street to get sandwiches from a deli. Then we ate lunch together, sitting on the floor of the living room. After that, Lucy played in her room, and I got back to work. Grace helped again."

"What did Lucy play?"

"I don't know, she was quiet, though."

"Then what? What time did you leave?"

"Late. I guess around nine. I went to K-Mart and got two pairs of jeans, a polo shirt, and sneakers. I guess I was there for about an hour or so. I came home, took the trash bags and the big can from the living room out to the trash pile, and took the can to the shop. That's when I saw the calendar."

"And that's when you got mad?"

"No, I went out to stand at the lake for a bit, and then went inside." Her eyes clouded over as the emotion and events came back to her. "That's when I got mad."

"Let me see if I've got this straight. You had a fun-filled day with Grace and her daughter, Lucy, while you worked on the house they rent. Then you spent money on yourself by getting new clothing and new shoes. You've been cleaning house if you had trash bags in the living room, so you must be feeling better there."

"And then wham! There was Anna and her death, and the damn mess."

Kelly felt the bitterness returning.

"She just popped your little happy bubble."

"Yes, dammit. I had a fun day with a beautiful woman and a kid! Me and a kid! We went for a walk, ate sitting on the floor. I felt like I belonged, you know? Then there came that bitch."

"Kelly, look at your right hand." Dr. Tower nodded toward that side of the bed.

Kelly had gripped the railing so hard her knuckles were white. Veins stood out on her forearm, bulging from the vise-like grip, blood was on the fresh bandages. "Shit."

"Exactly. That anger, that rage, that you let free last night is still there. I think you have a better grip on yourself, and I don't believe you'll go berserk like you did earlier. However, you're a risk to yourself." Dr. Tower pushed off from the wall and went to stand by Kelly's side. "I think you need to move in with someone while you and I work through this. You shouldn't be alone for now. You need someone safe around you whom you can talk to, someone who'll listen. If you can't do that, then I'll consider having you admitted to the psychiatric ward."

"What? You can't do that! I'm not..." She lowered her voice. "I'm not crazy."

"I know you're not. But, Kelly, what if you were driving when this hit you? What if you hadn't had friends come by? Until I believe you're in control of that inner demon, I'll not release you to live by yourself. Do you remember wrestling the orderlies and fighting with the nurses?"

"No."

"The leftover medication from the surgery probably has erased that. But that is exactly what I'm talking about now. That rage was still there, even after the surgery, even with all those medications, even with all that pain you must have been in."

Kelly turned her head to stare out the window. She knew Dr. Tower was right. "I'll talk to Kaye and Annette, see if they can put up with me for a few weeks. I can't be on my own right now anyway, not with this." She shrugged her left shoulder, wincing at the pain.

"There is that. Kelly, you've had a lot go through you, mentally and physically. Trust me, and your friends, to take care of you."

Kelly turned to face her again. "Okay, I'll agree to that." She said it as if she had a choice.

NIKKI AND HARRI arrived at Kelly's little house at the same time. They went inside, pausing in the living room to view the damage in the kitchen.

"She made one helluva mess," Harri muttered.

"Yep, she sure did."

The two friends began cleaning up the house. They swept up the glass and debris, washed the blood from the wall and nearby surfaces, installed a new wood back door, and put plywood over the broken window. After a break to rest and plan, they began patching up the holes.

Chapter
Seventeen

KELLY SAT OUT on the deck. She was wrapped in her heavy cotton robe and a blanket. She was watching one of the goat herds play king of the hill on a huge boulder. She suspected Annette had it put there just for this game. She'd been out of the hospital for two weeks but had only recently started coming out of herself. Behind her, inside the house, she could hear her friend making their lunch.

"Kelly? It's ready." Kelly stood and tried to fold the blanket one-handed. Knowing Annette was watching, she gave up and tossed it over her shoulder as she walked through the doorway into the house. "I made burgers."

"Beer burgers?" Kelly looked like a kid, her face all lit up.

"Yep. Are there other kinds?"

In the warm kitchen, Kelly got the plates and utensils to set the table while Annette started unloading lettuce, tomatoes, and ranch dressing from the refrigerator. Kelly carried the skillet to the table, the meat still sizzling.

"Those goats are a hoot." Kelly began building her burger.

"I had Kaye and Nikki move that rock six or seven times. I wanted it in just the right place, so I could watch them from inside. I think Nikki was going to put it on the deck if I had asked her to move it again."

"She would have, too. Cut this for me?"

"Half or quarters?"

"Half. Crap, I forgot drinks. What do you want?"

"Chocolate milk. You make it better than Kaye."

After lunch, Annette drove Kelly into town for her daily appointment with Dr. Tower. Kaye would pick her up afterward and drop her off at the library, picking her up again after she was finished with work. For the previous sessions, Annette had waited for Kelly and taken her straight home. But today, Kelly wanted to spend some time alone and do some reading at the library.

KELLY HAD IMPROVED in her ability to think of Anna and not show signs of her anger. Dr. Tower decided Kelly could come in every other day for the next week, but gave her "homework" to do. Kaye was waiting in the lobby when Kelly came out of the office.

After the short drive to the library, Kaye parked the vehicle in the drop-off zone in front of the library. "I may wander down to Malaprop's and get a coffee. Meet you there?" Kelly looked across the Jeep at her friend.

"Don't do too much on your first day out of the sanatorium. But sure, I'll meet you there, then. You have money, little girl?"

Kelly had left her wallet at the house, so Kaye gave her some money for coffee. Kelly waved goodbye and went inside the Pack Memorial Library. She went first to the newspaper and magazine racks. She decided to read the papers, starting with the *Wall Street Journal*, spreading it out in front of her on the table. After devouring that paper, she got the local one, going straight to the comics.

Next, she went to one of the computer terminals and entered in her search keywords. She found what she was looking for and went to get it from the shelves.

"Need any help today, Kelly?" One of the librarians, a young cutie, was going through the stacks, putting books away and straightening up. They'd met before, since Kelly was a regular visitor of this branch.

"Not at the moment."

She'd been thinking about the tiny desk Lucy was using in her bedroom. The kid had a microscope on it, using the sunlight for the mirror. The room was big enough for a larger desk, and Kelly wanted to build her one, but first she needed to look over other designs and get ideas going.

She admitted to herself that viewing the images was all she was capable of right now. She couldn't draw very well with her right hand, nor could she take notes. Not only was she physically compromised, she was still emotionally off kilter. Dr. Tower had shown her how she'd used her work to hide behind. By keeping busy until she was exhausted, she didn't have leisure time alone to sit and remember. Now, she had all the leisure time she could stand.

Today, she and Dr. Tower had talked about the desk and decided it would be a good project for her to research. It would occupy her mind but not enough that she could retreat behind it. It was also a feel-good project, which would help with her self esteem.

"Kelly Walker? It is you!"

She turned to see Rain Moon and Jake coming toward her. "Hey, Rain, good to see you."

"Good to see you, too. What on earth did you do to yourself?" Rain asked when she saw the bandages and cast.

"Um, I lost a fight, I guess you could say." She used her right hand to move books out of the way, so Rain could park across from her. Jake, ever the obedient dog, wagged his tail like mad but never approached her. Kelly used her foot to rub his chest.

"Okay, I can live with that answer. What are you looking up?" She nodded toward the book Kelly had been reading.

"I'm thinking about building a kid a desk. I need it to be big enough to be usable but not so big it's overwhelming."

"Yeah, right. You craft folk like to speak in riddles." Rain lightly touched the finger tips on Kelly's left hand.

"What are you here for?" Kelly felt tingling from the touch.

"Pure boredom. I'm between jobs at the moment and getting tired of staring at the same walls, so Jake and I went for a walk. My reward is seeing you."

Kelly knew she was blushing. "Isn't it just a might too cold to be out for a walk?"

"Just a might bit. It doesn't bother me much, and goodness knows, Jake couldn't care less."

They talked some more, keeping their voices low, so they wouldn't disturb others, but when Jake started snoring, they decided it might be best to go elsewhere.

"I was going to go to Malaprop's for coffee. Join me?" Kelly smiled as she made the offer.

"Sounds like a splendid idea."

Outside, the wind blew the heat right out of Kelly's light jacket. Luckily, the bookstore and coffee shop was only a block and a half away. As soon as they were in the door, the smells of the coffee and pastries made their mouths water. They got drinks and muffins and found a table near the window, which Jake could look out to keep himself entertained.

"You know, I thought maybe I would talk you into taking me out on a date." Rain grinned as she sipped her coffee.

"Oh? Changed your mind?"

"In a way. I like you, I'd like to spend time with you, but I don't think I want to date you. Nothing bad, honest! I just don't feel that connection, that special something I'm looking for."

"No problem. I considered asking you out, too, but, well, I guess I didn't feel a connection either." Kelly leaned forward. "I used to hate it when girls would say 'You are so nice' at the end of a date. That meant the 'I like you as a friend' bit was next."

"I've heard those lines before, too! Do you have problems finding a date? Surely not."

"Oh, yeah, lots of problems! They either wouldn't have anything to do with me because I was 'promoting the stereotype of dykes and not lesbians.' Or they wanted me to be more of a dyke — one even asked me to put a sock in my jeans."

"Are you serious? I knew a few women who packed, but only because they were transgendered." Rain leaned forward. "I was actually attracted to you because you were so butch. But also because you were so confident. You knew what to do and did it."

"Looks can be deceiving. I am butch, very much so, and damn proud of it. But confident? No, not me."

"You are when it comes to your work. I don't know about your real life." She reached out and touched Kelly's right hand. "Have a fight with yourself, perhaps?"

"Yeah. I taught my kitchen wall a lesson." *It's almost as if Dr. Tower paid Rain to say this.*

"Ouch. I take it you didn't win. So, back to the feeling of connection. Do you believe in love at first sight?"

"No, not exactly. I believe when soul mates first meet, there's a pull there, something that starts the spark, at the very least."

"Me, too. The right woman is out there for each of us, somewhere, waiting for us to show up." Rain watched the people hurrying by outside the window.

"Which is why you go to the library?"

Rain laughed and had to set her cup down to keep from spilling it. "It's better than the laundromat!"

"Now, produce sections can be interesting. You can have veggie sex right there in the aisle, and no one will know."

"Veggie sex?"

"Yeah, like phone sex except not with a phone." Kelly grinned as Rain tried to figure it out. "See, you go there, and you spy another lesbian. You circle each other, making eye contact as you sniff the various fruits and veggies. Depending on her size, you pick up either an apple or a cantaloupe, sniffing it as you squeeze for ripeness."

"Oh...my..."

"Exactly. Try it some time."

"I just might. Hmm. There are plenty of possibilities."

Kelly saw Kaye come into the bookstore and waved her over. "I got done early and hoped I would find you here." Kaye took off her gloves.

"Kaye, this is Rain Moon. Rain, this is Kaye, Annette's partner."

"Oh! I've heard so much about you!" the two women said together.

"Sit down, Kaye, join us."

GRACE'S CAR HADN'T started again, and she'd taken the bus. Lucy was at a Christmas play practice and wouldn't be ready to be picked up until six. She had made arrangements with one of the other mothers to bring Lucy home. She clocked out, put on her coat, and went to stand at the bus stop. A few minutes later, the purr of a familiar engine slowed down, and the car came to a stop.

"Hey, want a ride?" Deb called out, leaning over the passenger seat and opening the door. "I promise to behave."

Grace paused, knowing she shouldn't, but the wind blew harder, chilling her legs through her old jeans. "Sure, if you behave."

The car was warmer, the heat blasting at her feet. Deb shifted gears, and the car pulled back into traffic. "I can't believe how cold it is this early."

"The heating bills are going to be high."

"Pretty sad when two beautiful women start talking about the weather." Deb grinned at her but made no move.

Grace knew she had a bad habit of attracting and going after difficult women. She used to take love in whatever form she could find; usually that form was sex. She wanted out of that habit, wanted to stay in one place and set up a circle of friends. But resisting Deb's charms wasn't easy. The smooth, butch woman was good — too good.

Grace chewed her lower lip and wondered what to do next: tell Deb that she wasn't interested? Or just not respond?

"How about we get some coffee? Just the thing to warm us up."

"No, I need to get home. Lucy will be home soon."

"Surely the kid can go play with someone or something."

"No, she can't. She's only nine and —"

"That sounds old enough to me."

"You don't understand —"

"I understand that you need to get out more." Deb got off the bypass at Charlotte Street and turned toward downtown.

"Stop the car, Deb. I don't want coffee, I want to go home."

"Come on, it's just for a minute or two."

"Stop this car. Now."

Deb started cursing as she slowed the car and pulled into a space near the courthouse. "Look, I'll take you home. You —"

"No. Unlock the door, dammit." Grace grabbed the handle and pulled as soon as she heard the click. She got out, slammed the door, and started walking. She could hear the car slowly following her. So Deb thought she would change her mind? When she reached the corner of College Street and Spruce, Grace turned right, hearing the car turn, as well.

Once the car had completed its turn, Grace spun around and ran down the sidewalk, heading back up College Street. The move didn't give Deb a chance to turn the car around fast enough. Just a short block to Market Street and another to Broadway. Grace went inside the second business she came across, figuring Deb would assume she went into the first. She saw her drive by twice, and, after a long wait, Grace left the store and continued walking toward the center of town.

"I RECKON WE need to get to the house. Rain, you need a ride?"

"No, Jake and I need the walk. He does the walking, I do the looking, but thanks." She woke Jake and let him put his front feet on her lap as she checked his harness and collar.

"All right, then. Let's head out, cowpoke."

"I ain't no cowpoke. I'm a cow tipper." Kaye and Kelly sauntered out of Malaprop's, getting laughs from other customers.

"Where'd you park?"

"Would you believe right down there? It's darn near impossible to get a parking spot on the street, at least a legal one, but I, Kaye the Great, got one." They headed back toward the library to get into Kaye's Cherokee. "I'm to pick up dinner from Tripps. Want some, too?"

"Sure. You buying?"

"Nah, Annette is." They laughed as Kaye drove down Haywood, merging onto Flint, then onto Hiawassee before heading up Lexington, basically making a wide U-turn.

"You ever gone into these antique places? Nikki's dragged me into several of them." Kelly cradled her left arm. It was beginning to ache. She was trying to avoid the pain medication, but by the end of each day, she usually gave in.

"Only once. I had to go get a gift for her." She slowed the Cherokee and stopped at the light at College Street. "Hey, isn't that Grace Owens?"

Kelly squinted as she looked at the hunched-over person Kaye pointed to. "Yeah, I think you're right. Circle the blocks again. I'll meet you back here." Kelly got out of the SUV and crossed the street. "Grace?"

Grace looked up, surprised to see Kelly coming down the sidewalk toward her. "Hi, Kelly."

"Hi, yourself. I haven't seen you since I left the hospital." Kelly pushed aside the memories of that time, not wanting to revisit that raw anger she had to fight.

"How's your arm?" She reached out to touch Kelly's arm.

"Starting to hurt. What are you doing out walking in this cold?"

"It's a long story, and one I don't want to talk about. What are *you* doing walking in this cold?"

"I'm not. I was with Kaye. She's circling around in the Jeep. Need a ride home?"

"Do you think Kaye would mind?"

"Hell, no! Come on. We'll meet her on the other corner." Kelly took Grace's hand, and they ran across the street. "So, how's Lucy?"

"She's good. She's at school for a play practice."

"Sounds like fun. What's her role?"

"Today is just the try-outs." Grace was beginning to get colder now that she was standing still.

"Ah, here comes our taxi."

"SHE DIDN'T TELL you why she was out?"

"Nope. She had no bags except for the one she takes to work." Kaye pushed buttons on the microwave.

"Odd." Annette opened the refrigerator.

"She was freezing cold. I'd say she'd walked several blocks." Kaye watched the dinner plate spin 'round and 'round inside the microwave.

"What was she doing out there like that?" Annette put the soda cans on the table. "She's such a private person. When they were here, she didn't open up much."

"You mean she wouldn't answer all your nosy questions." Kelly turned from the window to wink at her friend. "Something is up with her, and this idiot who gave her a ride home from work once or twice. I saw her the Friday I was bringing in the drywall."

"Do you think she was offered a ride again and then got dumped downtown?"

"Something like that." Kelly sat down at the table and began eating.

Later, Kaye pushed her plate away and sighed. "Best damn meal I've had in a long time."

"Kaye!" Annette reached across the table to hit her.

"You two are dangerous." Kelly laughed and tried to stay out of the way.

After the kitchen was cleaned up and the dishwasher was running, they went to the living room to sit around the fireplace. Annette stretched out on her recliner to read a book. Kaye sat in her wingback recliner near the lamp to look at a magazine. The only sounds were the occasional sniff or cough, the fireplace cracking and popping, and the shuffling of pages.

Kelly sat on the love seat, her feet up, her left arm propped up on a cushion. She was becoming mesmerized by the fire, watching the delicate red and yellow flames dance across the logs to consume them bit by bit. She was thinking about Grace's situation, trying out different scenarios in her head. "Kaye, what say you get off work early again tomorrow? We can go cruising down around River Road."

"Oh? Think perhaps we might be needed?"

"I'm thinking it might not be a bad idea." Kelly still watched the fire.

"I usually follow your judgment." Kaye watched as her friend smiled.

"I guess I'll check the accounts to make sure we have enough bail money." Annette didn't bother looking up from her book.

Chapter
Eighteen

GRACE'S DAY WAS not going well. The tension from the obvious hostility that emanated from Deb was palpable. They avoided talking, avoided eye contact.

When it came time to punch out and leave, Grace hung around her station for a few minutes, pretending the tip of her iron needed changing. After clocking out, she went outside to stand under the awning, watching for Deb. With about ten minutes to go until the bus arrived, and assuming Deb was already gone, she left the safety of the building to go stand by the bus stop sign.

But she had underestimated Deb, and her need for payback. Grace had just reached the bus stop when she heard a too-familiar car approach and come to a stop. The woman got out of the car and literally swaggered over. "Well, well, if it ain't Miss High and Mighty."

"Look, I don't want any trouble—"

"Too damn late for that now. You think you're too special to be seen with me? You think you're too good for me? Tell you what, bitch. You're not special, and you sure as hell aren't better than me." Deb came to a stop, their faces a few inches apart. "You should be happy that someone even wanted to date you. You're used goods, Grace. Some man done had you and made a breeder out of you. Think many women want to go down on that?" She grabbed Grace's arm, squeezing and twisting it, dragging her toward the car.

"Let me go!" Grace tried to get away but she was not strong enough.

"Deb, I suggest you let her go and back off." Kelly stood there, big, tall, impressive.

But Deb wasn't impressed. "What's the matter, Walker? Mad I touched the goods before you could?"

Grace stood there, frozen in place. Deb twisted her arm harder. But Grace had seen Kelly's rage. There was no way Deb, although strong in her own right, would survive a fight with the bigger woman. But Kelly chuckled, surprising Grace.

"You sure haven't changed any over the years. That's the difference between you and me, Deb. I don't see her or any other woman I want to date as goods. I see her as a woman. You need to get your head out of your own ass and grow up." She stood there, grinning. But her eyes revealed the simmering anger inside her.

Grace saw Kaye walking toward them, flipping her cell phone closed, her facial expression revealing she knew Deb, too. As Kaye approached, the sounds of screeching tires drew everyone's attention but Kelly's. A flatbed tow truck stopped in the street and another woman, shorter but wider than Kelly, got out of the cab, the thicker half of a pool cue in her hand.

"Looky here now. If it ain't Deb Kawalski. I should have known it was your piece of trash I was to pick up."

"What?" Deb was thrown off kilter. She was outnumbered, surrounded by long-time enemies, and now her precious car was being threatened. Kelly took the opportunity to pull Grace away from her, putting her arm around her, protecting her.

"Yep, I got a call from the police to pick up a car that was blocking the bus stop. Ah, here's the officer now."

The next few minutes moved fast for Grace. The officer, another woman, turned on her lights and siren as she pulled in behind Deb's car, blocking her in. The tow truck driver put the end of her pool cue, the one with the metal flange, on the hood of the car and leaned on it. Deb's face was getting redder as the brass pushed in the hood.

Kelly took that moment to gently squeeze Grace's shoulder as Kaye took her arm and led her toward the Cherokee parked across the street. Grace let herself be led away, in shock over all that had happened. Behind her, she heard Kelly speak to the tow truck driver and the police officer. All of them ignored the fuming Deb.

"SO HOW DID you know?"

"Aw, it wasn't too difficult to figure out. It was the only one that made sense. Then earlier, when I was describing that fancy car to Kaye, she knew who it belonged to. So, on our way there, we made some phone calls and pulled some strings."

"It's good to have friends in the right places." Kaye grinned. They sat around Grace's kitchen table, sipping fresh coffee. An ice pack lay on the table near Grace's elbow. Her arm would have some nasty bruises.

"How do you two know Deb?"

"Nikki and Harri, the woman with the tow truck, went to high school with her. And I'd met her long ago and once since I moved here." Kelly refilled their cups. "She's known as a predator. Loves to go after what she thinks are the weak members of the pack. She about got more than she bargained for when she caught you."

The sound of the school bus and yelling children grabbed their attention. Lucy, dragging her big book bag, charged down the sidewalk, through the open gate and up the walk to the porch. "Mom! I'm home!"

"I hear that. So does everyone for two blocks."

"Only two? I'm losing my touch. What's for...Miss Walker! And Miss Gillpepsi!" Lucy gave Kaye a quick hug and ran and jumped in Kelly's lap. "What are you doing here? Where's your big white truck? How's your hand? I get to play an elf in the Christmas play, but Tommy's a rat."

"How can a rat and an elf be in a play together?" Kaye dared to interrupt.

"No, he *is* a rat. He told Miss Simpson that I stole his pencil, but I didn't, but I still got in trouble. Then later, he said I took it again, but Melissa said he was lying, and—"

"Breathe, Lucy." Grace considered recording that phrase and playing it over and over to save her own breath.

"...and Miss Simpson believed me this time 'cause he had all his pencils, and I had just one."

"You have just one now?"

"Yep. I lose them or they run away, or I know, they get taken by aliens."

"Lucy, darlin', you're something else, did you know that?" Kelly hugged the young girl.

"Yep, but no one knows what that something is." Lucy hugged her back and went to take her book bag into her room.

"No wonder you're tired all the time. Listen, I need to get to the house. Grace, you need anything, just holler. Even if it's just to ask what we know about someone you meet, okay?" Kaye stood and kissed her on the top of her head.

"I will, now that I know you really do know everyone." She stood to walk them to the door.

"Miss Walker, I got a ninety-eight on that math test." Lucy peeked out from her bedroom.

"Good for you! I knew you could do it."

"Me, too!"

GRACE SAT IN the quiet living room, letting the weirdness of the day drain from her. Lucy was sound asleep, the dishes were done, and the laundry was all folded, ready to put away in the morning.

She still couldn't believe what had happened. How all those women, all strangers, had come to her rescue. And she didn't even ask! What was it she was thinking the other day? That she wanted to settle down and have a circle of friends. Perhaps she already had one.

As she remembered the events out on the street, she heard what Kelly had said. *"I don't see her or any other woman I want to date as goods. I see her as a woman."*

It brought all sorts of thoughts rushing into her mind. *What did she mean by that? Does she want to date me? Or was I just the example? Do I want to date her? Duh!*

Grace shook her head and stood, ready to go to bed. She had no reason to believe Kelly Walker would want to date someone like her.

Chapter
Nineteen

GRACE HAD HER daughter's lunch put together even before Lucy was out of the shower. Once Lucy sat down to eat her breakfast, Grace joined her. "Lucy, we need to have a talk."

"Uh oh. What have I done wrong now?"

"Nothing, honey, not you. I'm quitting my job today."

Lucy paused, the spoon halfway to her mouth. Drops of milk splashed down onto the multi-colored cereal in the bowl. "Why?"

"It's a long story, sweetheart, one that I can't tell you. I'm going to go out looking for another one today, so don't worry."

"I don't want to move again. You promised we wouldn't."

"And we're not. I'll work something out with Kaye. I can get a job, don't worry about that. I just wanted you to know what was going on."

Lucy put the food in her mouth and scooped up another spoonful. "Is that why Miss Walker and Miss Gillpepsi were here yesterday?"

"Part of it, yes. But I made the mess myself. They just helped me clean it up. And it's Gillpesi, Gillepsi—crap, Lucy! Now I can't say it!" Grace laughed as she poured milk onto her own cereal, feeling better having told her daughter about her decision.

Once Lucy had gone to school, Grace cleaned up the house, although there was not really much to clean up. Most places weren't open until nine, so she needed the busy work. At 8:45, the phone rang.

"Grace, this is Annette. I've heard of a job you might be interested in. Didn't you say once you used to be a secretary of some sort?"

"A clerk. I suppose you figured out that I wouldn't return to work, huh?"

"Yeah, it did occur to me you were smart enough not to. Anyway, the job is with Thompson Construction. They're out here in High Pond, or at least the warehouse is. The pay is good, and I've heard he has great insurance. Want his number?"

"Um, sure." Grace used a crayon she'd found under the couch cushion and wrote the number down on the back of the envelope from the power company. "I'll let you know how it works out."

"I'd appreciate it. How's the kid? Kaye said she was at a play practice."

"Yes, she's going to be an elf. Now I've apparently got to remember how to sew."

"Don't ask me! I've never learned. Anyway, I need to go. You call him, and let me know, okay?"

"Sure, I will. And thanks."

"You're welcome."

ANNETTE HUNG UP the phone and pushed Kelly away. "I don't know why you didn't tell her."

"Because I didn't want her to think of it as charity. Coming from you it's less painful. How'd she sound?"

"Oddly, she sounded a lot like Grace Owens." Annette left the table and rolled down the hall to the library room.

"Thanks, Annette, for calling her." Kelly stood in the doorway, watching as Marley helped her friend out of her chair and onto a recliner.

"I just hope Clarence Thompson and his Neanderthal crew won't scare her too badly."

Kelly laughed. "Don't worry. I've met her inner Mama Bear. I almost feel sorry for Clarence."

GRACE CALLED THE number and spoke to a rough-sounding man who, while saying he was glad she called, also made it seem as if she was bothering him. The car decided to start, and she drove out to his facility in High Pond.

She went inside a long metal building full of supplies and equipment of all sorts. A group of men, most of them covered in dust, lounged around several trucks parked in the back just outside two big garage doors. As soon as they heard the door shut, the whistling and flirting began.

"Hey there, little lady, you lost? I'll help you find your way."

"Ain't you a cutie pie?"

"Boys, boys, whatever happened to southern hospitality? I'll call all of y'all's mamas, and tell them just how you're behaving." Grace shook her finger at them, her other hand on her hip. Assuming she would run into guys like this, she had dressed as androgynously as possible. The loose t-shirt she wore was tucked neatly into her jeans. She had decided that casual would be better than over-dressing for this interview.

"Now, don't go get all hostile on us and threaten to call our mamas." One of them raised his hands in surrender. The other men laughed, and they began teasing each other instead.

"Grace Owens?"

She turned to see a man standing in the doorway of what must be the office. The hair on the top of his head scraped the door frame when he turned to go back in. She wished someone had thought to tell her she might be working for Bigfoot.

ALL THAT WAS forgotten when she stepped into the office. The past nine years of being a parent had taught her just how messy a room could get overnight with very little effort. But this...this had taken years. Boxes of unorganized papers were haphazardly stacked along the wall. Rolls of blueprints were scattered about, as were balled-up pieces of paper that had been tossed but never made it to the trash can. The only cleared path went from the door to the time clock, and from there to another door, further to her right. Magazines, catalogs, more paperwork, several jackets, three boots, and an umbrella were spread around the room.

"Over the shock yet?" Clarence Thompson's deep voice startled her out of her inspection.

"Almost. Um, not had a secretary before?"

"Nope, ain't never seen the need for one. Not until about three years ago when the business really started taking off. Then it became more than I could handle. This is the main office," he said as he pointed toward the other door, "and through there is my office, although I'm so rarely in it I don't know why I bother having one."

"I suppose the job only lasts until I get this cleaned up?"

"Longer'n that. You think I want this to happen again? No, this is a permanent full-time job. You got experience?" He leaned against what must be a desk underneath all the stuff.

"I was a file clerk for a while, basically taking what I was given and filing it in the appropriate place. I've not been a secretary, although I'm adult enough to be allowed to answer a phone. I've got a nine-year-old daughter, so I'm used to balancing schedules."

"Good answers. When can you start?"

"Tomorrow morning?"

"No, why don't you wait until Monday? Start the pay week off right. We have no uniform here. What you're wearing will be fine. You'll be here all by yourself. During the summer, you're welcome to bring your kid if she stays away from the equipment. I wouldn't want her to get hurt." He took a folder that was balanced on a box and gave it to her. "Here's all the paperwork you need to fill out. Now, let me show you where everything is."

"DID YOU DO the homework assignment?" Dr. Susan Tower sat down, folding her legs under her.

"Of course. And I think I did it right."

"There is no right or wrong, Kelly. There's just doing it. Show me." She held out her hand and watched her client silently stare back. At last, Kelly reached into her front shirt pocket, pulled out a crumbled slip of paper and gave it to her. Dr. Tower smoothed it and squinted at the writing. "What chicken scratched this out for you?"

"I did it. I did it right-handed. I'll never do it again." Kelly's eyebrows bunched together, her sign she was not joking.

"Why didn't you just use a computer?"

"A what?" Again, she wasn't exactly joking.

"A com...I see. You read it, then. Out loud so I can hear you."

"Doc, you're crazier than I am."

"Yeppers." She waited as Kelly took the paper back and glared at it, as if it were all the paper's fault.

"'Name at least five things I've advanced with since Anna died.' That's the top line."

"What were your first two?"

"I started my own business, and I bought my own property."

"You consider them advancements? Why would they not have advanced if Anna was still alive?"

"For one, I wouldn't be here. For two, she didn't like me to get dirty, you know? She wanted me to go to architect school. I worked the construction job, but only because she said it would show me the basics."

"Sounds like she really ruled your life."

"It does, but it didn't seem like it then. It felt more like she knew better than I did, so I listened to her advice."

"If it were only advice, why wouldn't you have started your own business?"

"Like I said, it's a dirty job. She wouldn't have liked it if I did a blue-collar job."

"She wouldn't have liked it, but would she have stopped you?"

"Most likely. I realized something as I was writing these out. Anna had been telling me what to do for a while. She thought she knew more, she thought she was better, and that's just not right." Kelly shifted so one leg was crossing the other.

"Ah. So perhaps you can say that the mess was all Anna's fault and not yours?"

Silence.

"That's the goal here, Kelly. We aren't out to crucify her. We're out to show that you are not as bad as you think."

"I thought of that, too. If she hadn't died and I found out about it, at least then I could get angry. But with her dead, it didn't feel right, getting angry and blaming her, I mean." She smoothed out the paper on the arm of the chair then folded and refolded it.

"If a person is a bitch, she's as much a bitch dead as she was alive. Anna didn't immediately turn into a saint when she died. She treated you badly. She's worthy of your anger — then and now."

"It just doesn't feel right, blaming her. It's like — it's like it's sacrilege. You honor the dead; you don't throw stones at them."

"True, we're taught to respect those who have died. Perhaps you can look at it this way: respect Anna, but get pissed at what she did."

"Love the sinner, hate the sin?" Kelly grinned at that, something she hadn't done all session.

"In a way, yes. Anna herself is gone, but her actions continue. She was a stone, of sorts, that got tossed into a lake. The ripples from that toss continue long after the rock's on the bottom."

"So if it's her actions that are the problem, not necessarily her, then I wasn't as big a fool as they said I was."

"Right. And anyone who would tell you that, so soon after her dying, wasn't showing you respect. You were still alive, and they treated you as if you didn't matter. Even the two women who came forward. Did they need to do that? Why did they do it at the service? Talk about gall."

"I've thought of that, too. I think that the ideas — like I was a big stupid fool — settled into my concrete head so solidly because I was so torn up inside."

"Now that you've gotten mad, now that you let that pressure out, what do you think of Anna now? It's okay to say it out loud, you know. Really."

Kelly stopped fiddling with the paper, but kept staring at it instead of looking up. "She...she did me wrong. She had two affairs while I thought we were basically married. I loved her more than I loved anything else. I still do, but I don't respect her anymore."

They sat there, silent, letting the words echo around the room. "There now. No poltergeist came out of the floor to scream and yell. And you're the better for saying it. How does it feel?"

"Odd. Really odd. I didn't realize how much I had sunk into that idea that she was an innocent, and I was so guilty. I got to where I actually believed what they'd said, that I was an idiot and a fool."

"I think you're a wonderful, talented woman. You're intelligent, and you retain knowledge well. You respect others. You must be good at your job because your client list keeps growing. How can someone like that be an idiot and a fool at the same time?"

"I see your point. I never really saw my ability to fix things as an intelligent thing. I see it as something that I do. Nothing important."

"Now, what is the next thing on your list? What, thought you were getting away with just telling the first two?" Dr. Susan Tower laughed at the look on Kelly's face.

WHEN LUCY GOT home and heard the news about her mother's new job, she danced from the living room to the kitchen and back again. "When do you start?"

"Monday. I have to be there at eight in the morning."

"So we have the weekend together? Cool. What're we going to do?"

"I don't know. You got any ideas?"

"Let's have a movie weekend — eat nothing but snacks and watch movies."

"Sure, we haven't done that in a while. Tomorrow, while you are at school, I'll go get the snacks and pick up the movies. We can start as soon as you get home. What do you want for supper today, though?"

Mother and daughter went to the kitchen, and as Grace started their evening meal, Lucy took out her homework.

"Did you know that you should wash your hands for as long as it takes to sing 'Happy Birthday'?" Lucy looked up from her health book.

"No, I didn't. So if I hear you singing in the bathroom, I'll know why. Speaking of cleaning up, get your books off the table and we'll eat."

FRIDAY MORNING, KELLY and Annette were in the living room watching game shows on television. They were both startled when Kelly's cell phone rang. "Walker." Since news had spread that she was out of commission for a while, it had stopped ringing, but out of habit, the little phone was always attached to her belt.

"Just who I wanted to speak at. Listen, I was wondering if you'd help me with something." Clarence Thompson's deep voice sounded in her ear.

"What you need, Clarence? Someone to show you the difference between a rip saw and a hack saw?" She stood to go get two more cans of soda.

"Funny, but close. I got some plans that need going over, to make sure they're consistent with the changes list. They're projects I've already done and I just want to make sure I got the right copies."

"Can I do it one-handed?" She handed a can to Annette and returned to her chair.

Clarence actually chuckled. "Walker, you could do it no-handed. No drawing, just comparing. Come by the office Tuesday or Wednesday evening when I get done, and we'll discuss the details. Oh, I hired that girl you sent over. I think she'll work out just fine."

Chapter
Twenty

AFTER HER SESSION Thursday, Kelly had been given the okay to live on her own, even drive, if she wished. She wouldn't be able to drive the big truck with its manual transmission, so Harri loaned her one of the many vehicles she had and brought it over Friday afternoon. Sitting out in Annette and Kaye's driveway was a '72 Dodge Dart. The hood was green, the two driver's side doors were white, the two passenger doors were red and primer gray. The roof was another color of green, faded to almost a yellow. The trunk lid and the right back corner panel were black, also with primer gray. The opposite corner panel was mostly rust, with fist-sized holes. All four tire rims were different, and the front and back bumpers were gone.

It was the ugliest car they'd ever seen, but the engine was in great shape; it was easy to steer and was an automatic.

"Not the prettiest thing on the planet, but it runs." Harri handed Kelly the keys and drove off in her flatbed truck.

"Are you going to be staying with us longer?" Annette finished her roll around the Dart.

"I was hoping to, yes. I don't think I'm up to taking care of myself yet. Besides, you're a good cook." Kelly rested her hand on the push handle as they headed back up to the house.

"Good. We don't think you are, either, but we didn't know how to tell you and not hurt your butch-girl feelings."

"My *precious* butch-girl feelings. You always forget that word."

"On purpose, of course. What will you do, now that you're a free woman?"

"I thought I'd go to the shop and do some clean-up work there. Empty out the truck and get it cleaned and all that."

"Sounds horribly boring. Heading out now?"

"Soon. I thought I'd try to talk you into a sandwich before I left."

SUNDAY AFTERNOON, GRACE made a deal with a teenage girl two blocks down to meet Lucy after school the next day and stay with her until she got home from work. She figured her first day would be long, and she wouldn't be able to get back home in time. Lucy wasn't happy to know she was going to have a baby-sitter, but she preferred it to the after-school program.

Grace arrived at the warehouse at ten minutes 'til eight. Some of the men were already there, gathering their equipment for the day's work. They called out to her, still teasing her but she took it in stride. She leaned against the wall, watching them, and they did their best to show off for her.

"Boys, y'all gonna give yourself a hernia pulling crap like that." Big Clarence came in, tossing his jacket over a crate. "Grace, they bothering you?"

"Nah, just keeping me entertained. Ready?"

"Yep, step on in here."

"Careful nothing bites you!" one of the men called out as Clarence opened the door.

Grace didn't consider the comment to be a joke. The office area looked as bad as she remembered. Clarence sighed as they looked it over. "I reckon the best way to get started is to just throw you in and see if you learn to swim."

"That might be a good way, yes."

He put his briefcase down on a box on the desk, clicking it open. "All right then. This is the company credit card. The one with your name won't be here for a few weeks, but you can use this one. This is the card for the office supply store and the warehouse store. Here's a cell phone for you. I'll get you a newer one in a few days. Here are all my numbers. Don't hesitate to call, but don't expect me to be friendly. I'm a grouch at times. We'll sit down and go over all your questions at once when we're done for the day."

"That sounds like a good idea."

"Good. I called the office supply place already and spoke to a man named Mitch. He knows you're gonna call or come in to get some office type stuff. Get whatever you need, file cabinets, desk, chairs, whatever."

"Mr. Thompson, how —"

"Call me Clarence, or I'll call you fired."

"Okay. Clarence, how can you trust me with all this on my first day at work?"

"Several reasons. One, where would you go with all this? Everyone knows me and my company. Second, what would you do with all this? The credit card company would freeze it if they saw I went on a spending splurge at a dress shop. Third, and most important, I trust anyone that Walker recommends."

"Who?"

"Walker. Kelly Walker. I told her a while back I needed some-one, and she said she'd look around. She's the only one I told, so you had to be someone she knows. Now, I don't mind at all what Walker does in her private life, just as she don't mind what I do in mine, so don't worry on that account. Now, I gotta get these boys to work, or they'll get into even more trouble." Clarence patted her shoulder and went out to the others, his deep voice barking orders.

Grace stood in the office, wondering how she felt about this. *Did I get this job on my own, or did Kelly make him hire me?* She shook her head and took off her jacket. Even if Kelly did ask Clarence to hire her, she would show him she could do the job.

First, she poked around in some of the boxes, getting an idea of what was in them. Then she went out to the warehouse and asked one of the men if there were any empty boxes she could use. He got several broken down ones from a space over the office. "There's duct tape hanging on a hook behind the door." The man, young enough that his beard was just starting to grow, grinned and ran to join the others by the trucks.

With the boxes reassembled, she began sorting. It was like sort-ing clothes, actually. If it had to do with employee records, toss it into that box. If it had to do with projects, toss it in that other one. If it had to do with equipment, over in that box. There were three other boxes for paperwork: one for paperwork that fit more than one category, one for those that she hadn't a clue what to do with, and the last for those that had to do with the vehicles.

She decided that clearing off the desk would be the best place to start. It was a harder task than she thought. She had gotten most of it done when she stopped for lunch.

KELLY HAD SPENT the weekend with her friends, putting off working in her shop until Monday. Now she turned on the lights and the heater and looked around the building at her tools and equipment. She tried to keep positive and considered her time off as time to clean up, do repairs, and to work on some ideas she had. She'd promised to go slow and not move any of the larger equip-ment without assistance. One of her friends must have come over to accept the delivery when the architect store had brought over the desk. It sat against the wall near the door. Nikki was coming by as soon as she was done with work to back the big truck into the shop so Kelly could go through it. For now, she wanted to start an inven-tory.

She couldn't write all that well yet and was never good at writ-ing right-handed. She thought it over and took some labels, a good pen, and got to work. As she went through a box or drawer, she stuck on a label for each type of part and an approximate count. The work took longer since there were plenty of parts—screws, bolts, nuts, etc. that were in the wrong drawer or box.

It had been a long time since she'd not had anything to do. She had gotten too used to being busy almost every hour she was awake. Now she could look back and see that it was a way for her to push Anna and that mess to the back of her mind where it sat and festered.

She worked until her stomach rumbled. She got out the lunch Annette had packed for her and ate it while sitting out on the dock. The lake took up roughly three hundred acres of the property, making it one of the largest privately-owned lakes in the area. When she was younger, she and her brothers came here for the summers, and the lake was their biggest toy. She learned how to swim here, as well as how to fish and snorkel. Only a few parts of it were deep enough for decent SCUBA diving, but she always thought about someday she would learn that, too.

Out in the distance, she saw a fish jump up out of the water to catch a bug. If it weren't careful, it would be caught by the hawk that was sitting in the trees somewhere nearby. Kelly had heard it call out earlier. To her right, a small rabbit, brown with black flecks in its fur, came out of the tall, dead grass and stood on its back legs to look around. It saw her and darted back, moving faster than she could believe. She made a note to herself to plant a winter garden next year for the winter critters.

She decided she wanted to go for a walk, and after putting her trash in the can outside the shop, she got her walking stick—in case she came across any snakes—and headed west toward the old homestead. Along the way, she saw many cardinals and blue jays, several more rabbits, and even a turtle making its way across the path. The trees, all bare and standing silent in the cold, looked like the x-rays she'd seen of her hand: twisted bones against a dark background.

Over another ridge and below her stood what was left of the old house. Originally built in the late 1700s, the house had burnt down once before her great-grandfather had been born. They rebuilt it, other generations making it smaller or larger as their current need dictated. Its second fire had been just a decade ago, right after her grandfather had been moved to the nursing home. The arson expert suspected kids had come to swim in the lake and had started a fire to get warm. The house, with its dry, old wood, was burned to the ground in less than half an hour, just long enough for the fire trucks to arrive and keep it from spreading.

All that was left was the tall chimney made from the original stones saved after the first fire. Even the sidewalk had become overgrown, and from up above, she could just make it out. Perhaps someday she would rebuild it, maybe making it look the same as it did originally.

The wind blew cold down her back. She turned and headed toward the shop, ideas rumbling through her mind.

It felt good to be thinking again. She was doing much better, facing Anna's death and her affairs. Annette and Kaye, in their gentle manner, didn't push but would set aside everything to listen. That had helped more than Kelly realized.

She got back to the shop and sat near the heater, her sketch pad balanced on her knee. It was hard to draw, but she found that if she moved the whole arm, it wasn't completely impossible. She sketched the idea she had for a desk for Lucy and later moved to her new drafting table to do the more detailed plans. Nikki came by but only had enough time to move the truck into place for Kelly before she was gone.

She was figuring out the lumber list when her cell phone rang. "Walker."

"May I speak with Kelly Walker, the fix-it lady?"

"This is she." The voice was familiar.

"Oh, hi, Miss Walker. This is Lucy Owens. Um, I need help with my math homework again. I have a test coming up I need to study for."

"Fine, when's the test?" Kelly leaned back in her chair.

"Tomorrow."

"Oh. Well, I reckon I can be over in an hour or so."

"No! I mean, can you come now? I'd like to get it done and over with."

A little orange light of alarm flashed in Kelly's mind. "Sure. I can be there in less than thirty minutes. Can you wait that long?"

"Yes ma'am! I'll watch for you."

After she hung up, she stared at the phone, wondering why it was so important that she be there now to help with Lucy's homework. Maybe the kid was really concerned about the test and was afraid of a low grade. She supposed that would explain it. She gathered her briefcase and her large note pad, turned off the heater, and locked up the shop. On her way to the car, she called Kaye and Annette to tell them she'd be getting dinner elsewhere.

KELLY PARKED THE car in front of the house on Oak Street and got her briefcase out from the passenger side. She knocked, but the front door was opened slowly, a timid Lucy peeking out. "Hello, Miss Walker. Come on in."

"Hello, yourself." She noticed how quiet the house was. "Lucy, where's your mom?"

"At work."

"And you're here alone?" Kelly sat on the edge of the couch.

"Yes," she whispered, "The baby-sitter never showed up."

"And you've been here alone since you got home?"

"Yes. I thought I could do it—show Mom how mature I am. But then it started getting dark."

"I guess we'll make the best of a bad situation. Have you eaten?"

Lucy shook her head. Her eyes were still wide, and she chewed on her bottom lip. Kelly could tell the girl was frightened but was trying not to show it.

"When I was your age, maybe a little older, we were helping my uncle move. We had a station wagon and a moving van. We got everything loaded and were getting ready to leave. The moving van was on one side of the apartment building and the car on the other. Mom told me to go ride in the truck with Uncle Jim and his son, my cousin Mark. But when I got there, they said there wasn't room because they'd had to put plants up front with them. So I went back around the building, but Mom and my brothers were gone. I ran back around again and my uncle was already down the hill and out onto the highway. They had no idea I was left behind."

"Were you scared?"

"Heck, yeah! I mean, I tried to be brave and not cry. I knew I had to think and find some way of being safe until they figured it out."

"What'd you do?" Lucy's body was more relaxed, and she was no longer chewing her lower lip.

"I went to find the security guard. He took me to his shack, and we called both the houses. But he had to get back on his rounds, so he took me with him. We must have walked several miles, checking all the buildings and the other gates. It was fun, and spending time with him made me feel better. He had a little girl, younger than me. We got a call on the radio from another security guard that Mom had gotten the phone message and was on her way back to get me. He took me to the guard shack at the main gate, and I got to help him raise and lower the gate until my mom arrived."

"Was your mom mad?"

"Nope. More mad at herself than me. So, what say you and I go see what we can make for dinner? I'm a lousy cook, but I reheat like a professional. Then we'll get to your math homework, if that part was true."

GRACE PARKED HER car near her house and noticed the ugly rust bucket of a car parked by the gate. She got angry, thinking the teenager had invited a boyfriend over.

When she opened the front door, she smelled burnt food and heard giggling coming from the kitchen. She stood in the kitchen doorway, unnoticed, as Kelly and Lucy sat together at the table. In front of them was a short stack of pancakes. One side of each pancake was burnt black. The two were laughing as they used butter knives to scrape off as much black as they could.

"Mom never burns the pancakes." Lucy kept giggling.

"I told you I couldn't cook. Besides, you distracted me."

"Don't blame this on me!" Lucy stopped scraping, poured syrup on her pancake, and took a small bite. "Ew. I need to scrape off more."

"My first question is what are you doing?" Grace finally spoke, startling the two at the table.

"Mom! You're home! How was your first day at work?" Lucy spun around in her chair to kneel on the seat.

"My first day at work was interesting. Hello, Kelly."

"I guess you want to know why I am here, huh?" Kelly also turned in her seat, leaning on the back of her chair.

"Yes, that's one of my questions." She came into the kitchen and put her lunch bag on the counter by the sink.

"It's a long story. How about I take you two cuties out to eat, and we'll discuss this?"

"That sounds like a marvelous idea. Lucy, go change clothes and wash your hands." Grace waited until Lucy was out of the kitchen, then turned to face Kelly. "What happened?"

"Lucy called me and said she needed help with homework. I guess that was around 5:30. I got here, and she told me the baby-sitter never showed."

"Never showed? Why didn't you call me?"

"Why should I? I mean, Lucy was safe with me. We talked about being scared and stuff like that. I knew you were at work on your first day."

Grace rubbed her temple. "Okay. Next time, let me know anything that has to do with my daughter. I appreciate you staying and not freaking or anything. I think it's great she trusted you enough to call you." She looked up. Kelly had stood and was piling the burnt pancakes onto one plate.

"I'm sorry I didn't call. I'm not familiar with parental protocols."

Grace took the three steps to stand in front of Kelly. She put her hand on the woman's forearm, stopping her movements. She leaned her forehead on the big but soft shoulder. "My daughter is my life. The idea that she was here alone..."

She had felt Kelly stiffen when she had leaned against her but soon felt strong arms wrap around her. "It turned out okay. She's a tough kid but got scared when it started getting dark."

"She's always been afraid of the dark." Grace sniffed, the only outward sign of the tears that had threatened to flow. She smelled Kelly's aromas of the outdoors and sawdust and burnt pancakes. "You really can't cook, can you?" She straightened up and took a step back.

"Nope. I tell folks, but they never believe me 'til the first time." Kelly reached out and rubbed her arm. "See what's keeping the kid, and we'll go out to eat where folks cook for a living."

AS GRACE LEFT the room, Kelly took a deep breath. Her body was shaking. *Embarrassment? Failure? No, from holding Grace in my arms.* She hadn't felt—hadn't allowed herself to feel—that level of attraction in far too long. She dumped the burnt pancakes in the trash and rinsed off the plates. She made a mental note to buy Grace a new fry pan.

Outwardly, Kelly appeared to be calm. Inside, however, she was running in circles. She'd held in that anger for two years, and look what it did. She glanced at her arm and hand, covered in plaster and bandages. She knew she needed to be herself, to face herself again. *What was it Dr. Tower had said? That I needed to trust myself again?* Could she trust herself, or was this just an infatuation with the first woman to come along? *No, Rain came first.* She put her hand down and turned toward the doorway. *Am I ready for this? For more?*

"We're ready when you are," Grace called out from the living room.

Chapter
Twenty-one

"BUT INSTEAD YOU faced it and moved on. What do you think you'll do about it?"

"I'm not sure. I mean, the feelings were there, but is the common sense? I'm thinking of asking her out on a date. But, well, I'm afraid to. Afraid of myself, mostly. Will that anger come back at me? I don't know." Kelly sat on the end of the couch.

"Didn't you say that it was Grace who pulled you out of the rage in the hospital?" Dr. Tower had read the nurse's report.

"Yes. I still don't remember much of it. Only that she was telling me to do something and I did it, just for her."

"Why do you think you did?"

"I guess there was a sane part of me that responded to her inner Mama Bear." Kelly grinned.

"Do you think that you could hurt Grace? Or Lucy?"

"No, never." Kelly knew it was true.

Silence.

"I keep wondering if the attraction is there because of the timing thing."

"What about this other woman you met recently? Didn't you say the two of you discussed attraction versus like?" Dr. Tower leaned on the arm of her chair, resting her chin on her palm.

"We did. If it weren't for that conversation, I don't think I would be taking this attraction seriously."

"Have you asked Grace out on a date?"

"No, but I am thinking about it." Kelly stood and went to the window. "I'm afraid, though. I feel as if my insides are so vulnerable, that it wouldn't take much to crush them."

"So it may be that you're not feeling you're moving too fast, but that you don't want to be hurt." Dr. Tower waited. "Is that such a bad thing? You can't live the rest of your life and never get your feelings or emotions hurt."

"I know, I just...I feel so...open and exposed."

GRACE LOVED HER new job. She liked the men, even their silly, ritualistic flirting. She especially liked big Clarence who sounded rough and mean but was actually far from it. She'd met his wife, Helen, and immediately saw she had her husband wrapped around her finger, right where he wanted to be.

The space was beginning to look like an actual office. Each evening, the men would return to the warehouse and crowd the door to check out what she had done that day. Of course, they also had to give her their advice, at least until Clarence made them all go home.

She'd organized their time clock and cards on her second day. She got a long rug that went from the clock to the door. It helped cut down on the dust almost immediately. She went to a thrift store and bought several old couches that she had placed in the warehouse. Her object was to get them to gather out there and not in the office. Clarence grumbled that she was softening up his crews, but she saw him sitting there, too.

The new coffee pot became the most used item. These guys loved their coffee in the mornings. She was going to tell them she wasn't going to make it for them, but they surprised her by doing it without her asking.

Almost everything was filed or stored in the cabinets and shelving she had purchased. Clarence presented her with her own filled tool box one morning after he realized she was bringing in her odd collection of tools from home to assemble the furniture.

He was also teaching her the basics of his business so that she understood the language that went along with it. By the end of the second week, she was able to start answering the phone knowledgeably, leaving Clarence to do his job out at the various sites.

The biggest problem with the job was that she spent so much time alone. She had brought in a radio and some CDs to listen to, which helped, but some days it was just not enough. When Kelly had called, offering to take her out for lunch, she jumped at the opportunity.

KELLY DROVE THE ugly Dodge down the road toward Thompson Construction's warehouse. She felt nervous and anxious but also excited. She was prepared for Grace to say no, but she was really hoping it would be yes.

First, she was going to take her out to lunch at the local diner. After that, she'd ask her to go to the Goat Farm Thanksgiving Gathering.

When she pulled up in front of the warehouse, Grace was waiting. "I hope you weren't standing out in the cold for long."

"No, I just stepped out, actually. Have I told you how ugly this car is?"

"Yes, you and everyone else. Harri says it's not looks that count but what's under the hood. I think that's just her way of saying 'beggars can't be choosers.'" Kelly did a U-turn in the lot and got back onto the road.

"She's the tow truck driver from...the other day, right? But she's more than just that, isn't she?"

"She's trying to be. She's got this side business of restoring old classics and antique cars. I think she's going to make that full time soon."

"So how come you're driving this ugly Dart and not an ugly Model T?"

"Funny. But Harri's right. This thing has a fantastic engine. I'd love to drive over to Tennessee where the speed limit's seventy."

"I bet. You just be sure to keep Harri's number on speed-dial."

"You're such a smart ass today!"

"I spend far too much time by myself. I love this job so far, but I don't like being alone all day."

Soon they arrived at the little diner, its parking lot full of trucks of all sizes, shapes, and conditions. When they entered, many of the patrons called out.

"Hey, Walker, finally crash that truck of yours?"

"My gosh, Walker! Could you get a car that was any uglier?"

Kelly just waved them off and found a table against the wall. "Y'all just jealous 'cause this Dodge runs better than your Fords." That comment earned her both boos and laughs.

The waitress approached their table. "Howdy, Walker. Ain't seen you here in a while. What'll you have?"

"Y'all get those actual menus yet, or do I have to squint at the board?"

"Honey, the board ain't changed in ten years, so if you don't have it memorized by now, holding one in your hand won't help any." She clacked the napkin-wrapped utensils down on the middle of the table.

"Friendly person," Grace dared to comment.

"That's one way to describe her. Everything here is good, although most of it's greasy and not good for you."

"What do you usually have?"

"The bacon double cheeseburger and fries. Sometimes the BLT 'cause they believe the B should be as noticeable as the LT."

"So if I got the single patty burger it would be safe?"

"Yep."

"Y'all ready to order yet?" the waitress called out from where she sat with two burly farmers.

"Yeah. Double bacon cheeseburger, single burger, two fries, two sweet teas. Got that?"

"I can hear your arteries complainin' all the way over here." She got up and went through the swinging doors to the kitchen.

A THIN, SMALL man wearing sawdust-covered overalls came to sit at the table next to them to talk with Kelly. He began discussing a job with her, something about wood piles. Grace took the opportunity to look around the diner. The walls were whitewashed cinder block covered in posters and old calendars from tractor, feed, heating oil, and well drilling companies. The waitress's uniform of simple but too-tight jeans, t-shirt from a gospel singing, and a canvas nail bag from the local feed store seemed to fit right in with the rest of the room. The smell in the air was a mix of fried food, cigarette smoke, cigar smoke, and cow manure — and oddly, not repulsive.

"What are you thinking?" Kelly spoke softly, hoping not to startle Grace.

"I was thinking about the smells in here."

"They are rather eclectic."

"You come here often? Silly question, I know, based on the reactions of everyone when we came in."

"I'm part of the morning crowd. I don't come here every morning, but often enough that everyone knows my name. Or at least my last name."

The waitress came over with two huge plastic glasses of ice tea. "We all know your first name; we just think the last one fits you better."

"Funny. I'm surrounded by comedians."

"While I'm here, they're placing bets about how you broke your arm and hand. We've heard all sorts of rumors, and I figure we might as well get it straight from the jackass's mouth."

"The basic story is I got mad and hit a wall with my fist."

"Dang, lost five bucks." One of the men slapped a bill on the table, and the man across from him snatched it.

"What'd you think?" Kelly asked him as she laughed.

"That you hit it with a hammer."

"What the hell made you so mad you hit a wall hard enough to break your hand?" The waitress looked closer at the fingertips that showed at the end of the bandages beyond the cast.

"Something in my past. You know, an old wound that hurts at certain times of the year."

"Ah. I got one of those. I send her checks every month." The other betting man's remark made everyone guffaw.

Soon after, the waitress brought out their lunch, refilled Kelly's glass, and slipped the bill under the salt shaker.

"So they all know you're...you know." Grace began eating.

"I believe so. I think that's why they call me Walker. It's their way of adjusting to it."

"I guess that makes them all think I'm your...what? Fluff chick?"

Kelly choked on her tea. "Um, well, um, some may wonder, but no one'll ask you. But they'll all know your name by seven o'clock."

"How will they know that?"

"Someone will say they saw me drive back down that road, and another will say I pulled into Thompson's lot. Then someone will remember he just hired some woman. If they still had party lines, it'd be known within half an hour of me dropping you off."

"Oh. Small town ways."

"Yep. How's the food?"

"My food is great. So, am I your fluff chick?"

Kelly choked on her fry this time. "I haven't asked you yet, so I'd say no."

"Oh. Shy butch girls and their silly ways."

AFTER THEIR LUNCH at the diner, Kelly drove on, past the warehouse, until she came to an area with a fallow field on one side of the road and rolling hills on the other. She pulled over and parked in front of a cattle gate. "I thought I'd bring you here to meet my other set of friends. This is one of the most peaceful places I know."

"Here? Where are they?"

"They should be coming over that little hill any second now."

The two of them leaned against the hood of the car and watched the crows overhead. The sound of a bell came with the wind, and the first cow came lumbering over the rise. She was using the same worn trail she and the others walked every day they were out.

"That's your friend?"

"Wait, there's more." She pointed as another cow crested the top and came down on their side. Then another and another until there were well over two dozen cows milling around the round hay bale.

At first Grace didn't understand what was so peaceful about them. They lifted their tails and pooped wherever they were, peed with even less concern, and didn't watch where they stepped. They'd pull a mouthful from the round bale, and then chew with most of the hay still hanging from their mouths. As she watched them, she began to feel calm, bemused.

"What is it about them that's so peaceful?" she asked aloud.

"I think it's their lack of concern for what anyone thinks of them. None of them cares that someone just shit on their foot. They aren't concerned with the mud on their knees. They just exist. What happens will happen, so why bother worrying about it?"

"Interesting philosophy. You don't follow it too often, do you?"

"No, no, I don't. I try, but some things just make me all nervous and twitchy."

"You come here often?"

"When I'm in the area, or when I've had a particularly bad day. Soon, they won't be this far out. They'll be kept in a field closer to the barn. But by then, it'll be too cold to sit out here, anyway."

Grace stared at Kelly, not the bovines. "You're such a complex woman, do you know that?"

"Me? No, I'm plain and simple."

"Far from it. You can be so gentle with Lucy. You come here to find peace watching cows, of all things. You work steady and do a good job, even if it takes longer. Yet...yet I saw you taking on two orderlies. Sometimes getting those images to merge into one is difficult."

"Ah. I keep meaning to talk to you about that day, but I've been afraid to." Kelly turned her body away.

"What were you afraid of?" Grace took Kelly's shoulder and turned her around. "That I'd be terrified of you?"

"That, and disgusted with me. I'm nothing special, Grace. I work hard for a living. I get dirty and sweaty. I tend to hold things inside, letting them either go away or get all moldy in that dark corner of my mind. Yes, I have a temper, but when I get mad, it's for a good reason." She paused, staring at her shoes. "I don't go ballistic like I did that night. I never have before, and I don't think I ever will. I wouldn't hurt you or Lucy."

"I'm not afraid of that happening. Nikki told me the condensed version of what set you off." Grace couldn't resist reaching over to cup Kelly's cheek.

"It's a long story. The short of it is I had a partner who died. When she died, I found out she had two other relationships. All our friends knew. Even the other two women knew. But not me. Her friends called me a fool. My friends there called me naive. I pushed it all inward and didn't deal with it. After all, who can get mad at someone who just died?"

"And that date was important to you, wasn't it?"

"Yes. It was the second anniversary of her death."

"That must really hurt. Not only did your partner die, but you found out some terrible secrets she held. You must have felt betrayed by all your friends. You weren't here then?"

"No, up north in Ohio. I moved in with my parents for a few months, and then moved here."

Grace touched Kelly's face again. "I repeat, I trust you. I even trust you with my child. Want to know why? Because I saw you in that rage. You weren't trying to hurt them; you were just trying get free. When I yelled at you, you stopped immediately. You trusted me, even in your madness. The least I can do is trust you back."

Kelly looked down into the eyes of this woman. She desperately wanted to swoop Grace up and kiss her. Instead, she crushed her cap in her hands. "Grace, I asked you to lunch 'cause there's something I wanted to ask you. Something else I wanted to ask you, I mean."

"Okay. Go ahead."

"Would you consider going out on a date with me? You know, a dress-up kind of date?" *The Thanksgiving gathering can be our second date. Yeah, that's it.*

"I'd consider it, yes." Grace smiled up at her and winked.

The wink relaxed a part of her but fired up others. "Okay, smarty. Grace, will you go out on a date with me?"

"Yes, I will."

Phew. That was easy. "And I know that Lucy will come with us, so I've got a good place in mind."

"Lucy's coming with us?"

"Yeah, you're a package deal. I'm assuming she has to like me, or you won't date me again."

"Something like that, yes. Call me later tonight at home, and we'll set the time."

"Speaking of time, I need to get you back to work." Kelly opened the passenger car door and walked around to the other side.

"SHE WHAT?" ANNETTE didn't believe her.

"You heard me! She asked me out on a date!" Grace held the phone to her ear with her shoulder while both hands sorted a pile of papers.

"Our Kelly? Wow. I don't think she's been out on a date since she moved here. Congratulations."

"And she told me about her partner who died. No wonder she's so quiet and nervous around me."

"Yeah, you and all the other women who have thrown themselves at her. I personally know of four who all but stripped naked to attract her attention."

"Hey! I didn't throw myself at her!" Grace laughed, trying to imagine shucking her clothes there on the side of the road.

"Do you know where she's taking you?"

"No, I told her to call me tonight at the house. By the way, Lucy's going with us."

"Okay, it's official. Our Kelly has been abducted and replaced by aliens."

"LUCY, HOW DID play practice go?"

"It went okay. Oh, and one of the moms said she'll do all the elves' costumes. Patty and Cathy are her kids, and she said since she was going to do two, she might as well do two more, 'cause there's four of us."

"Good! I'll have to give you a note to pass along to her. Got your social studies done already?"

"Yep. It was easy enough. And you're off the hook for math homework tonight. I did it in class."

"Speaking of math homework...I got asked out on a date."

"A math date? That's totally weird."

"No, silly pumpkin. Kelly Walker asked me out on a date."

"Way cool! I like her, Mom. Date her all you want!" Lucy jumped up and down.

"She wants you to come along, too, at least for the first one."

"Wowzers. Really? On the first date? Have I ever done that before?"

"Um, I think once but you were very young."

"Was I so young I drank from a bottle?"

"Not that young. But you still wore diapers." Grace grinned as she remembered her date's face when Lucy had filled a diaper with some wondrous toddler poop.

"Ew. I don't even want to think about it. When are we going?"

"I don't know. She's supposed to call later to finalize the plans."

Chapter
Twenty-two

"THIS IS A nice place! Look at all the stuff on the walls!" Lucy sat on the bench in the lobby of the restaurant, her gaze flickering from wall to wall as she looked over all the artifacts on shelves or attached to the wall itself.

"I thought you might like it. It's all stuff from the fifties and early sixties. Wait until you meet the staff."

"Walker, party of three." The hostess, wearing a leather jacket, held menus in her hand as she scanned the crowd.

"Here." The three of them stood and Kelly rested her cast-covered hand on top of Lucy's head.

"Follow me, please." The hostess, a cute young thing probably not even out of high school, led them past the chrome doors and down the aisles to their table near the raised bar where a young man in a starched white uniform and hat was making milkshakes and sundaes. "Your waitress will be right with you."

Kelly watched her leave. "Wonder if she even knows who Joan Jett is?"

"I doubt it." Grace laughed as she opened the large menu. Lucy had a smaller one, geared toward kids. "Wow, check out the names of everything."

"Mom, who's Rosie the Riveter?"

"She was a poster girl from World War II, who promoted women going to work in jobs that the men used to do." Grace pointed out the poster over on a nearby wall. "The women went to work doing all sorts of things because most of the men were away at war. They were riveters, welders, assembly line workers, and did all sorts of other jobs that needed to be done."

"So why did they name a meatball cheese melt sandwich after her?"

"Because it's on a torpedo roll, I suppose. Is that what you'll have?" Kelly asked as their waitress approached.

"Hello, ladies, I'm Dot, and I'll be your waitress for the evening. What can I get y'all to drink?" Dressed in a uniform that could have been worn by Alice or Flo at Mel's Diner, the middle-aged waitress pulled a pencil from behind her ear.

"I'll have a sweet tea." Kelly motioned toward Grace.

"I'll have a sweet tea, as well. Lucy, no caffeine."

"Can I have a lemonade and Sprite? Mixed together?"

"I can do that for you, Sugar. I'll be right back with your drinks and to take your orders."

"Everything looks good, Kelly. Do you recommend anything?"

"I've had almost everything on the menu, but I really like their burgers. And the fries are great, too."

Grace looked over Lucy's menu, too. "What about you? Know what you want?"

"They have a Wimpy Burger Special. I think I'll have that. Can I have a milkshake after?"

"If you have room, sure. Kelly's buying." She elbowed Lucy and winked at Kelly.

"Oh, in that case, Lucy, why don't you try the soup?"

"Funny. Veeery funny."

They all wound up ordering burgers, but in different styles. Kelly got a huge bacon cheddar cheeseburger; Grace ordered a burger with swiss cheese and spicy sauce; Lucy ordered the Wimpy Burger Special: two small burgers stacked with cheese, lettuce, and tomatoes.

As they waited, Grace noticed how Kelly talked mostly to her, but also aimed the conversation toward Lucy, including her in their discussions. She never would have thought Kelly to be as educated as she sounded. Despite what she knew about her job, she had this stereotype of the apartment superintendent in her mind, one that Kelly no longer fit into.

"I think Mom is zoning."

"Is that what you call it?"

"Yeah. She gets that look in her eye when she's off thinking. Let's just hope she doesn't start talking to herself."

"It's not like I didn't hear you say that, little girl."

"I think she means you, Miss Walker. She always calls me 'little lady.'"

They all three had a good laugh just as the waitress returned with their food. The two large platters each held a hamburger sitting open-faced with the hot meat on one side and the cooler lettuce and tomato on the other. The fries—browned with their peels still in place—were spread around the two halves, leaving no part of the platter uncovered. The smell from the fresh combination was enough to make a vegetarian drool.

"How am I supposed to open my mouth wide enough to eat this?" Grace picked up her assembled burger.

"You can smoosh it." Lucy put both hands on the top of her own burger and pressed down.

"Gross, Lucy. A good idea, but gross."

"You just kinda aim the top or bottom then wiggle the rest in." Kelly demonstrated by holding the burger one handed, using her cast to support it, but managed to squirt a tomato out the opposite side when she bit into it. "Only you do it while leaning over your plate."

By the time they had the burgers eaten and the fries nearly gone, even Lucy was saying she was full. "But I really wanted a shake."

"Tell you what. We'll come here again, if it's all right with your mom that is, and just have dessert."

"I think that would be a splendid idea. As long as I get to come, too." Grace laughed as she put her napkin on her plate.

"I guess it's okay. Is it okay with you, Miss Walker?"

"I think it would be okay with me, too. She might have to sit at another table, though."

Kelly was saved from a comment by the waitress coming up to the table. "Can I interest you ladies in some coffee?"

"Yes, for me, please." Kelly put her utensils and napkins on the plate so the waitress could take them away.

"Hot tea?" Grace hoped they had some.

"We have Earl Grey, Lady Grey, and green tea."

"Green tea, please. And little bit here will have chocolate milk."

"I'll be right back with your drinks." She picked up their plates and left, balancing them in her arms.

"SO HOW DID it go?" Annette didn't even say hello when Grace answered the phone.

"It went well, I suppose. There wasn't much difference between this and the other time she took us out to eat. Only she got the doors and held my coat while I put it on. Butch girls and their weird habits." Grace wiped the kitchen counter off after making the meatloaf. She'd thought a lot about the date she'd had with Kelly the day before.

"Do you think it was because Lucy was there?"

"I don't know. Probably. I think Kelly doesn't know what to do on a date. Dating. I'm thirty-four and dating."

"It could be worse. You could be fifty-two and stuck in a thirty-year marriage. Ouch!"

"I take it Kaye threw something at you?"

"Yes, her shoe. Now she wants Marley to bring it back."

"Reloading!" Grace loved those two women. They were perfect together, representing that level of partnership most lesbians only dream of obtaining.

"Don't give her any ideas. If you need a baby-sitter for Lucy, we'll do it. Kaye can pick her up at your house when she gets off work, and then you can pick her up here after your date."

"No, that would be too much trouble for you two. Lucy is a handful and very hyper."

"So are Marley and the goats. We can always lock her in the pen if she gets to be too much."

"I'll think about it. We don't even know if Kelly'll ask me out again." Grace set the timer and went to the living room to read some in a book she'd gotten from the library.

LUCY WAS IN her room playing with her microscope, and Grace was well into the book when the phone rang. "Hello?" Grace answered on the fourth ring.

"Grace? Kelly."

"Hi, Kelly! How was your day?"

"Not too bad. I'm still doing little stuff around here. How was yours?"

"I think I may actually have that office under control." Grace leaned back onto the sofa.

"I met that office once. I admire your attitude. What'd you do? Dump it all in the stream out back?"

"No, but I considered it."

"Anyway, I called with a reason. Kaye and Annette have a gathering at their place next week. We call it the Goat Farm Thanksgiving Gathering. I was hoping you and Lucy could go with me." She heard Kelly clear her throat. "There's games for the kids, and there'll be all sorts of dogs to entertain them. There's adult games, too, like board games and charades and other stuff. I've never paid that much attention."

"Hmm, I already bought a small turkey for us."

"Oh. Maybe we can do something else later then."

"Wait, Kelly, I wasn't finished. I haven't set it out to thaw yet, and I can cook it for us later. I'd love to go. What time?"

"It starts the night before and goes through until the next day. But most locals only come for dinner on Thursday and breakfast on Friday."

Grace shook her head. Kelly really didn't know about things like this. She'd have to call Annette later and get details. "So what time will you be here to pick us up?"

"I was thinking about two or so. Is that okay?"

"Fine with me. I look forward to it. Oh, do you have your calendar out? We were hoping you could come see Lucy's play at school."

"Of course! When is it?"

"Two weeks after Thanksgiving. It's the last day before Christmas break."

"I've marked it. How'd Lucy do on the health test?"

"She did good, eighty-eight, I think. I don't believe she takes it seriously like she does math."

"We all have our weaknesses."

WEDNESDAY AFTERNOON, GRACE was surprised when Kelly came walking through the office doorway. "Howdy."

"Howdy yourself! What are you doing here?"

"I've got business with the big man himself. Not God, Clarence." Kelly grinned.

"Oh, they aren't due back for another hour at least."

"Would I disturb you if I waited here?" She cocked her head to one side.

"Just keep quiet and don't touch anything." Grace laughed with her.

"Actually, I think I might be safer out with the sharp tools than in here. Although seeing parts of the floor is interesting. I don't think I've seen it before."

"I don't think Clarence has, either. He was surprised it was wood." Before too long, Grace had put Kelly to work taping shut boxes of old files and documents.

When Clarence and his crew arrived, he and Kelly took a stack of rolled-up plans out to a workbench. "These are the ones I was talking about. They're from way back when I didn't keep as good care of the plans as I do now. I know you're probably about bored out of your mind, so I thought I could solve both our problems at once."

They spent the next half hour going over them, revealing the validity of Clarence's concerns. Kelly's architect schooling would come in handy as she went over the diagrams. "For now, I reckon just make notes of which are salvageable and which may be beyond it."

Grace watched the two as they hunched over the table and went over the multiple rolls of blueprints. Hearing Kelly use the axioms and terminology as easily as she spoke to Lucy about multiplication, Grace was quite impressed. It was easy to forget that under that humble butch exterior was an intelligent woman who was good at her craft.

Chapter
Twenty-three

"DO I HAFTA wear this shirt? It itches!"

"It's a nice shirt. I let you wear your pink jeans. Get over it." Grace once again fixed the back of the collar on the pretty blouse her daughter disliked.

"I won't know any of the kids there."

She tried to not grind her teeth any harder as Lucy whined. "I won't know any of the adults there. So we're even."

"What if I don't like them?"

"You can come sit with me, and we can not like anyone together."

"I like that shirt." Lucy reached up to flip one of the ties on the front.

"Me, too. I don't wear it often enough." The blouse was white with flowing wide sleeves that were gathered at the wrist with two buttons. The front had a deep v-neck that tied with cloth strings. Tiny embroidered roses lined its hemmed edges. "Now, behave yourself today. Be sure to say 'please' and 'thank you.'"

"Yes, ma'am."

"And be nice to the other kids. No showing off."

"Yes, ma'am."

"Now, go sit by the window, and let me know when she arrives."

"Aren't you nervous?"

"Of course! What if I don't like them, either? What if they don't like me?"

"You can come sit with me, and we can dislike them together."

"I will. Now scoot to your post."

Lucy stood on the coffee table to watch out the window. Grace could hear her singing one of the songs from the Christmas play.

"Mom! She's here in that ugly car! But, wow, she looks good!"

Grace went into the living room to look out over her daughter's shoulder. "Think so?"

"Now who's being silly?"

"Okay, I'll agree then." They watched as Kelly walked down the path toward the house. She wore what must be new jeans along with a crisp cream oxford shirt and a heavy leather jacket. Her shoes were also new, polished and dust free.

Kelly came in after Lucy opened the door. "Hey, ladies. You look nice, Lucy. I like that shirt."

"It's an adult conspiracy, I just know it." Lucy crossed her arms and glared at the two women.

Kelly came further into the room toward Grace. She leaned forward and gave her a quick peck on the cheek. "You look decent, too."

"Thank you." Grace felt her face redden. "You got your cast cut down."

"Yes, I have an elbow again. I was getting tired of my jacket always falling off the shoulder."

AT THE GATHERING, she was introduced as Kelly's date, and she didn't argue. Lucy went to join the kids and fit in rather well, despite her initial fears. Grace and Kelly found a spot to sit in the kitchen where Annette ruled. As each person came in, Kelly would whisper in her ear about each one.

The wide assortment of people who came and went through the kitchen was not a complete surprise to Grace. There were lesbians, persons who were transgendered, several drag queens, several good ol' gay boys, and some persons she wasn't sure where they fit into the mess of things. There were also a good number of heterosexuals who seemed to be quite comfortable with the crowd around them.

Grace and Kelly went from room to room, meeting everyone and discussing whatever came up. Grace met the parents of the other children and was immediately welcomed by them, sharing the common bond of being gay parents.

During most of their wanderings through the house as they met and talked with everyone, Kelly held onto her hand. She decided not to question it or analyze. She'd just enjoy the company of this handsome woman at her side.

KELLY CARRIED THE soundly sleeping Lucy into the house and stood aside as Grace undressed her and tucked her into bed. They went into the kitchen where Grace turned on the coffee pot. "I had a fun time."

"Me, too. You didn't seem to be too overwhelmed." Kelly grinned and leaned against the counter.

"Not too much. What an odd mixture of characters! And they all know Annette and Kaye?"

"Yep. Those two are like our matrons. They act as surrogate parents, role models, counselors. They wear all sorts of hats. They really helped me when I first arrived. I stayed with Nikki for a while until I got the house fixed. They provided a lot of my initial furnishings, including plates and bowls. I needed someone that solid, rooted to the earth."

"I can see that. They are two amazing people." Grace poured coffee into a small mug for Kelly. "Shall we go sit in the living room for a bit?"

They sat on opposite ends of the couch, turned to face each other. It was a comfortable silence, each sipping her coffee. "I enjoyed your company today."

"I enjoyed yours, too. It was nice having your hand to hold when I was meeting all those strange people."

"This is usually the part where two people lean together to kiss and grope." Kelly grinned at her over the edge of her cup.

"I think I remember that stage."

"I...I don't think I'm ready for that yet. It's not you, trust me. You are a beautiful, sexy woman. I'm still sorting through things in my head. I'm afraid I would either freeze and freak or tie you up and have my way with you."

"The second option doesn't sound too bad." Grace sounded so normal.

Kelly was glad she hadn't any coffee in her mouth. "I'll have to remember that."

"Come here, Kelly." Grace patted the back of the sofa near her.

She didn't hesitate more than a second. After putting her cup down on the table, she slid over closer to Grace.

"Turn around and lean back."

They settled together, Kelly leaning into Grace's chest, Grace's hands stroking Kelly's arms. They didn't speak, just lay together touching. Kelly let Grace explore her arms, felt her stroke her bicep muscle. Her soft hands felt the back of her arm down to the cast. She then explored her right arm, again feeling the muscles and stroking down to the hand.

"You're a strong woman."

"Do you find that a turn-off?"

"Hell, no! My gosh, woman, your body is wonderful! At least what I have seen and touched so far. What woman wouldn't like to be held by those arms, feeling secure and safe?"

"Some women don't like it. They think it's too manly."

"Hmph. They have a hang-up that's no fault of yours. I've never liked scrawny women. I like something to hold onto in a storm." She grasped both of Kelly's upper arms.

"It would take one heck of a wind to blow this body down." Kelly flexed her right arm, showing off her muscles.

"Oh, I bet I could knock you down with a mere breeze."

"Stop it, you damn tease." Kelly laughed and kissed Grace's arm where it lay next to her cheek.

"Okay, just this once."

"On that note, I'm going to head to the house." Kelly stood and took her cup to the kitchen. She was tempted to dunk her head under the cold water tap.

Grace joined her in the kitchen. "I've never seen your house." Grace rinsed both cups, and turned them upside down on the drainer.

"It's not much to see, just a little one room shack. I added a bathroom, so I guess you could say two-room shack. Why don't you and the brat come over tomorrow? We can go for a short hike and have a picnic."

"That sounds like a plan. How do I get there?"

"It's easy. You know where you turn off of Spring Highway onto Mountain Pass?"

"Yes, the four-way-stop intersection."

"Instead of turning left, go right onto Lake Road. It makes a big sweep around, passing some new developments. Anyway, about two miles up, there'll be a right called High Lake Road. When that ends, make a right onto Sneaky Creek."

"I thought you said it was easy."

"To me it is. Okay, here's an easier way, I suppose. Go down Spring Highway. Before you get to the post office, there'll be a right for High Lake Road. Keep going up High Lake — it drops down a bit in the beginning but climbs back up rather quickly. When you come to the stop sign, continue straight, except now you're on Sneaky Creek. About a half-mile later, you'll see my place on the left. I'll park the truck at the end of the driveway, so you'll see it. If you come to a fork in the road, you've missed it."

Grace finished writing it down. "Okay, we'll be there. Noon-ish?"

"Sounds goodish. Can't waitish." She leaned down and kissed her on the lips, a light kiss, and was gone.

"DOES SHE HAVE farm animals like Miss Gillpepsi?" Lucy sat on the floor while she tied her shoes and did a good job of it.

"I don't think so. But I'm sure there will be something for you to do. Just in case, you can take your hand-held game. You're doing a great job with your shoes. That's the fourth time in a row, isn't it?" Grace watched as Lucy worked on her newly-refined skill since Kelly had determined her to be ambidextrous and would do better to learn shoe-tying as a left-handed person would.

"Yep. I keep practicing. Tommy's a lefty, and I told him I was ambidextrose like Miss Walker, and he said that was weird, but he's showing me how to write with my left hand."

"You talk about this Tommy a lot. Should I be concerned?"

"No way! He's a rat!"

"Okay, just wondering. Make this your last tie then go get your stuff ready."

"Okee-dokee smokey."

"FOLLOW THIS ROAD until you get to the fork. Next, it says to follow Sneaky Creek Road for about a half-mile. Her house is on the left." Lucy read off the directions as they turned off the main road.

The road did go downhill for a bit, passing a cinder block garage with a collection of disassembled cars scattered about in front of it. The road soon began going back uphill, higher than when it started. As it leveled off, Lucy pointed out the lake that was now visible.

"Wowzers, Mom. That's a pretty lake."

"It is, isn't it? I wonder if there are any fish in it."

"I wonder if they let people swim in it Oh, here's the next road." She pointed out the sign for Sneaky Creek Road. "What a weird name for a road. How can a creek sneak?"

"If a sneaky creek could sneak creeks, how many creeks can a sneaky creak sneak?"

"Bet you can't repeat it."

"Bet you're right."

"So her house is on the left? She must live close to the lake."

"She must. Now, Lucy, Miss Walker lives in a very small house. She works hard, but I'm sure she doesn't have much money, just like us. So don't make comments about the looks of things."

"Like if the couch has holes like the green one had?"

"Exactly. There's her truck." She slowed the car and turned into the driveway. She drove slowly to avoid spinning her tires in the gravel.

"Wowzers. That is a small house."

"Remember, be nice."

"Yes, Mom, I'll be nice. I won't put my feet on the table, and I'll cover my mouth when I cough."

"Good girl." Grace saw Kelly walking toward them.

"Ladies, you made it. Get lost any?"

"Nope. We spooned right by the fork." Lucy leaned out the open window, so that Kelly could pull her out.

"Did you knife through the pass?"

"All right, you two, don't start the puns again. You make me dizzy."

"She's just jealous," Kelly whispered to Lucy before going around the car to help Grace with the basket. "What did you make? Anything good?"

"Nope, it's all bad, nothing good at all. Bunches of green stuff."

"You better be joking. Come on, I'll show you around."

She held the basket in one hand as she led the way along the short path to the front door. "The tour will be short, so pay attention." She opened the door and ushered them in. "This is the living room, kitchen, dining room, and bedroom. That door leads to the bathroom. Okay, tour over."

"Wowzers. Is that a real TV?" Lucy bent over to examine the front of the small television.

"Yes. I water it every day, but it doesn't seem to grow."

"Not bad, Kelly. From what you said, I expected much worse." Grace looked around the two rooms, noting the lack of decoration. It was clean enough, although there were two pizza boxes balanced on top of the trash can, and, by the couch, were two overflowing laundry baskets. She noticed the patched areas along one wall in the kitchen.

"You should have seen it a while back. The health department would have condemned it."

"Where do you sleep?" Lucy went into the kitchen.

"On the couch. I put a sheet on it and lay down with my blankie. Sometimes I don't bother with the sheet."

"Making your bed is easy, though. Your kitchen is way clean." Lucy peeked around the counter.

"It stays clean 'cause I don't use it. You know better than most how well I cook."

"I didn't forget. Where's your closet?"

"I don't have one. All my hang-up clothes are behind the bathroom door."

"Efficient." Grace peeked into the bathroom.

"You mean boring." Kelly winked at her. "This is where I sleep and read. The real fun place is the shop." She opened the back door and stepped outside again.

"Wowzers, Mom! It's the lake! Miss Walker has a lake in her backyard!"

"The rent here must be high." Grace wondered if she should ask Kelly how her finances were.

"Rent? No, it's not too bad. This is High Lake. It used to be bigger than High Pond, hence the name difference. But High Pond was dammed about twenty years ago and is now bigger than High Lake."

"Why are they called high?"

"You're standing at about 3000 feet above sea level. Hence the high."

Lucy went down to the dock. "Is that your canoe?"

"Yes, I haven't used it much, though."

"Where's your shop?" Grace looked back up at the house.

"Just over the rise." Kelly led them down a paved path leading to the other building. "Lucy, there's equipment in there that's not to be touched. Some of them can cut your arm off, and others can sand it off. There are some hand tools that are almost as bad. So ask before you touch or pick up something, okay, kiddo?"

"Yes ma'am." Lucy stuffed her hands in her pockets.

Grace was impressed with how Kelly spoke with her daughter. She was even more impressed that Lucy listened to her. When she stepped inside the shop, she was pleasantly surprised. The building looked large from the outside but seemed even larger inside.

There was a not-so-small fortune in equipment on the benches and carts. She had seen similar things at the warehouse.

"Where's your 'puter?"

"I don't have one."

"What? Are you still in the twentieth century? Everybody has a computer!" Lucy was appalled.

"Not me. But I do have two sets of encyclopedias."

"THAT WAS FUN, Miss Walker!" Lucy's cheeks were red from the cold air. They'd taken a trail along one side of the lake then looped back by going through some of the woods.

"I'm glad you liked it. There are trails all over this property. Maybe in the spring, you can come back, and we'll do more plant identification."

"That would be cool! Okay, Mom, let's eat!"

"Yeah, Mama Bear, what's in the basket?"

Chapter
Twenty-four

THE FIRST SNOW of the season didn't come until early December. As usual, it was gone by noon in town but hung around the shadier parts of the hollows and hills.

Kelly stood outside on her doorstep, looking at the hills around High Pond. Her family had once owned almost the whole area, including High Pond itself. Her great grandfather had sold huge chunks of it in order to entice other farmers to join him in this odd valley, and it had worked almost too well. She was glad her brothers had offered her their shares in this property, allowing it to remain intact while so many of the other larger farms in the area were being divided up and sold. Kelly was no farmer, but she knew enough to understand what needed to be done. She leased the lower fields across the road to a produce grower. A steeper section further to the northeast was rented out as sheep grazing land. Another large field was leased out for hay.

And then there were the trees, something her grandfather had started. There were stands of huge walnut trees he had planted in his youth that now were worth a lot of money as boards and veneer. She needed to go see them and do a survey of their width and height, as well as the count. But the storm that had come through earlier had left the tall, dead grass too wet to walk through.

Kelly was startled when her cell phone rang. "Walker."

"Kelly? It's Mrs. Maples, dear. I have a problem!"

"What's up?"

"That old apple tree fell on my rabbit hutch. I think I have all of them, but their house is smashed. Can you come out and fix it?"

"I suppose so. I'll be there soon." She couldn't fix the hutch one-handed, though. Her cell phone rang again.

"Kelly? What are you up to this evening? Lucy and I were wondering if you wanted to share pizza?"

"Actually, you called at just the right moment. You and Lucy get over here as soon as you can. I need your help with something."

"YOU BROUGHT A work crew, Kelly." Mrs. Maples held open the back door as they came in.

"I needed the help today. Mrs. Maples, this is Lucy. She's going to help you with your rabbits while Grace and I fix the hutch." The young girl grinned and held up three old towels and a pair of leather gloves.

"Oh, good! I need to check them over to make sure they're okay. Grace, nice to meet you. How did you and your daughter get conned into this?"

"I'm not quite sure, ma'am."

"Kelly does that to people. If you need anything, just holler. You know where the hutch is?"

"Yes, ma'am. I'm going to drive the car through the yard, so I can get it closer."

"Just miss the house this time." She laughed and began talking to Lucy as she directed her out of the mud room.

"This time?" Grace flipped her sweatshirt hood up over her head.

"Once, just once, I miscalculated and hit the corner of her house. I was trying to pull up under a window. She's never let me forget it."

Kelly backed the car up to the enclosure. She and Grace stood near the fence, looking over the mess.

"We could cut the tree up into pieces, moving it a little at a time."

"Cut it into pieces?" Grace's voice squeaked.

"I could if I had two hands. I don't guess you've ever used a chain saw?"

"Funny, Kelly, very funny. No, I have not used a chain saw." Grace was beginning to consider this might not be possible. "Why didn't you just tell her the truth?"

"I couldn't. You saw her face. These rabbits are like her grand-children." Kelly turned back toward the mess. "Okay, here's the plan."

Kelly taught Grace how to use the reciprocating saw to cut the larger branches from the main trunk. Once Grace had it going, Kelly then used a long handled lopper to take off the smaller branches. She had to brace one handle of the tool on her thigh and push down with her good hand in order to use it. Once most of the branches were off, it was easier to move the tree by rolling it until it was free of the rabbit hutch.

"There. Now, to get to work."

"*Get* to work? What was that? The warm up?"

"Yep. Ouch, what a mess. She's lucky the rabbits got out alive." Kelly surveyed the damage, most of which was to the door and the middle part of the roof.

"So what's first, boss?" Grace watched the clenching of Kelly's jaw and the narrowing of her eyes as she thought.

"We need to measure and cut wood for the door, using the wood from the busted door to fix the roof. First, I need to show you where everything is in my tool boxes."

They took apart what was left of the door, setting aside the usable wood to reinforce the roof. The scrap pieces of plywood Kelly had tied to the top of the car were just the right size to patch the holes. Rebuilding the door would take more effort.

The full sheet of plywood had to be cut down to fit. Kelly snapped the lines then talked Grace through the process of using a circular saw run from an extension cord. Next, Grace used a hand saw to cut the two-by-four braces and frame. Kelly hammered it all together, although it was awkward for her to use her right hand, while Grace continued to remove debris from inside and around the pen.

"Kelly!"

"What?" She rushed over, afraid Grace had impaled herself on an old nail. Instead, she was kneeling in the corner, pulling something from the hay.

"I think it's dead."

Kelly squatted next to her and looked at the small rabbit in her hands. She felt the ears and was surprised they were still warm. "Not yet. They shock easily and freeze in place. Put it inside your shirt against your skin. The warmth may revive it. But I doubt it will. Rabbits can actually die of fright."

They reused the hinges, using a battery drill to get the old screws out and put new ones in. Kelly even had a small pivoting wheel she put on the corner of the door to help it swing open and closed. "I'll come back in the spring and fix it better."

"Kelly, it moved," Grace whispered as she felt a movement inside her shirt. Her eyes were open wide, and she was slightly hunched over. "I forgot the poor thing was in there."

"Then let's take it in to its grandma." Kelly grinned.

GRACE DRIED HER hands at Kelly's kitchen sink. Lucy was still chattering on about everything she'd learned about rabbits. Grace leaned against the sink, listening and watching them. She'd learned a lot, too, all about Kelly, and now she now understood the woman much better. She knew how she thought, how she was at work, and how she was so good at what she did. Grace's hands and shoulders ached from the work, but Kelly seemed to be at ease. Her doctor was not going to be pleased to see the cast wet and dirty again.

Am I falling in love with this woman? Surely not, we've only had one date and the party. Maybe falling in like was a better term. Yes, that was it.

Kelly looked up to see Grace watching her. She'd learned a lot about this little woman this evening. Grace was willing to at least try everything Kelly asked, well, everything except the chainsaw, but that was understandable. Kelly knew her arms and hands must be aching from the work.

"Excuse me a moment, Lucy." She went to the kitchen and knelt down at the cabinet under the sink. "Here, this is a good rub. It doesn't smell too good, but it does wonders for aching muscles and joints. I use it on my hands a lot." She stood back up, rocking on her heels. "You know, you did good today. You didn't hesitate and jumped right in there. Not many women would have done it. Thank you for your help."

"You're welcome. I've never done anything like that before, other than assemble furniture. And thanks for the cream. Do you need me to put it on your right hand for you?"

"If you don't mind. I can always go and have Annette do it."

"No, I'll do it."

Kelly stood still as Grace rubbed her hand, massaging the knuckles, the fingers and even the wrist.

"There, did I get it all?"

"Yes, thanks." She wondered if Grace felt as electrified as she did.

"Ew, that smells!" Lucy wrinkled her nose."

"Here then, get closer." Kelly chased the girl around the small house, trying to get her hand up to her nose.

KELLY COULDN'T HELP it. She kept comparing Grace to Anna. She supposed it was natural, but it made her uneasy. The two women could not have been any more opposite. Anna, with her Jewish ancestry, had been tall with tan skin and jet-black hair. Her face had sharp angles that she softened with expertly applied cosmetics. Her hands had been thin, with long fingers that were perfect for lovemaking.

Grace, on the other hand, was several inches shorter than Kelly, had strawberry-blonde hair and a round, soft face. Her hands were small, with calluses from her work at the factory. But Kelly was sure those hands were capable of lovemaking.

They were opposites in behavior, too. Anna had always been aloof, her mind more on appearance than anything else. Kelly was kept around because her square size and height complimented Anna's slender, tall body. Grace was always dressed neatly, although rarely more than blue jeans and nice women's blouses. She cared more about what was going on in Kelly's head than how well the two of them looked together.

Anna never would have helped her with a job like Grace had with the rabbit hutch a few days earlier, and she hadn't hesitated. She asked questions as though she were really interested in Kelly's approach to her work.

She looked across the room to where Grace sat reading a book. Lucy was out making snow people with Kaye. Annette was in the kitchen making another batch of cookies.

Grace looked up and made eye contact. A slow smile came to her lips, more erotic than amused. Kelly felt herself responding to that smile, and without thinking about it, she stood and crossed the room. She put one knee on the couch, her good hand on the back, and leaned down toward Grace. The smile was magnetic. Kelly lowered her head, and they kissed.

Their lips barely touched, but the response was there. She kissed her again and again, just small little touches that caught fire. Grace reached up and pulled her down closer, and their kiss became deeper, harder. She felt Grace moan at one point, the sound vibrating her lips. At last, she dragged herself from Grace's lips to kiss her forehead. She stayed there until her breathing leveled off.

As she straightened up, she saw Grace's face and wondered if her own was that flushed. Were her lips as red, too? Grace let go of the front of her shirt, and Kelly stood up the rest of the way. She walked backward to her seat, falling into it. They were still looking at each other, with identical smiles, when Annette rolled into the room.

"Who wants a hot, soft cookie?"

GRACE BIT INTO her second cookie, still willing her heart to slow down. She'd been kissed before, of course. But never like that. Never with such intensity. If she were capable of thinking, she might be able to remember one or two kisses during sex that might rank this high, but they had been part of a whole.

She dared to look up toward Kelly. The woman was staring into the fireplace, the half-eaten cookie on her knee. Grace didn't often study her face, mainly because the woman always seemed to be in motion. But now, sitting still, her feminine side was evident. Her facial features were relaxed, although there was still a red blush to her cheeks. *Did our kisses affect her as much as they did me?*

Kelly turned her head toward Grace at that moment as if to answer the question. When she saw Grace watching her, she smiled and winked. It took most of Grace's mental strength to keep from jumping up and dragging her down the hall to the guest bedroom.

Lucy charged into the house and jumped up onto Kelly's lap. She leaned back onto that broad shoulder and stole the cookie. "Mom, whatcha doing?"

"Thinking. Did you get the snowman built?"

"We built a snow goat 'cause the snowman kept falling over."

"That happens sometimes."

"Miss Walker, whatcha doing?"

"I guess I'm thinking, too."

"You two ought to think the same thing and get right to it."

Chapter
Twenty-five

A FEW DAYS later, Kelly was in her shop drawing up some plans when her cell phone rang. "Walker."

"Miss Kelly Walker?"

"Yes, this is she."

"This is the nurse at the school. Your name is on the list of people to call. Lucy Owens is sick and needs to be picked up."

"Crap. She okay?"

"She's running a slight fever. I tried to reach her mother, but there was no answer. Are you able to come get her?"

"Yes, yes. I'll be there as soon as I can. Tell her I'm coming."

Grace had put Kelly's name down on the contact list back when she was having so much trouble with her car. That way, if needed, someone Lucy knew could take care of her. Kelly pulled up in front of the school and went in.

"Hey, kid." Lucy lay on a bed, curled up in a ball.

"She's asleep, I think. Here's a sheet of instructions for you. If the fever isn't down by morning, or if she vomits again, she'll need to see the pediatrician. Were you able to get in touch with her mother?"

"No, I tried. She must be out of range. Is there anything else?"

"Not that I can think of. Just let her sleep, and she should be fine. Kids are tougher than they look."

Kelly bent and picked up the little girl, who woke just long enough to put her arms around Kelly's neck and lay her head on her shoulder. The nurse went with her and helped buckle her into the back seat where Kelly had tossed a pillow and some blankets.

She considered taking her to Annette's where she could easily be free of this frightening responsibility. But she knew that when Grace got the messages, she'd expect Lucy to be home. She would be panicking and would want to see her daughter. Lucy had a key in her book bag, so Kelly would use that to get into the house.

Once inside, she lay Lucy down on the couch and undressed her, putting one of her big undershirts on the little girl. After tucking her under the covers, she'd gotten from Lucy's bed, she went to the kitchen to get herself a drink.

"HELLO, GRACE. WHAT are you—?"

"How is she?" Grace took off her jacket and sat to take off her shoes.

Annette looked at her a moment. "It depends. Who?"

"Lucy. I got the call from the school."

"I haven't a clue what you're talking about. Lucy isn't here."

"They said Kelly picked her up. I assumed she'd bring her here for you to—well, where the hell are they?"

"Did you try your house?"

GRACE CAME INTO the house to find an interesting scene.

Lucy lay on the couch. She had kicked the blankets most of the way off. She wore a large white t-shirt that was threatening to swallow her whole. Kelly sat on the floor, the back of her head leaning against the arm of the couch. Lucy's head lay on Kelly's shoulder, her hand curled around the collar of Kelly's shirt. Both were asleep.

On the coffee table sat two soda cans, and a glass half full of water. A bottle of children's analgesic lay on its side near a pack of crackers and a wet washcloth.

Grace wondered if she should cry from joy or from relief. Kelly had brought Lucy here to take care of her herself. She'd taken on that responsibility with ease it seemed. Lucy, even sick, was comfortable enough with Kelly to fall asleep like that.

She watched as Kelly awoke, blinking in confusion. She saw Grace, smiled, and closed her eyes again.

"I DIDN'T DO anything special, Grace. I followed the sheet from the school nurse." She pulled the paper from her back pocket. "It was easy enough. Lucy asked where you were and went back to sleep."

"Still, you did a good job. Good enough that her fever's down."

"It's all Lucy's doing, not mine."

"What's with your t-shirt?"

"When I was a kid, whenever we got sick, Mom put one of Dad's undershirts on us. It was special, you know? She even took one and embroidered the collar for me. When I got the call and was getting my coat, I thought about what she would want or need, and the first thing I thought of was the t-shirt."

"You're so sweet." Grace leaned over and kissed her on the cheek.

LUCY WAS BETTER in time for the Christmas play, although her voice was still squeaky from laryngitis. She didn't get to say her lines, but she did get to stand up there with the others. The teacher let her be the one to walk across the stage carrying a box.

Kelly felt odd sitting in the audience. She was there to see Lucy, sure, but she felt no connection to the people around her. Grace, on the other hand, knew several of the parents and had gotten sidetracked into several conversations, the topics of which were out of Kelly's league, names and events she had never been a part of.

The play was good, and Lucy carried the box well. In several places, Kelly had let her mind drift off as she fixed several problems they were having with the stage and set, then someone would laugh, or they would all clap, or Grace would reach over and touch her in response to something on stage.

When it was over, Kelly took the Owens women out to dinner. Even then, she felt out of the loop as they discussed the various cast members by name.

This world of kids was something she'd not paid attention to nor thought she'd ever experience. If she continued to date Grace, it would mean taking another step further into the reality of parenthood, albeit secondhand.

Lucy was tired much earlier than usual, most likely because of her recent illness. Kelly took them home and waited while Grace tucked her daughter into bed.

"You've been quiet tonight." Grace leaned against the kitchen doorway.

"I suppose I have." Kelly paused, not knowing what to say next or even if she should. "I felt like such an outsider. I didn't know the parents or their kids or who Lucy's friends were or nothing. I stuck out like a sore thumb."

"No, you didn't. Mr. Minelli and his yellow plaid pants stuck out like a sore thumb. You, sweet woman, were more like a taller duck amongst the others."

"Flattery will get you everywhere." Since their kiss at the Goat Farm, it had been difficult for them to keep their hands to themselves. Kelly was hesitant to go further. She didn't know why, only that she needed to go slow.

GRACE AND ANNETTE sat at the kitchen table to cut carrots and potatoes for the stew. Kelly was putting a shelf back up in the library, and Kaye and Lucy were out at one of the goat sheds.

"Kelly says she went to a Christmas play at Lucy's school."

"Yes, she did. She said later that she felt out of place, but I think I convinced her otherwise." The large knife she wielded cut through the long carrots easily, making a *clack* as it hit the cutting board underneath.

"Kelly feels out of place in a lot of situations. Her self-esteem isn't all that great to begin with." Annette peeled the potatoes, dropping the peels into a bucket on the floor.

"Lucy adores her, you know. She doesn't often like the women I date."

"Anyone else ever go to a school event?"

"Yes, Lynn, a cute butch woman who was horribly uncomfortable around kids."

"What was she like?"

"What a goofball! She was very out of place, all right! She clammed up and wouldn't talk, ignored the kids, and ticked off a few parents, too, by looming like some big, silent giant. Some of them knew I was gay, but they all knew by the end of that experience!"

"Wow. I can't imagine Kelly doing that."

"I couldn't, either. Want me to start on the potatoes now?" Grace put the carrot slices in the sink.

KELLY FINISHED GLUING the peg into the end of the shelf. She replaced the broken one and added another in the middle to help it handle more weight. The broken peg had been fairly thick but must have had a crack. But these weren't bookcases she had built, so there was no telling what the problem was.

The little battery drill was charged just enough to do the five new holes. It took some fancy pushing and pulling to get the shelf back into place, but once it was done, she was sure it was not going to come down again.

She stuffed the drill, the glue, and the leftover doweling into the pockets of her smaller tool belt. As she sauntered toward the kitchen, she could hear the ladies talking. Grace's crisp voice was louder than Annette's softer one.

"What a goofball! She was very out of place all right!"
What?

"She clammed up and wouldn't talk, ignored the kids, ticked off a few parents too by looming like some big, silent giant."
Is she talking about me?

"Some of them knew I was gay, but they all knew by the end of that experience!"

Shit.

"Wow. I can't imagine Kelly doing that."

"I couldn't, either."

Kelly didn't hear anything else. There was a roaring in her ears, and her vision was blurred by unshed tears. Everything was blocked out except the repeating thought of "Run. Leave. No one wants you around."

She dropped the tool belt on the deck on her way out and started walking. She knew roughly where she was going. About three miles southwest was her house. She knew where to find the old path.

She was thought to be a fool again. A looming, silent giant. She'd missed something somewhere. Something that should have told her what was going on. She'd missed the signs with Anna, but she'd been sure she'd missed nothing with Grace, but apparently she was still just as big a fool. An idiot, stupid. She was a big goof-ball. Too tall and too big and too naive to see the truth blinking its neon lights right in front of her.

She found the trail easily despite her roaring thoughts. She felt the branches snapping back and hitting her face and arms as she plowed through. She kept her eyes on the obscured trail at her feet. Twice she walked into trees that had sprouted and grown since she was last through there.

Are Annette and Kaye thinking the same thing? Are they like Jennifer and Kate and the others? Do they whisper and laugh at me behind my back?

It had been a while since she'd thought of her alleged friends in Ohio. She could still hear their bitter voices as they gave her their prepared speech. They had told her of how they had hinted, but Kelly had ignored them. How she'd seemed to turn her eyes away from the facts. She deserved the pain of finding it all out after Anna died.

She was slowly coming back to her senses now, realizing she had to have a plan of sorts. How was she going to handle this? She needed to get away to think this through. Perhaps she'd already done enough thinking. Maybe she'd thought so much she'd missed the warning signs.

The trees thinned, and she left them behind and began crossing an open field. She was high enough now to see her house down below. Near where the meadow started sloping downward, a rock outcropping faced the sunset. She sat down almost too hard and lay back, putting her left arm and its cast under her head.

I just ran rather than get into a rage. I don't even feel any anger, other than at myself.

A raptor circled over head, scanning the meadow for a late afternoon snack. She watched it sail around twice and fly over to a tall naked pine. Now that she wasn't crashing through the woods, the wildlife began making their own noises. Another bird sang out from somewhere, getting an answer from way over on her left. If it were summer, she'd hear the crickets and the cicada. But this time of year, that brink near true winter, the air was quiet.

The air smelled crisp, though, as if snow were coming. She sat up and looked around, seeing the clouds looming to the east. *If I'm going to head out to think – or run away – I need to do it soon.*

Chapter
Twenty-six

GRACE WENT TO the glass doors that overlooked the deck and saw Kelly's tool belt lying near the steps. She went outside but couldn't see her anywhere, so she picked up the belt and went back inside.

"Has anyone seen Kelly?"

"I thought she was putting up that shelf." Annette rolled down the hall and peeked into the library. "The shelf's up, but she didn't tidy up. That's not like Kelly."

"Maybe she went out to Kaye and Lucy. I'll be right back." Grace felt something was wrong. She didn't know what; she just felt it. She wasn't surprised when the two told her they'd not seen her, either. "Kaye, do you mind watching Lucy longer while I go look for her?"

"Sure. We've got some more to do here. Call us."

She drove the back way to Kelly's house. She knew where it was, more or less, but had never actually driven to it herself from this direction. When cresting a hill several miles later, she happened to look to her right and saw a person walking across a meadow. Grace pulled the car over to the side of the road and looked closer. She couldn't tell if it was Kelly or some farmer out checking on cattle. Then she saw the flashes of white as the person's left arm swung.

"What the hell are you doing, Kelly Walker?" She mumbled as she got her gloves from under the seat. Hopping the fence, she got a general idea of where Kelly was headed and started walking.

Kelly was startled to see Grace step out of the tall grass and shrubs. They walked along in silence before Grace spoke. "Taking a walk-about?"

She grunted. "Yes, you might could say that."

"Cool. I brought money just in case we needed some."

"We?"

"Yeah. Surely you weren't going without me? Or at least without telling me?"

Kelly's steady pace slowed a notch. "I was considering it."

"Why? Do I smell bad? Or perhaps you heard I snore?"

"Perhaps I discovered I had you figured out wrong? That I had me figured out wrong?"

"I'd hope that if you did, you would present facts to back up your discovery. A hypothesis needs to be tested."

"I got the test results just fine. Listen, Grace, you don't have to act anymore." Kelly stopped and spun Grace around, keeping a tight grip on her arm.

"I'm not acting, I'm reacting. What discovery did you make?"

"In your words, 'looming like a big, silent giant' and I think the word 'goofball' came up. Just tell it to my face, okay? Don't do it behind my back, dammit."

"What the hell are you talking about? Goofball?" Grace felt her eyes widen. "In the kitchen. You heard part of the conversation."

"Exactly."

"Kelly, sweetheart, we weren't talking about you. We were talking about an ex of mine. She'd also gone to a school function, and unlike you, she really did stick out like a sore thumb." She put her hand on Kelly's cheek. "I know trusting is hard for you, but you need to trust me. I can't promise to never hurt you, but I can promise to try not to."

Kelly's eyes flickered over Grace's face, trying to see the truth. Grace tried to put the truth as far out in front of her as possible, not wanting to lose this wonderful woman's trust again.

She was swept up into Kelly's arms, her ribs crushed in the hold. Lips smashed against hers to the point of pain. Kelly lowered a hand and grabbed Grace's crotch, lifting her off the ground before kneeling and laying them both on the grass.

Grace knew Kelly needed this. This level of physical contact. She needed it as badly as she had needed to smash the kitchen wall. Part of her was afraid Kelly would accidentally hurt her. She tried to relax into the kiss, even moving her hips against the hand at her groin. That seemed to slow Kelly down enough to let up the pressure on her mouth. Sucking her top lip, then the bottom one, Kelly shifted her body off Grace. The hand remained in place, and Grace naturally spread her thighs apart and was rewarded with a moan.

What happened next was sex. Raw, hungry sex. No clothing was removed, but one button was lost forever. Kelly's hand was rough against Grace's sensitive inner labia. How the hand got there, she didn't know. The first orgasm was quick, the second hard. She lost track after that.

Kelly was good. She knew where to touch when, and how hard and how gentle. She kept coaxing one orgasm after another until Grace reached down and grabbed her wrist. They paused, each of them catching their breath.

"MOM, WHERE'D YOU go? We had dinner without you."
Lucy didn't get up from her seat on the floor.

"I went looking for Kelly."

Annette looked over the top of her book, seeing the mud on the
back of Grace's jeans. "Did you find her?"

"Yes, she needed a ride to her house, so I drove her home."

"Good. I put a bowl of stew in the nuker for you."

Grace sat at the kitchen table and ate in silence, even after Kaye
came in and sat down across from her, sipping coffee.

"You need to talk about it?"

"I'm not sure I know what to say."

"Is Kelly okay?"

"Yeah, she's okay. She needed space to think. She overheard
something and thought we were talking about her."

"Mmmm. She tends to think too little of herself." Kaye got
them both more coffee. "She's strong and capable, yet she thinks
she's but a worm of a woman. I don't understand it."

"Me, either. Inside of her is a passion that can burn."

They drank their coffee, the only sound coming from the living
room. The kitchen still smelled of the stew and the bread Annette
had made in the machine.

"I wish I had some advice for you, but Kelly is a different kind
of beast. I'd think slow would be best, but then, maybe not."

"I don't know, either. I think I'll just let her call the shots. It's a
good thing I don't have control issues, eh?" Grace raised her cup in
salute.

Chapter
Twenty-seven

"MOM? TELL ME about my father."

Lucy was sitting on one end of the couch, chewing on her fingernail. Grace was on the other end reading a book. She stared at the book, afraid to move, afraid that if she did, Lucy would repeat the question.

"Mom? Did you hear me?"

"Yes."

"Can you tell me about him?" She used the remote to turn the television sound off and turned to face her mother.

Grace closed the book. "It's complicated, really. We made a mistake of thinking we could get married. I left when I realized that mistake. I found out I was pregnant with you later. After I left, I never spoke with him again."

"Did you tell him about me?"

"No. I considered it but decided my child didn't need to be exposed to him."

"Oh. So he didn't leave because of me? Because you were going to have me?"

"No, baby, no, he didn't. He didn't even know. Lucy, why all the questions?"

Lucy watched the silent sitcom stars.

"Why all the questions?" Grace repeated.

"You know Travis down the street? His mom has to go to court next week, so he can stay with her and not go with his dad 'cause his dad just found out about him and wants to take him away."

Grace scooted across the couch to scoop Lucy up into her lap. "Lucy, there's no way the man who is your biological father will ever come to get you. I promise." She kissed her on the forehead. "Travis and his mom must be pretty scared, huh?"

"Yeah. He said some lady with a briefcase came and inspected his house, his bedroom, his toys, and asked him all sorts of questions, like does his mom spank him and does he eat dinner every day."

"Wow. That's a lot for them to go through. How old is Travis?"

"Thirteen."

"He's old enough that the judge will listen to what he wants, too. But, Lucy, it won't happen to you. It can't. Okay? Don't think about it or worry about it."

Dear Mrs. Higgins, Esq.

I am writing in regards to file no. 493-22. I spoke with you just over eight years ago about him. I still have the same concerns and wish to know the status and location.

Sincerely,
Grace Owens

THE MONTH OF December flew by. Kelly had dropped by late Christmas Eve to give them each some gifts. She gave Lucy a new handmade wooden chess board and pieces and an Appalachian-crafted dancing man. She gave Grace a creche, complete with shepherds and little animals. She also gave her a handmade recipe box that included several recipes her mother had mailed to her.

Grace and Lucy spent that night with Annette and Kaye, something Lucy had been looking forward to. Lucy awoke Christmas morning, momentarily confused about where she was. She found her mother sprawled across the bed in the other guest room, sound asleep. First she stared at her, knowing that often woke her up. It didn't.

Next she coughed once, twice. Not a move.

Then she went to the door and opened it and shut it. Nothing.

Finally, she stuck her finger in her mother's ear.

"If you don't stop, I'm gonna take them all back to the store."

"Will not."

"Will so."

"Get up."

"No."

"Why not?"

"'Cause the sun's not up yet."

"So? Get up."

"Nope." Grace rolled over, sticking her head under the pillow.

Lucy lay down and put her head under the pillow, too. "You asleep?"

"Yes."

"Can I drive the car?"

"No."

"Then you aren't asleep. You always let me drive the car when you're asleep."

"Nice try."

Lucy got an idea. She'd seen Annette do it to Kaye once. It was different and far from the other methods Lucy had tried over the years. She left the room to find Marley. The large dog was lying in the hallway, munching on the last of a large dog cookie. "Marley, will you do me a favor?"

Marley looked up and stared as if saying, "Sure. What is it?"

"Come with me."

Marley got up and followed Lucy back down the hall to the guest bedroom. The dog automatically got up on the bed. When she did, she saw the human under the covers, her head under the pillow. Marley knew this game. She liked playing it as often as she could.

She crawled over and put her head under the pillow, too. This human reacted much better than any other. The screaming and laughing was loud. Marley, even more excited than usual by the game, just licked more, standing up so she got the entire face in one wet swipe.

Kaye and Annette could be heard giggling in their bedroom. Kaye came in first, trying to call Marley down, but she couldn't stop laughing. Annette rolled into the room laughing just as hard.

NOT MUCH SNOW came to the mountains, at least not much that stayed on the ground once the sun was up high enough. On Lucy's second day back to school after the holidays, it was starting to snow when Grace walked to the mailbox after work.

Dear Ms. Owens:

In response to your inquiry about the status of file no. 493-22, the status should be closed. The person in question was in the Ohio prison system when he was killed during a fight with another inmate.

Based on this information, I will be closing file.

If you have any questions, feel free to contact me again.

Dorothy Higgins, Esq.
Higgins, Higgins and Paul
Attorneys at Law

Grace was glad to have gotten the reply so quickly. She had assumed it would take longer to dig out the old case files. By the time she reached the porch, the grass was already getting white from the snow, although the sidewalk was still just wet.

"Hey, Mom! It's snowing!"

"I can see that." Grace went into the house and started their dinner.

The next morning, there was just enough snow to cancel school. Grace had an agreement with Clarence that allowed her to take snow days off to be home with Lucy. Mother and daughter spent most of the day curled up on the couch watching movies.

She was in the kitchen when the phone rang. "Hello?"

"Hi. You two behaving yourselves?"

"Hi, Kelly. Nope. We have been watching movies and being slugs."

"Gross."

"We like having slug days. We don't do anything or move much, just be slugs."

"Oookay, if you say so. I'm just making sure you two were safe and sound."

"Yep. And you?"

"Bored silly."

"Poor baby."

"Does Lucy ride a sled?"

"Not since she was a toddler. There's not enough snow out there to ride a sled."

"No, but there might be the next time. Can she ski?"

"No, she's never tried. Neither have I. I've not done much playing in the snow."

"Not even a snowman?"

"Um, maybe a snowman."

The phone line clicked. "Miss Walker?"

"Hey, Lucy! What's up?"

"Nothing. Just wanted to interrupt your phone call 'cause I can."

"You are in so much trouble, little lady."

"She means you, Lucy."

"Don't be a smarty pants, Kelly."

"Oh, she's after both of us now! Hey!"

Kelly laughed as she heard the yelling and the laughing in the background. She finally heard Lucy yelling uncle. "Kelly? You still there?"

"Yes, did you kill her?"

"Nope, I just taped her up with duct tape."

"Ouch. Well, my job here is done. You two slugs stay away from the salt, and I'll call you later in the week."

Chapter
Twenty-eight

KELLY SPENT THE next day in her workshop. Each year she assisted the staff at the YWCA by providing all the wood for a birdhouse project. The kids at the center would make the houses, which would be sold at a spring event.

She had gotten the head count on the kids who had signed up for the first class, scheduled for in the morning, and she always provided plenty of extras. There were bound to be kids wandering in. Kelly laid out all the pieces to confirm she had enough of everything.

She was sweeping the floor when Beth from the Y came by to pick up the wood. "Hey, Kelly!"

"Hey yourself, Beth. That time of year again, huh?"

"Yes. And there's a bump in the road."

"Oh? What's up?"

"I no longer have a truck. I traded it for a car in the spring and just figured there would be someone around this time of year who had a truck. No one I know is available. Even Nikki Rogers has other plans. I came here to ask you to volunteer yet more of yourself and to help you load, knowing you couldn't say no."

"I can bring them over, I guess. You're just so full of yourself, aren't you?"

"Well, yeah! Duh!"

"All right then. I'll go pull the truck around. You finish boxing the bundles. I'll have to unload the bed, but that's no problem. Be right back." With most of the bandages off her palm, Kelly was able to drive her manual transmission truck.

She backed the truck up against the large doors. Kelly and Beth began unloading her tool boxes and supplies.

"I never realized you had so much stuff to do your job. And you also have the van, right?"

"Not any more; it died last summer. I decided not to replace it and instead just got more tools and boxes. I only take the tools I need for the job that day."

"Oddly, that makes sense."

"Scary, ain't it? Anyway, once a month or so I unload the boxes and compartments, go through all the stuff, and then reload."

"When you lived in Ohio, did you keep your car this cluttered?" Beth had looked inside the cab of the truck.

"Yeah, but Anna made me clean it out all the time." Kelly stood still, remembering. "She used to count the number of french fry containers."

"There were that many?"

"THAT'S THE FIFTH one! My gosh, woman, no wonder you're so rotund!"

"What? I am not!"

"Are so! Take off your shirt and I'll prove it."

"Nice try, Princess, but it ain't gonna work. If I do you'll be over here attacking my personage."

"Yes, but it's all to prove how rotund you've become."

"Woman! Don't be so rude!"

"Six."

"What?"

"Six. There's one right there."

"You already counted that one."

"No, I didn't. I couldn't see it around your fat – "

Anna couldn't say much more; she was being chased from the garage and up the stairs to the apartment.

"SO, YOU'LL BE there at eight?"

"Yes. I can't guarantee I'll be communicative by then, but I'll be there. You owe me." Kelly shook her finger at her friend.

"Yes, I do. Maybe I'll let you take me out to dinner some night."

Kelly looked up at Beth, knowing what she meant. But she felt nothing but friendship for her. "You'll let me take you out as repayment for your debt to me? Gads, that's proof you work in either social services or for the government."

"WOWZERS, THIS IS going to be fun!" Lucy was dancing in place at the bus stop.

"It better be, 'cause you're driving me nuts." Grace yawned. She'd had weird dreams and had sat up most of the night.

"Am not."

"Are so. I'm the mother, don't argue with me." Grace put on the worst scowl she could muster, but she couldn't hold it and started laughing.

The bus pulled up, and they got on board to go for the first part of the YWCA's birdhouse project.

"KELLY, YOU DID make it!" Beth came over to the truck window.

"Ugh. Me drive truck. Me drink coffee."

"Ah. You weren't kidding, were you? Just pull around back, and we'll unload it from there."

"Ugh. Me drive truck. Me drink coffee." Kelly did as she was told and drove around the building. By the time she got there, a small platoon of volunteers were ready to start unloading. She got out of the truck, coffee cup from Krispy Kreme in one hand and her cap in the other.

"Go on inside where it's warmer. You going to stay for a while or just head right out?"

"Me drive truck. Me dr..."

"Yeah, yeah, I get it. Page, take this person inside to the lounge. She can stay there till she wakes up."

"WHAT DOES YWCA spell?"

"Young Women's Center of America, I think. I'm not sure. We'll get some brochures while we are there."

"The song goes Y-M-C-A, though."

"That's the men's version."

"Gotta share everything, huh?"

"Yeah, something like that. Now, you remember that I'm not staying, right?"

"Right. Which is good 'cause you'll mis-measure something and screw it all up."

"Puh-leeze! I will not!"

"It's probably pre-cut anyway. Miss Walker says pre-cutting and drilling makes assembly easier on the site."

"She did, did she? Well, she should know." Grace watched the town of Asheville go by the bus windows. Other than a few phone calls, it had been a while since she had heard from the infamous Miss Walker.

"Mom, earth to Mom."

"Yes? What?"

"I think we're getting there."

"Oh, yes, we are."

They got off the bus and walked up the hill to the Y. There were already several dozen children running around. A handmade sign on poster board directed them to the sign-in desk. Grace let Lucy do it all, knowing her daughter needed to.

"Lucy Owens."

"Yes, here you are. This is your first year it says."

"Yes, ma'am."

"Here's your t-shirt. Here is a permission form for your mom
or dad to sign. And here is the instruction sheet for the entire class.
You do know this is just one of several steps, right?"

"Right."

"Good. Now, have your parents give this to your group leader.
Your leader will be Page, and she's through those doors to your
right."

"Thank you, ma'am."

KELLY WATCHED THE organized chaos that normally happened right before such a big undertaking. She did what she knew
would be of most use—she stayed out of their way.

Most of the kids were around Lucy's age. Kelly was curious
about how she would feel if she interacted with them. *Would I feel
all nervous and cautious and act as if I were a clumsy elephant among little cute mice? Probably not.* Lucy had taught her that kids were more
than just pests.

As the groups came into the gymnasium, she sat in the office
that overlooked it. Kids from about six to twelve years of age came
in. They formed their little groups with their group leaders and sat
on the floor to await introductions and instructions.

Kelly put her feet on the floor and sat up when she recognized
a thin child in Page's group. Lucy. Automatically she spun around
to look toward the side wall where the parents were assembling.
Yes, there was Grace. *I'm not sure how I feel about seeing her here.
Pleased? Surprised? Annoyed?*

She sat back, thinking about what to do. She could just leave.
Grace would never know that she was the one who cut the wood
and even delivered it. Or she could go out onto the floor and volunteer as if she'd planned to do it all along. She'd spoken to Grace on
the phone several times, but she hadn't had the nerve to ask her out
again since their romp in the field.

All of those thoughts were interrupted when Beth started
speaking.

"Good morning, kids!"

"Good morning!"

"Welcome to the first class of the yearly birdhouse building. If
this is your, oh, fourth year of doing this, stand up." She paused as
about ten children stood. "Good! Welcome back! Now, if this is
your third year? Your second year? And now all you first years."
She paused between each one, given them the chance to stand and
be recognized. "I see we have more of second year group than any
of the others. That's good! We didn't scare you away last year,
huh?"

The kids all laughed.

"This is actually our seventh year of doing this. It started as a thought, a plan discussed over coffee. Then it grew to what it is now. It used to be a small little thing we did, but, two years ago, it grew when we sweet-talked someone into joining us, Miss Kelly Walker."

Beth turned and waved for Kelly to come out of the office. Against her better judgment, Kelly did, but as she approached Beth, she whispered a death threat. Beth laughed but kept going. "Miss Walker is the one who cuts up all the wood pieces that make up the birdhouse. She was also the one who came up with a design for all of you to use, as well as most of the decorative ideas we'll work on later."

Kelly wanted to sink into the floor. She hated being put in the limelight. She could feel her face burning. In front of her were all those faces, turned to look at her and wonder about her. She decided not to look toward Lucy, not wanting to single her out from her new potential friends.

"Miss Walker is also a good example to all of you girls, and you, too, boys, of what you can do with a thought. Miss Walker fixes and builds things, from broken pipes to enlarging a desk. She does it because she went to school, several schools, to learn her trade. Her example should show all of you that any of you can do anything, if you set your mind to it. Thank you, Miss Walker."

"Thank you, Miss Walker," All the kids sang out.

GRACE WATCHED HER daughter on her own for the first time. She saw Lucy lean over to giggle with another girl in her group. Lucy was going to be just fine.

She decided to wait and hear what the head teacher had to say. She wasn't prepared for it. Out came Kelly Walker, coffee cup and all. On her head was perched the usual cap. Kelly said something to the teacher, but it wasn't repeated; Grace could only imagine what Kelly would have muttered. As the woman went on about everything that Kelly did, Grace realized there was even more to this woman than she thought. She was complicated underneath that stoic face.

She watched as Kelly shuffled her feet, obviously uncomfortable being there. Was this the first time she'd been introduced? Surely they had acknowledged her contribution before. When Kelly was finally released from her torture, Grace pulled out the information brochure about the class. On the back was a list of supporting businesses. And there, under the large bank and car dealer logos, under the radiator shop and the others, was Around-To-It Services.

KELLY LEFT IMMEDIATELY and got into her truck. She'd get Beth for pulling that stunt. She'd wanted to get her more involved, but Kelly had refused, insisting on staying in the background. She had consented to having her company name on the supporter list, but only if it didn't say anything else.

She sat in the truck to let her face cool before she went home. She had no plans for her Saturday; she just wanted to not be there. She drove back around the building. As she came around the front, she saw someone standing on the sidewalk, thumb out as if hitchhiking. It was Grace.

"Got any cookies?" Grace asked as Kelly stopped next to her.

"Huh?"

"If you have any cookies, I'll get in the truck with you."

"Um, I got half a donut."

"That'll do." Grace opened the door and hopped in. "Now, is there anything you can't do?"

"Huh?"

"You fix things, you build things, you can do fourth-grade math, and you volunteer at the YWCA."

"Yeah, well, it may look that way."

"What're your plans for the day?"

"Huh?"

"Is that all you have to say?"

"No, I usually just say 'ugh' but I'm more awake now."

"Ah. Listen, let's go get something to eat. Like coffee and biscotti. I can afford that."

Kelly grunted, but she put the truck back into first and pulled away.

Chapter
Twenty-nine

GRACE WATCHED THE world around her slip by. Large fields of tobacco stubble, scattered with the stalks; a tractor pulling a large piece of machinery that paused, shook, and spit out a huge round bale of hay; and a field dotted with black and white cattle. She realized they were heading toward High Pond. She was surprised, though, when they pulled up in front of Kelly's little house.

"Come on." Kelly got out of the truck and stood in front of it as she waited for Grace to catch up. "Go down to the dock while I get coffee."

Grace walked down the woodchip path toward a deck-like structure that extended out onto the lake. She heard footsteps and turned to see Kelly coming down the path, holding two cups with a paper bag under her arm and a blanket slung over her shoulder. "Take this, please." She turned, so Grace could reach the bag and blanket.

"We can sit on the edge and dangle our toes at the fishes."

"This is beautiful. It must be nice to have this as your backyard. Is High Pond as secluded as this?" Grace refolded the blanket, so it was thick enough to protect them from the cold wooden dock.

"Not so much anymore. That lake wasn't owned by one person, so it's a little more crowded."

"How has this lake remained so private? Is it owned by a club?"

"No, by a single individual. What do you think of it here? Do you think the owner should share this beauty by selling off property or building rental property?"

"Hell, no! This needs to be preserved! It's far too beautiful to ruin with other houses polluting the skyline."

"You don't think that's selfish?"

"Not really. There's too much of nature being swallowed up by developers. I guess as a mother, I want to leave something behind for Lucy and her friends, you know?"

"Good point." Kelly opened the bag and pulled out a package of cupcakes. "Sorry, no biscotti, but this should do."

Grace opened the package and put the plastic in her pocket. The water was only a few inches from her toes. By pointing her foot, she could touch the water, making little ripples form and expand. A recent warm spell had melted the ice from the shallow water along the shoreline.

"I like living here. It's peaceful, quiet, and not crowded by life." Kelly nodded toward the lake.

"It must be nice to have a place to escape to."

"You can come here any time you want, you know." She turned toward Grace.

"I wouldn't feel comfortable without asking the owner first. I'm weird that way."

Kelly turned back toward the water, looking out over the miniature waves caused by the constant breeze. A series of thoughts made its way into Grace's consciousness. She began putting the pieces together and came up with a surprising picture.

"You own this, don't you?"

Kelly didn't speak, but finally nodded, still looking at the lake.

"Why didn't you just say so?"

"You didn't ask."

"How did you get it?"

"This land's been in my father's family for generations. My grandfather left it to me and my brothers, who then sold their shares to me a few years ago. One of my brothers is a lawyer, and the other owns his own supply business."

"And your brothers willingly sold you the property?"

"Yes. Neither of them wanted it, but they didn't know what to do with it. When I mentioned I was thinking of moving here until I got my head together, they offered me their shares."

"Is the house the original one?"

"Heck, no. The old house, or rather its chimney and foundation, is over that way, past those trees. The barn still stands, though. It was made of chestnut logs, so it'll be here long after we're all gone. My house was an old cabin I renovated to make it livable."

They sat in silence for a while, drinking their coffee. "Want to go on a walk? The old house is over that ridge. It's got a great view of the lake."

"Sure. I even have on the right shoes." They stood and walked together past the shop. The path they were following wasn't much more than a crease in the grass, unlike the more defined trail they had used on Grace and Lucy's first visit.

"At one time it was a road, but this is all that's left." Kelly began the tour by discussing the trail they followed. "These trees sprung up once they stopped haying this field. It was too steep for that, anyway."

"Is any of it worked now?"

"I rent out a hundred acres or so. Some for hay, some for sheep, and some to a produce farmer. They keep up their parts, and I get all the hay I need for my projects from the hay guy."

"Why would you need hay?"

"Reseeding a yard, water blocking or redirecting, stuff like that."

"Wait. You said a hundred acres or so? Just how big is this property?" Grace stopped walking and stared at Kelly.

"We had it surveyed when I bought the place. It hadn't been done in decades, and I think it came out to be about 1500 acres or so. Most of it's the mountain."

"Wow. Taxes must be a bitch."

"Yes, they are."

In silence, they continued along the trail, both watching the birds flit about. Once Grace reached out to take Kelly's hand, to silently get her attention, so she could point out a rabbit. She never let the hand go.

The trail kept slowly going upward and then began going down a bit before ascending again. When they crested the second ridge, they were overlooking a valley.

This hill went down quite a distance, to just above the lake's water line. It continued upward in three directions, forming a bowl. Down in the bowl stood a lone tower of brick and stone. Scattered about were other stone formations, hinting at the foundation.

"Is that the original house?"

"What's left of it."

"Wow. It was big."

"Yeah, it was. I've only seen a photo and some sketches. It was burnt down once, a long time ago, then again about ten years ago."

"And your grandfather left you and your brothers all this?"

"Yep. I don't know if he did us a favor or not. This time of year the humidity is lower, so you can see further. See that stand of trees? That's walnut. My grandfather planted that when he was just a boy. They're the right size to sell for boards. I have three other groups of them. I figure they're kind of like a nest egg or retirement plan."

"I've heard that walnut wood is expensive."

"It's the grain. The layout and texture of the wood." They turned, going back a different way. "Plus the color is so rich."

"That woman this morning said you took a lot of classes."

"Yeah, a lot! Four different community colleges, two universities, and one short apprenticeship. I was considering becoming an architect when...I moved here." Kelly's voice faltered and Grace squeezed her hand. She was rewarded with a genuine smile from Kelly, followed by a kiss on her forehead.

PAINTING A ROOM can be rather Zen-like. Dip the brush into the paint, swipe it, brush up, brush down, make the 'W', then fill it in. Kelly preferred the brush for small areas like this. She didn't like this particular color, but to each their own.

This was her first job since breaking her arm and hand. She still had the two surgeries to look forward to, but they wouldn't happen for a few more months.

The ceiling was already done. She'd gotten to work on that first thing. Now, painting the narrow wall space between the window frames, she could let her neck relax. She still had six windows to do, and she needed to get them done today. The walls, all six of them, could wait until tomorrow, although she was certain that if she worked late, she could get them done, too.

"Paintin' in the mornin', paintin' in the ev'nin', paintin' at supper time..."

ANNA HAD HER nose pinched shut when Kelly got out of the shower. "Take those clothes out to the dumpster."

"They'll clean right up. The smell goes away with the soap."

"They're not going to stay in this apartment. Get them out."

"Hon, we painted today. The fumes just stuck onto the clothes. They'll be just fine with a wash."

"I said, get them out." Anna spun around and left the bathroom.

KELLY PAINTED THE last of the window frames and put the brushes in the water to soak. Tape had to come off the windows; the newspaper on the floor that was wet with paint droplets had to be picked up and replaced. After this was done and the brushes were washed, she took a very late lunch break. She sat out on the homeowner's back lawn and watched the birds at the feeders.

She'd been thinking a lot about Anna lately. Not many of the memories were painful, at least not as bad as they used to be. She also realized, as she watched a blue jay chase off a cardinal, that she had been thinking of Grace more. Maybe she would ask her out again.

Lunch break over, she returned to the painting, losing herself in the movement of the brush.

Chapter
Thirty

"IS THAT UMPIRE blind? How can he say he wasn't safe?" Kelly sat back down, slapping her cap back onto her head.

"Does that mean the guys in the white pants didn't get their touchdown?" Grace bit into her chili, cheese, onions, and mustard hot dog.

"Yes. I mean no. They didn't get the home run." Kelly saw the far too innocent look on Grace's face. "Funny. Veeery funny. You have to get the next round of beers."

Behind them sat Annette and Kaye, with Marley's head on Lucy's shoulder. "This is kinda fun. It's going to get cold, though, when that sun goes down."

The Asheville Tourists were up four to two in the bottom of the sixth inning. Kelly and Grace were having fun, teasing and joking with each other, and with Kaye, a diehard baseball fan. While the early April day had been wonderfully warm, there was frost predicted for that night.

KELLY DID HER usual duty of carrying Lucy into the house and onto her bed. She started the coffee pot as Grace got her daughter undressed and tucked in.

"I kept meaning to ask you—I may need you to pick Lucy up from school, and keep her with you for a few hours."

"Not a problem. I'm still not able to do much with this arm yet." She resisted the urge to scratch the bandages covering the stitches from the surgery a few days before.

"I may go out to the job sites with Clarence one afternoon this week to get a feel for what they do out there. He's wanting me to try to do more of the scheduling and thinks I can do it better if I understand what their jobs are."

"I agree." Kelly nodded and put her coffee cup down. "It'll also be good for you to get out of that lonely office."

"Amen to that! But I love my job. It's even more fun now that the office is officially finished."

"I heard! He was telling me you handed him a briefcase the other day and proceeded to tell him how to use it."

"He looked like he was going to have a heart attack! It was priceless, especially when I introduced him to Mr. Folder and Miss File Drawer."

"You're a mean woman."

Grace looked over at Kelly, wondering if she should make the first move. They'd not had more than a few simple kisses since that event out in the field several months ago. She could almost see the sparks fly whenever they touched.

"Grace, I... I need to apologize for something. I acted inappropriately that day after Lucy's play. I keep wanting to say it, but..."

She couldn't say much more since Grace launched herself from her end of the couch and onto Kelly. She put one hand behind Kelly's head and held her in place as they kissed. Kelly scooted down, so she was lying flat with Grace on top.

The kissing continued for several minutes, much to their enjoyment, until a voice, hoarse from sleep, said "Gross" just before the bathroom door shut.

"Ah, the joys of having a child." Grace laughed as she rested her head on Kelly's shoulder.

"It could be worse, like a farting dog in the room."

"Gross."

"I WAS TALKING with Kaye, and we agree that if you don't mind, we would love to have Lucy for a sleep-over." Annette handed Grace another set of books.

"Really? She's not had one before. I think it would be great. But what would you two old crones want a hyper child around for?" They were doing some cleaning in Annette's library.

"Old crones? You're so in trouble for that one. Actually, we were wanting to do it more for you. If Lucy has a sleep-over, maybe Mama can have one of her own."

"What?" Grace stopped wiping the shelf. "Oh. Oh! Good idea!"

"SO, LIKE, THAT means we'll be, like, alone?"

"Yep, from beginning to end."

Kelly took in a deep breath and clutched the phone harder. "I need to know what you're thinking."

"Thinking? As to what I want?" Grace took a deep breath and clutched the phone harder. "I want you to spend the night with me. Even if all we do is cuddle and sleep, that'll be fine with me. I want to feel you, touch you, get to know you."

"Oh, good, 'cause that's what I was hoping for."

THEY DECIDED NOT to go out to dinner or even rent a movie. Instead, they went to Kelly's and went for a walk. Grace learned how to skip stones. Kelly was taught how to make a whistle from a blade of grass.

They watched the heron swoop in for the night as they sat on the dock, listening to the sounds around them.

"You'd think that Mother Nature was quiet. She's not, is she?"

"Not in the least. Farther up, over the hill and away from the road, it's just her and her noises. It can get loud at night."

"You've camped there?"

"Not there, but up at a nice flat spot just below the top of the mountain. A stream is close by, too, so it's perfect. We used to go up there on weekends and camp out."

"Speaking of camping out, Lucy was excited about going over to Annette and Kaye's alone. She gave them a list of kid movies she thinks all adults should see."

"That's either a good or a bad thing. I am not sure which."

"Me, too. I didn't ask to see the list. I let her do it all by herself. Someone named Pat was coming over to play chess and watch the movies, too."

"Good. Pat needs to get out of the house more. Pat runs that store down close to Nikki's. Listen, want to go in and warm up? I got a hot chocolate recipe from Mom earlier today."

"Is it something even you can't mess up?"

"Yep. Come on." Kelly stood and put her hand out to help Grace up off the cold wooden dock.

They continued to hold hands as they walked up the path toward the house. "Kelly, may I ask you something?"

"Sure. I may not answer, but you may ask."

"Was Anna ever here?"

Kelly stopped walking and looked down at Grace. "Never in the house, never in my shop since it wasn't built then. She stood out on the dock once until a bug flew by. I think we were here for, like, three minutes, maybe."

"Good. I want this night to be all me."

THE HOT CHOCOLATE recipe turned out to be a box of packets from Swiss Miss, complete with the little marshmallows. "I hadn't planned on us being here this late. My house is so small."

"No, this is fine. I prefer it actually. I'm not sure why. Maybe because I don't want to keep thinking Lucy is going to say 'gross' again."

They sat on the couch, sipping the hot chocolate, listening to a CD Kelly had recently bought. They talked about the singer, about the chocolate, and about Mrs. Walker's passion for cooking. At some point, they positioned themselves, so Grace could lean against Kelly.

"I've never had sex on a sleeper sofa before."

"What?" Kelly was startled with the sudden change in conversation.

"I've done it in cars, a movie theater, and once under the bleachers in high school."

"Really? Let's see, I've done it in a parking lot, the back of a truck, and once on a kitchen table."

"Must have been cold!"

"I don't know. I was sitting in a chair."

"Oh. My."

"If I remember correctly, from your temper tantrum not too long after we first met, you don't like tongue kissing."

"I don't. It's gross, to quote Lucy."

"I agree. I'll do a lot of things, but I never understood that. Especially in romance books. It's always about 'invading' or 'dancing' or something. I'm sure lots of people like it, but I don't."

Grace turned around. "You've read romance novels?"

"Many. Mom and I used to swap them. I like that they're always so happily-ever-after."

"Hmm, I never would have thunked it."

"I'm a woman of many talents."

"I'm beginning to understand that. Show me some of them."

For all of the time they had spent building up to this moment, their lovemaking was slow. They learned each other's likes and dislikes without speaking many coherent words.

They made love on the sofa, on the floor of the living room, twice in the shower, and again in the morning in the kitchen against the counter.

Chapter
Thirty-one

GRACE AND LUCY were at home, each with her nose in her own book, when the phone rang.

"Hi, Annette, what's up?"

"There is a big snow storm on its way."

"Oh, really? We've not turned the television on this afternoon. Isn't it almost May?" She watched as Lucy got the remote and turned the set on.

"They're saying it'll be one of those heavy, wet storms that come this time of year. We were thinking maybe you'd like to come join our Snowbound Party."

"A what party?"

"We have a get-together here at the house since we have a generator. Usually Pat's here, as is Kelly."

"Do you have room for two more?"

"Yes, you'll have to share a room, though."

"Oh, darn, that doesn't sound like fun at all. Hee hee. We'll get packed and be over in a bit."

She hung up the phone and told Lucy the news. She had her get the cooler from her closet. "We'll empty the fridge and freezer, just in case the power goes out."

While Lucy was gone, the phone rang again. "Grace, it's already started here and it's nasty! This is going to be a mess by morning. Kaye's going to come get you in the Jeep."

"Okay, we'll watch for her."

But it was Kelly who arrived less than a half hour later. "Hey. Y'all call a cab?"

"Miss Walker! Hi!" Lucy ran across the room and jumped up into Kelly's arms. "We're going to Annette and Kaye's, and we're going to have a Snow Party, and we're gonna make cookies 'cause Mom got the stuff out of the cab'net, and I think we're going to...."

"Slow down, kiddo, I can't keep up with you. Yes, I know about the Snow Party, and I'm glad about the cookies, since your mom is such a good cookie maker. You got your stuff together?"

"Yeppers! I got Bear and my books and my underwear. Oh! I can't forget my game board." Lucy ran to her bedroom, and Grace came out of the kitchen.

"What have you been doing today? You're a mess!" Grace looked down at Kelly's lower legs covered in a thin layer of mud.

"Oh, I had a broken pipe and had to dig a hole. A dyke's work is never done." Kelly looked down at her boots. "I didn't have a chance to shower or change. Sorry."

"No problem. It's your truck." Grace kissed Kelly gently on the lips. "I'm having to take some dirty laundry with me. If you have any, I can wash them at the same time."

"Actually, I do. I have to swing by the house to get my stuff. You don't have to do mine, though. It's all smelly."

"Yes, and?"

"And...it's smelly. You know, sweat and stuff."

"Yes, and?" Grace looked up at her. "I don't mind. It's you, so I'll put up with it."

GRACE TUCKED LUCY into the bed they'd made out of a cot in the library. Her daughter thought it was cool, like sleeping in a museum. "I'm going to be up for a while, okay? But you know which room we'll be in?"

"Yep. I promise not to send Marley in there again."

"You'd better not! Sleep good, Lucy."

"Nope. I'm going to stay up all night with my flashlight and read all the books within my reach."

"Yeah, you try that."

Grace shut the door on her way out and returned to the living room. Kelly, Annette, Kaye, and Pat were shuffling the cards for a few hands of poker.

"Shall we play strip poker?" Pat grinned, dealing out the cards.

"No way. Last time we did that, you scared us all." Kelly ducked as Pat threw popcorn at her. "Come on, Grace, you sit next to me, so we can pass aces back and forth."

"Get the munchkin tucked in?" Kaye leaned forward, so Grace could walk behind her.

"Yep. I told her to have a good sleep, and she said no, she was going to sit up all night and read all the books within her reach."

"Oh, that'd be an accomplishment. Our biggest books are down there. *War and Peace* in hardback, for example."

"That big dictionary is down there, too. The unabridged one."

"Ew! Is it legal to own one of those?"

"Would you believe I found it at a yard sale for a dollar?" Kaye cracked open her beer bottle.

"Now that should be illegal."

KELLY WAS IN the guest bedroom, sitting on the edge of the bed as she pulled off her socks. She opened the door to put them in the hall with her boots as Grace stepped out of the bathroom, wearing a long robe. She held the door open for her to walk past, shutting the door behind her.

She watched Grace put away her toiletries, watched her move and the flow of the robe around her. She felt the arousal rise in her, craving a repeat of their last time together. Grace turned then, as if she, too, remembered.

"You look...nice...in that robe." Was all Kelly managed to say.

"Thanks. Then you'll really like this." Grace opened the robe and pushed it from her shoulders to stand there in her long flannel night gown.

Kelly just grinned. "Oh, yeah, I really like you in that." She went toward Grace, reaching forward to touch a fold of the soft material. "Don't you know I'm into textures? Soft, cottony, warm textures?"

"That's just it. I don't know much about you. Especially not what you like in this room."

"Then let me tell you." She fanned her fingers out, smoothing the material over a breast. "Nice. I like this. Soft. I much prefer hints of a body to actual nudity. Nice jeans and a sweater is better than a bikini any day."

"Do you like the more flimsy garments?" Grace had to remember to breathe in, breathe out.

"No, not really. I have rough hands, and they catch on stuff like that." Kelly lowered her head to plant a kiss on the bare spot between the collar and her ear.

"Interesting." Grace put her hands up, touching Kelly just below her breasts. "What do you wear to bed?"

Kelly grinned down at her. "Nothing."

"You sleep in the nude?"

"Yep. If it's cold, I'll wear flannel pants."

"Oh. You need to get ready for bed then."

"I do, don't I? I brushed my teeth. I've put my boots outside. I've locked the door—"

"Locked the door?"

"I figure we won't want a little munchkin to come in here and learn some things before she's ready."

"Oh, there is that."

"You never locked the door?" Kelly started emptying her pockets into a wooden tray on the dresser.

"I've never had to."

"Oh." Kelly understood what that meant. That made her feel better somehow. "To hear Lucy, you've dated dozens of women."

"Date, yes. Have sex with, a few. Sleep with, no."

"Oh. I...is this arrangement okay with you then?"

"Yes. It's more than okay with me." Grace came to stand behind Kelly, wrapping her arms around her.

"Good—but I'll sleep on the couch if you need me to."

"Don't you dare!" She spun Kelly around and reached up to unbutton the top button. She continued down, unbuttoning the shirt to reveal the tight muscle t-shirt underneath. "Do you always wear these?"

"Most of the time. In the summer I can unbutton the top shirt and cool down. In the winter, it's another layer against the cold."

"And no bra?" Grace grinned up as she ran her hands over the t-shirt.

"No, I almost always wear one. Just not when I'm home or relaxing." Kelly was afraid to breathe, afraid taking air in would press her breasts further into Grace's hands, and she would lose all control.

"Darn." She took a step back. "I'm going to check on Lucy, and I'll be right back. Okay?"

"Sure. Want me to do it?"

"No, it's a habit to look in on her before I go to bed."

"Good habit. I'll keep the door unlocked while you're gone."

"You better."

After Grace left, Kelly shrugged off the over shirt, dropping it onto her laundry bag. She took off her belt next, rolling it into a coil and laying it on the dresser. She was unbuttoning her jeans when Grace came back into the room "Sound asleep with *War and Peace* on the floor next to her."

"Didn't get very far, huh?"

"Nope." Grace sat down on the bed next to Kelly. "Need help?"

"Nope."

"I see. May I watch?"

"Grace, sweet Grace, do you know what you're doing to me?"

"No, I don't. Why don't you tell me?" Grace batted her eyes, trying to look innocent.

"First, you shuck off the robe and make me feel how soft your granny gown is." Kelly took a step toward her. "Then you unbutton my shirt. Woman, if you just want to sleep tonight, you'd better let me know now." Continuing to take slow steps toward her, Kelly was just outside of Grace's reach.

Grace was quiet, staring into Kelly's eyes. She stepped forward and started pulling Kelly's shirt up over her torso. "I want to see if we can repeat what we did the last time."

"We need to not take so much time in between, that's what we need to be doing." Kelly pulled Grace to her and held her close, just hugging. Grace leaned into Kelly's big body, enjoying the strength that surrounded her.

Their lovemaking this time was slower, gentler, more exploratory. They needed to get to know each other, what the other needed and was willing to give. Kelly discovered that Grace loved to have her butt grabbed at just the right moments, especially when Grace was on top. Grace discovered that Kelly liked as much inside her as she could get. She also discovered that she liked the feel of Kelly around her hand, liked the power it gave her.

Chapter
Thirty-two

THE SNOW CAME down throughout the night. By morning, it was two feet deep against the side of the house. Drifts were six feet or more against the sheds. Lucy was up first, running down the hall, banging on the door to wake her mother up.

Kelly groaned and rolled over, untangling herself from Grace before covering her with the sheet and blanket. She got up, putting on her jeans and digging a clean undershirt out of the bag. She unlocked the door and left, shutting the door softly behind her.

"Shhh, brat, your mom's still asleep. What's with all the banging?" Kelly slipped on her boots.

"It snowed!"

"Shhh. Yes, we all knew it would. Come on, let's go to the kitchen."

Once there, Kelly pushed the button on the machine to start the coffee brewing. Walking to the large window that looked out over the goat pen, she pulled the cord for the blinds.

"Whoa! Look at that! It did snow!" Kelly picked up Lucy and put her on a chair, so she would be high enough to look out.

"Wowzers! Told ya!"

"It snowed asshole-deep to a giraffe! Oops. Guess I shouldn't use words like that around you."

"It's okay. I hear it all the time at school. But don't let Mom hear you; she goes bonkers." Standing on the chair, Lucy's head was even with Kelly's. She put her arm around her shoulders, and they stood there, watching the snow fall.

"Put your jacket on. Let's go outside. There's something I want you to hear." Kelly got her own jacket.

Lucy got down to put on her jacket and shoes.

"Here, hop on. You'll drown out there." Kelly squatted down, so Lucy could climb on her back.

She carried her up the driveway past Annette's studio. At the top of the rise, Kelly stood still. "Listen."

The snow meant no traffic sounds, not even a tractor in the

field. With their bells silenced, not even the goats were making noise. Lucy listened, not hearing anything, which she admitted to Kelly.

"In a way, there aren't any sounds, which is good. I like this quiet. But listen again. You can hear the snow fall."

Lucy rested her chin on Kelly's shoulder. Now, listening with a different purpose, the sound of the snow falling was quite loud. It was a kind of a hiss, like a radio off frequency. "Wowzers," Lucy whispered.

"Now, listen further. What else do you hear?"

"I hear snow falling from tree limbs," Lucy said a little later.

"Yeah. Sometimes, if you listen close enough, you can hear rabbits hopping in the snow, or a mouse digging a tunnel underneath."

"Really?"

"Yep. I like the quiet like this. True silence doesn't exist. Everything makes a noise, even a snowflake hitting another snowflake."

"I read a book about Indians, and it said they could hear really good."

"Their survival depended on them being able to hear that well. They needed to find food. They needed to find water, too. Let's go see if the coffee is done."

"I can't drink coffee."

"Why not?"

"I dunno. Mom said so."

"And that, my friend, is a very good reason."

"Can I ask you something?" Lucy put her head back on Kelly's shoulder.

"Sure."

"Can I call you Kelly? I'll still respect you as my elder, but I like you too much to call you Miss Walker."

Kelly spun the girl around so that they were face to face. "Sure, you can call me Kelly. I'd like that a lot."

GRACE WOKE UP and realized Kelly wasn't there. She stood and pulled aside the curtain on the nearest window. She saw Kelly standing knee-deep in snow, Lucy on her back. They stood there for quite a while, Lucy at one point putting her chin on Kelly's shoulder. When they turned around, Grace dropped the curtain, afraid of being caught spying on them.

Am I this lucky? This lucky to have come across someone as good as Kelly? Is Kelly real? Was she faking all this just to get to me? Surely someone as good as Kelly cannot really exist.

She put on a loose t-shirt and a pair of sweats, thinking she would meet them in the kitchen. She felt sad, afraid Kelly wasn't real after all. It was obvious Lucy liked her a lot. She didn't want her daughter hurt when Kelly turned out to be all wrong.

NIKKI JOINED THEM a short time later after skiing over from her house. They had a big breakfast, cooked by Kelly and Pat, of all people. Bacon, sausage, biscuits, scrambled eggs, and toast. Afterward, Grace was in the kitchen, watching Kaye, Nikki, and Kelly go check on all the goats.

Pat came up behind Grace to watch them, too.

"Amazing, isn't it?" Pat grinned and poured another cup of coffee.

"What is?"

"Butch mountain women. They can be calm, yet passionate, creative even. When I first moved here, I kept waiting for that other shoe to fall. I couldn't believe I was lucky enough to stumble right into the nest. These people, Kelly, Annette, and Nikki included, are not complicated. Those of us who've been away from here and know of the other types, we keep expecting them to do something to screw it all up. But they won't. What you see is what you get." Pat returned to the window. "I've watched you this morning, watching Kelly. Something is going on in that head of yours."

"I...I don't want to be hurt. I don't want my daughter to be hurt, either."

"It's going to happen you know. Even they aren't perfect, they'll do something that will disappoint someone. And everyone will survive. We'll work it through, and we'll survive. You need to decide what the bigger risk is: not experiencing her at all, or experiencing whatever happens as you go through life together." Pat paused, watching Grace. "I thought I loved once. I thought I was going to have the happy-ever-after we're all reaching for. But she wasn't honest; she wasn't who she said she was. That's why I moved here, to start over. I left the flat sand of Georgia for the mountains. Look at them." Pat nodded toward the scene outside: Kelly and Nikki were burying Kaye with snowballs. "They are just kids at heart, the big lunks."

Grace laughed. "You're right. They are lunks. And you're right in that I need to decide which is the bigger risk."

"Nikki may not have a human child, but she does have that big silly dog of hers. Whoever she dates has to understand that the dog is part of her life, and they can't expect her to get rid of the idiot. But I can't imagine what Kelly thinks of Lucy. I know that the dog can be left at home and that the dog can be put outside in all sorts of weather. But a child, that's a totally different thing."

"Kelly seems to genuinely like Lucy. She seems to care for her as much as any non-parent can."

"Exactly. You know, they say that kids and dogs know the true essence of a person. What does Lucy think of Kelly?"

"Oh, goodness!" Grace laughed. "I hear 'Miss Walker said' all the time!"

"There you have it!"

Chapter
Thirty-three

"YOU'RE AWFUL QUIET this afternoon. What's up?" Kelly had picked up Lucy from school and was taking her to Annette's.

"I got this from my English teacher. Mom has to sign it." Lucy handed Kelly a sheet of paper.

At the next red light, Kelly read it. "You were talking in class? Why?" She gave the paper back.

"'Cause Melissa gave me a note to pass to Will, and I didn't want to, and I told her so."

"Why didn't you want to?"

"I dunno. I don't like her."

"Ah. Your mom's gonna have to sign it. You'd better have your story straight by then."

"I'm not going to give it to her."

"Why not?"

"If I don't show it to her, she won't know about it. If she knows about it, she won't let me watch television, and I'll have to read some dumb book instead."

"So why did you show it to me?"

"I dunno."

"You know that if you don't show it to your mom, I'm going to have to tell her."

"Why? I thought you were my friend!"

"I am. That's why I'll tell her if you don't. Do you know how much trouble you'd be in if she hears it from me and not you? As it is, all you did was talk in class. Do you want to make it worse?"

"If you tell her, I'll tell her you're just being mean!"

"Who do you think she would believe? Why would I make up a story like that? Stop kicking the dash."

"No. You can't make me. You're not my mother OR my father."

Kelly took a deep breath. "You're right on both counts. But this is my truck. So stop kicking the dash."

"Fine. I'm glad I'm staying at Annette's instead of with you 'cause you're not my friend anymore, Miss Walker."

"Fine. You know where I'll be when you want to be my friend again."

GRACE CAME INTO the shop and tossed her jacket over the chair. "What did you do to Lucy?"

"I picked her up from school and dropped her off at Annette's. Why?"

"She's been pitching a fit all afternoon. She said you aren't her friend anymore and that you were mean to her."

Kelly knew she had to be careful here. "Did she tell you anything else?"

"No, I couldn't get her to talk to me. Annette said she won't talk to her, either. What happened on the drive from the school to her house?"

"I...I made Lucy mad at me."

"That's obvious. What did you do to make her mad?"

"I told her I'd do something if she didn't do something first."

"Okay, listen." Grace rubbed her forehead. "Lucy is nine years old. You're an adult. Now, tell me what happened in the truck on the ride from school to Annette's."

Kelly hesitated. If she told Grace, she'd lose Lucy. If she didn't tell, she'd lose Grace. "I think you need to talk to Lucy first. Get her side of the story."

"Just tell me, dammit!"

"Lucy got a note from her teacher, and you're supposed to see it and sign it. Lucy said she wasn't going to show you, and I said I was going to tell you if she didn't. She got mad at me."

"I see. I'm going to go get my daughter now, and take her home." She paused as she was turning to leave. "I'm not mad at you, Kelly. This is new ground for us both. I'm not used to the idea of sharing my daughter any more than she is used to the idea of sharing me."

"LUCY, I SPOKE with your English teacher, Mrs. Parham, today."

"Why? What did Ms. Walker tell you?"

"Nothing. I spoke with your teacher because she called me at work to tell me you were caught talking in class again."

"She did tell you!"

"No, Kelly told me that you had a note, not what was in the note. I had hoped you would tell me last night, and you didn't. Then you got caught again today, and I got a call at work." Grace sat down opposite her daughter at the kitchen table. "Now, tell me about yesterday's note."

"I didn't get a note."

"Lucy, don't lie. Just tell me."

"I didn't get a note! Miss Walker's the one lying to you, not me!"

"Go to your room. I'll come and ask you again later. I hope you'll tell me the truth."

KELLY PUT ON her boots and a heavy jacket before leaving the shop. She pulled her knit cap down over her ears and drove her truck across several fields. She first went to check the oldest stand of walnut trees, making measurements and using spray paint to mark each tree. From there she hiked to the second oldest stand. She hoped she wouldn't have to take this group, but she'd have the notes just in case.

She stood at the top of the ridge and looked down at the old homestead. From there she could tell where the old dock had been before it had rotted away. She could also just make out the old sidewalk, although not much of it was left, the stones long since covered in grass.

She took out her notepad and began sketching, using her practiced eye to gauge distances. When she was done, she had a good idea of what to do next.

"MOM?"

"Yes?"

"I'm sorry I didn't show you the note from yesterday."

"I'm sorry you didn't tell me about it."

"But I'm mad at Miss Walker for telling you."

"That doesn't matter at the moment. What matters is you telling me what happened. What was your purpose in all this?" Grace turned the TV off and gave her daughter her full attention.

"I dunno."

"You don't know." Grace waited, but she knew Lucy wasn't going to say much else. "Lucy, you talking in class is nothing. It's something that just happens. You lying to me about it is *not* something that just happens. It makes me not want to trust you."

"But—"

"There's no excuses for lying, none at all."

"What are you going to do to me?"

"I don't know. I'm too disappointed to decide right now. There's a sandwich wrapped in plastic in the refrigerator for you. Sit at the table and eat, then go to bed."

Lucy went straight to her bedroom.

KELLY MADE IT back to the truck just as it was getting dark. Her nose was running, and her hands were ice cold. She was almost warm by the time she reached the shop. After making sure everything was off or unplugged inside, she turned off the lights in the shop and returned to her truck.

She considered driving into town to see Grace but decided that perhaps it might not be a good idea until Lucy was out of whatever fit she was in. But she couldn't resist calling her on the cell phone.

"Hello?"

"Hi, Grace, it's me, Kelly."

"Hi. Where are you?"

"In my truck at the end of my driveway. Where are you?"

"Sitting on the couch. Lucy's in her room."

"Ah. Bad evening?"

"Not really. I have no idea what's going on."

"Jealousy, maybe?"

"Maybe, who knows?"

"I just thought I'd call to see what was going on."

"I'm glad you did. I'll call you tomorrow, okay?"

"Sure, tomorrow." Kelly turned off the phone and headed over to The Goat Farm for dinner.

"SHE WAS AN absolute brat yesterday." Annette handed Kelly the plate they'd kept warm in the oven.

"She was a brat in my truck. She told me she got the note, told me what was in it, then proceeded to pitch a fit." Kelly sat down to eat after getting a glass of milk.

"Maybe she just had a bad day." Kaye sat down at the table, too.

"I don't know. I got the feeling she set me up. Like she's trying to get Grace mad at me."

"Weird. Why would she do that?" Annette joined them at the table.

"Jealousy?" Kaye asked.

"That's what I asked Grace. She doesn't know, either."

"She'll find out sooner or later. Lucy's a good kid. She's just having a poor spell, I guess."

"So, Kelly, this is what life with a kid will be like if you and Grace get serious. You ready for it?"

"I don't know. It felt odd, telling someone else's kid to do something. I mean, I have for a while now, but this was way different." Kelly took a bite of the pork chop and a swallow of milk. "Lucy even said I wasn't her mother or her father, and she didn't have to listen to me."

"Ouch." Kaye winced. "You know, maybe she's just testing you, trying to find out where you two stand with each other. You're her friend, yes, but you're also dating her mother. I wonder if she did this with any of the others."

"Grace says no one has lived with them."

"If you're the most serious so far, then Lucy may feel threatened by you."

"Me? Whatever the hell for?"

"Her mom's time, space, attention, energy, all that."

Kelly thought for a bit as she chewed. "So what can I do?"

"I haven't a clue, girlfriend. This is beyond my experience."

GRACE WENT TO Lucy's school the next day and met with the guidance counselor and her daughter. "Miss Owens, Lucy's a good child. I've looked over her records, and she's been an excellent student. But in the past few weeks, she's been getting worse about her behavior in class, and her grades are suffering."

"I didn't know it had gotten that bad. Lucy, honey, what's up with you? What do you need?"

"Nothing."

"Lucy, your mother is asking you a valid question and deserves to know more than that. Let's start at the beginning." The counselor looked at her notes. "This began just a few days after the big snow storm."

"We spent the weekend at Kaye and Annette's, right, Lucy?"

"Yes."

"And Nikki came one day. And Kelly and Pat were there."

"Yes."

"Did something happen that weekend that upset you?"

Lucy was silent, just sitting and staring at the floor. "Yes."

The two adults waited for Lucy to continue.

"I heard you talking to someone in the kitchen."

"What were we talking about?"

"You were talking about how you didn't want Kelly to hurt you."

Grace began to understand.

"Yes, you're right. We were talking about that."

Lucy looked up. "You said that you wouldn't date any one that didn't like me, so if you were afraid Kelly would hurt you, I figured that, if Kelly didn't like me anymore, you wouldn't date her, and you couldn't get hurt."

"Lucy, honey, I don't think you understood everything you heard." Grace knelt on the floor to be even with her daughter. "I was afraid that Kelly wasn't being herself. That she seemed too perfect. She likes you, she likes me, she's sane, gentle, smart, easy-going. Just too perfect. I was afraid that I'd get my hopes up, and something would happen. But, baby, that's what life is all about, you know? You can't go through life not doing things because you're afraid something bad will happen because of it. We have to take risks. I was afraid to take that risk, not afraid of Kelly. I was afraid that loving someone that much would hurt me."

"I don't understand."

"If I may, Miss Owens?" the counselor interrupted. "Lucy, remember the big spelling bee last month?"

"Yeah."

"You were afraid to sign up for it, weren't you?"

"Yeah."

"What were you afraid of?"

"Afraid of making a mistake, of looking like an idiot." Lucy rolled her eyes.

"But you signed up for it. Why?"

Lucy paused, even her feet got still. "Because I wanted to be in the spelling bee. I'm a good speller."

"Right. So you decided that you would take the risk of looking like an idiot."

"Yes. Oh! I get it." She looked at her mother. "You were afraid Kelly might make you look like an idiot, so you were having to decide if you wanted to do that."

"Exactly. I think Kelly is worth the risk."

"And I thought the trophy was worth the risk." Lucy's smile faded. "Kelly's mad at me, isn't she?"

"Not mad, but confused and hurt."

"I gotta 'polagize, don't I?"

"Yes, yes, you do."

KELLY WAS AT the shop again, sitting at her drafting table, sketching out the ideas she'd come up with the day before. The CD player was on, this time with some bluesy jazz.

"Kelly?"

She turned to see Grace and Lucy at the door. "Come on in, ladies." She scooted over and turned off the music. The two came farther in, Lucy in front of Grace, her mother's hands on her shoulders.

"Lucy has something to say to you."

Kelly focused on the little girl.

"I'm sorry. I didn't mean to get you mad at me. I'm sorry for kicking the dash of your truck."

"It's okay—" Kelly couldn't say anything else because Lucy

launched herself at her, crying her heart out. "It's okay, Lucy, it's okay." Kelly closed her eyes, feeling herself start to cry, too. "I'm still your friend. I wasn't mad, just confused. It's okay." She rocked her, patting her back, both of them crying, neither of them noticing Grace was crying, too.

AFTER THEY DROVE over to The Goat Farm, Kelly and Grace had a chance to talk alone.

"And that's why?" Kelly had stayed calm as Grace had told her what the situation had been.

"That's why. She overheard me and Pat and assumed the responsibility of protecting me."

"I see." Kelly wondered if she should be glad or upset or just roll with it.

"What's in that head of yours?"

"I'm not sure." She took Grace's hands in her own. "Grace, are you saying you're wanting to take the risk? Are you wanting to make this relationship more serious? Make an actual relationship?"

"Yes, Kelly, I'm willing to take the risk. We've got some work to do, but I want to take the risk with you. Can you?" Grace held her breath, afraid of what she might say.

"Yes, yes, I think I can. Um, Grace, do you love me? I mean, love love me, not just like me a whole bunch."

"I love love you. I love love love you. I quadruple love you. And I like you a whole bunch. A bunch of grapes, a bunch of bananas, a—"

Kelly hushed her by kissing her. Kissing her on the lips, sucking her bottom lip between her own. They stood then, holding, hugging, kissing. Grace had her arms around Kelly, pulling her close, not wanting to ever let go. Kelly felt the same and had to force herself to end the kiss.

"I love you, too. God, how I love you."

They stood there for quite a while, just holding. Grace had her face turned toward Kelly's throat, Kelly had her cheek resting on Grace's head.

This is how Lucy and Kaye found them later.

"Gross," Lucy said, emphatically.

"Yeah, gross." Kaye agreed.

Chapter
Thirty-four

"WHAT ARE YOU going to do?" Dr. Tower rested her chin in her hand.

"I want to do things to test my trust. I trust Grace. I do. But I don't trust myself to trust her. Does that sound as weird to you as it does to me?"

"Probably." She laughed with her. "So what are you going to do to test your trust?"

"We're going to have a couple of weekends where I sorta live with her and Lucy. Feel it out to see how we get along. Except for that one time, Lucy has been a wonderful kid, almost too good. And Grace is almost as perfect. I need to find that imperfection, and deal with it. We need something more...tangible to deal with than a temperamental little girl."

"You mean like leaving your muddy boots on the carpet?"

"Exactly! See, it was those little things that Anna was good at using to cut me down. Things like my dirty clothes, or the way I tossed my Coke can into the bin from across the room."

"What about that bothered her?"

"I missed ninety-nine percent of the time. It would clang on the tile floor, and it really pissed her off. But I liked to see if maybe just that time I could make it. You know?"

"So you want to see how Grace reacts to that? To where you toss your empty cans?"

Kelly stood and went to the window. "Sounds weird, but yes." She spun back around. "I told you about the Band-Aid, right? How Lucy put one on and had Grace kiss it, and then she redid it? See, that's something Anna would never have done. There was this one time when I myself really bad, and all Anna could say was how the blood was going to be a bitch to get out of the carpet. I could have bled all over that floor, and I don't think it would have occurred to Grace about how to clean it. Because she was thinking of me, not the floor."

"And Anna didn't."

"Right. And I don't think she ever really did."

"THESE ARE THE plans for your client?"

"Yeah, what do you think?"

"Rough. Basic. But I can work with it." Clarence leaned back against the hood of the truck. "You're going to do most of the interior?"

"Yep, you do the shell, meaning the building itself, plumbing, electric, stuff like that, and I'll do the inside."

"Where's this house going?"

"I brought a map." Kelly unrolled it and pointed to the location.

"I see. And I bet the client doesn't want this to be widely known, huh?"

"You got it. So, can you do up an estimate?"

"Yep, I can do that. I'll need to go see the site, make notes. Is that old road still usable?" Clarence tapped the map with his big calloused finger.

KELLY WENT TO Thompson Construction to pick up Lucy. Off for spring break, she would be spending most days with Kelly at the shop.

"It's about time you got here." Lucy stood at the door, hands on her hips, one foot tapping.

"I do mornings about like I cook."

"Ew, and you drove?"

"Surprising, isn't it?"

"WHO IS THIS?" Lucy had been going through Kelly's music collection of old vinyls.

"That, my friend, is Joan Jett."

"Who?"

"What do you mean, who? You don't know Joan Jett?"

"Nope. She sing?"

"Girl, your mama ought to be slapped for not introducing you to the fabulous Joan Jett." Kelly knelt down and went through the CDs. "Here, we'll listen to some of her stuff." Soon the guitar and drum music, along with Joan Jett's wonderful voice, filled the shop.

"Hey, she's good."

"Come on, let's rock and roll." Kelly picked up Lucy, so she stood on the work bench. "Now, air guitar!"

"Do what?"

"Man, you've been sheltered far too long. Watch me." Kelly, big butch strong Kelly, proceeded to play air guitar to "I Love Rock n Roll." Lucy, still up on the table, joined in. The music was cranked up, the two of them were jamming and dancing, and it was the most fun Kelly had had in a long time.

"MUST YOU LISTEN to that so loud?" Anna came in, dropping her bag on the chair on her way to turn down the music.
"It's the only way to listen to this album. Bad day?"
"Yes, damn clients. Sometimes I wonder why I keep doing this." She went into the kitchen and poured herself a drink.
"Because you like — "
"Don't tell me what I like and don't like. Just, just leave me alone for a bit, will you?" Anna went to the bedroom and shut the door.
Later she came back out, dressed in a t-shirt and jeans. She sat down next to Kelly and kissed her cheek. "I'm sorry about yelling at you. I shouldn't take it out on you."
"It's all right. I know I should keep my distance at times. So, feeling better?" Kelly let Anna kiss her on the mouth, but she didn't like the taste of the alcohol. But she knew Anna used sex to release the day, so she pushed the taste aside and did what Anna wanted.

"YOU LIKE KELLY, don't you?" Grace put a serving of casserole on Lucy's plate.
"Yeah. She's cool."
"Do you think, maybe, you could have her around more often?"
"You thinking of letting her move in?" Lucy put a spoonful of her dinner in her mouth.
"We were thinking maybe just for the weekends for a while."
"I don't know, Mom. We never let anyone live with us before."
"I know, I know. I'm just thinking about it and wondered what your thoughts were." Grace sat down to her own dinner after pouring milk for them both.
"Would she be like my second mom?"
"Yes. That means that she would tell you to do things, and you'd have to do it, just as if I had told you."
"That doesn't sound very fair."
"No, I guess it doesn't. But that's how all the kids with two parents have to live."
"I do like her. She's nice to me and doesn't put me down. Margaret's mom is always putting her down. Says she's stupid and lazy and all that."
"That's not nice, no matter who the person is."
"Oh, Miss Walker said you ought to be slapped."
"What?" Grace dropped her fork.
"She said you ought to be slapped for not telling me about

Joan Jett."

"Joan Jett? Okay, back up. What's Joan Jett got to do with this?"

"I was going through her music today and found some of these big square cases with round things inside, she said it was records or something like that, anyway, I found one that had this lady in a white coat and she said it was Joan Jett, and I said Joan Jett who, and she said you ought to be slapped."

"I see."

"Then we listened to some of the music, and I got up on the table, and we did air guitars and danced, and—"

"Back up again. You did air guitars?"

"Yep. Miss Walker had to show me how 'cause I didn't know what she meant."

"Okay. And both of you danced or just you?"

"Both of us, but I was the only one on the table."

"Okay. And, no, you may not slap me. I may not have introduced you to Joan Jett, but you do know about Johnny Cash."

"Yeah, but I like Joan Jett better."

Chapter
Thirty-five

"GRACE, CALL WALKER and tell her I'm ready to get started on that project for her client. Have her call my cell phone when she's ready to discuss it."

"Sure will, boss. Anything else?"

"Not at the moment. How's that dang car of yours doing?"

"It's still alive. Amazing isn't it?"

"Yeah, I'd have pushed it into the creek a long time ago. My wife is wanting a new car, and she wanted to know if you wanted her old one. It ain't old, just four years, but she wants a new one. It's a four-by-four station wagon, one of those rice burners."

"I can't drive a stick shift."

"Hmph, neither can she—the wagon's an automatic. But you ought to learn how. Ain't Walker's truck a stick? Have her teach you how. I'll bring the wagon by tomorrow. We'll work out payments later."

"YOU WANT TO learn to drive a stick shift?" Kelly sipped her coffee.

"Yep. Clarence said I should."

"It's easy enough. It's too hilly here, though. We can use one of Kaye's big fields."

"Okay. Let's go do it now."

"Now? I gotta get my nerve up first. This isn't something you just jump right into."

"Get your nerve up? I'll get your nerve up." Grace began whomping Kelly with the newspaper they'd been reading.

An hour later, a bruised and battered Kelly sat with Grace in her truck out in a back level field. Lucy, Kaye, and Annette sat in the Cherokee providing moral support.

"Now, I'm going to do this as if you're an idiot, so that I don't assume, and you don't get confused, okay?"

"I'll keep that in mind."

"Now, this is the clutch, this is the brake, and that is the gas. The thing is, your left foot does the clutch, your right foot does its usual thing. Now, the clutch and the gas are never fully on at the same time, usually one is going on while the other is coming off. Watch my feet." Kelly slowly let up on the clutch while pressing in on the gas. "See how they're counter-balancing each other?"

"Yes."

"Okay, now we're rolling, and it's time to go from first to second. So I push down on the clutch, and let up on the gas. That part is much faster than the other. I put it into second, I push down on the gas, and let up on the clutch."

"Okay."

"There's a point where you'll feel the gas get stronger than the clutch. So, think you're ready?"

"Um, sure. Yeah, I can do this."

As Kelly walked around the truck, she saw Lucy sitting on the hood of Kaye's Jeep, cheering them on. Kelly wagged her finger at her, warning her not to be too rough on her mother.

"Okay. Now, to start the truck, you need to be out of gear."

"Why?"

"Ever seen a bucking bronco? Well, that's what it'll be like. So push the clutch and brake, put it in neutral, and turn the key. Now, put it in first, let go of the brake and ease on the gas while letting go of the clutch."

"You make it sound so easy."

"It is once you've done it for twenty-something years. There you go."

Slowly the truck began to creep forward.

"Ready to go into second?"

"No!"

"You gotta do it some time. You can't drive in first all the way to town and back."

"Sure I can."

"Not in my truck. Now, let up on the gas, push in the clutch, shift to second, and —"

The truck began to stutter, leaping forward several times before the engine died.

"That's the bronco part you mentioned."

"Yep."

With the engine off, they could hear laughter across the field.

"OKAY, YOU STILL love me?" Kelly held onto Grace's hand as they walked from the truck to Kaye and Annette's house.

"Yeah, I still love you. Do you forgive me for making your

truck make such noises?"

"Yep, not a problem. I'll send you the bill for the transmission repair."

"Funny. Will you take a trade?" Grace leaned into Kelly and looked up at her with a lustful look.

"Heck, yeah! Whatcha got to trade?"

"A nine-year-old girl."

"Nice try. I'll send you the bill." Kelly picked Grace up and threw her over her shoulder to carry her the rest of the way.

Chapter
Thirty-six

CLARENCE WATCHED AS one of his crews unloaded the earth-moving machinery. "Walker, this is going to take a few days, I reckon. We'll make this the working road and then make the official driveway later."

"All right. They'll probably wind up being the same. I'm not sure yet."

"We'll make the road, get it packed good, then start bringing in the materials."

"How long until you start building, after the foundation, I mean?"

"We've got a lot of prep work before we can even do the foundation—I'd say several weeks. I got two masons subcontracted to take the chimney down. They'll be starting that today, so it comes down as they plan rather than by vibration. We'll also be building a storage shed. I thought about bringing one in, but we're using both of them elsewhere."

"No problem. I'm going to wait 'til true thaw to move the water. The ground's too hard right now."

"Yep, at least I got these toys. All you got is a shovel."

"KELLY, WHAT'S A memorial?"

"A memorial is, well, it's when folks do something special to remember someone who's died. A funeral is a more official, formal thing." Kelly looked up from her drafting desk.

"Melissa's grandpa died somewhere else, so they're having a memorial tomorrow."

"That sounds tough for Melissa, to lose her grandpa. Is she okay?"

"He's been gone for over a year. He was an army policeman or something. She says it doesn't seem real, that he'll just come home like he always does."

"Do you remember your grandpa?"

"A little. Not much anymore. He died when I was in kindergarten. He had a good laugh."

"I think it's a good thing if someone remembers you the most for your laugh. You talked to your mom about this?"

"Nope. I figured I'd ask you 'cause you 'splain things better than Mom. You ever gonna get a real house of your own?"

"How'd you get from your Grandpa to me having a house?"

"I dunno. Who knows how a nine-year-old's brain works?"

Kelly laughed. "True! I hope to have my own home again soon. Maybe by fall."

"That long?"

"Yes, that long. It can only go so fast. I have to sell a few things first. But don't tell your mom. She'll want me to spend money on less fun stuff, like clothes."

"Ew."

"Exactly."

"KELLY, DO YOU know anything about my dad?"

Kelly wondered where these questions were coming from. "No, I don't. Do you?"

"No, Mom won't tell me. I thought maybe you knew, and you'd tell me instead."

"If I did know anything, I wouldn't tell you. It's something you and your Mom need to talk about. Why do you want to know?"

"I want to know who my dad is."

Kelly turned in her seat to face the young girl directly. "Lucy, there's more to being a parent than just making a kid. The man who was responsible for his part of that making is nothing more than a paternal parent, not a father, and certainly not a dad."

"Mom says he never knew about me, so how could he have even tried?"

"Maybe there's a reason she didn't tell him. Your mom is smart and would have had a very good reason."

"The teacher says that with some animals, the father doesn't even know his kids. That after mating season he goes away. And some animals are born and don't know either one of their parents, like sea turtles."

"True. And with some animals, it's the father who takes care of the offspring, not the mom, like the sea horse."

"But humans are different."

"Are we? If we were, then there'd be no orphanages and no single parents. Just because we wear clothes and stand upright doesn't mean we're smart."

Lucy looked at Kelly for a few seconds. "I think I understand."

"And remember, Lucy, sometimes when we ask questions, we don't get the answer we expected."

"MOM, I'M NINE years old, almost ten."

"I know, I was there, remember?" Grace pushed away her book.

"No, I don't. I don't remember that, silly." Lucy sat on the opposite end of the table. "Mom, I think I'm old enough to know about my panertal parent."

"It's paternal, and no, you are not." She raised her hand to stop Lucy from speaking. "Some things you are still too young to understand."

"Isn't there anything about him you can tell me? Like, where is he now?"

"You may not want to know. He died a few years ago." Grace watched her daughter, scared of what she was thinking.

"How do you know?"

"I asked someone where he was. Remember when Travis and his mom had to go to court? I wrote someone a letter and asked."

"That's when I asked you last time?"

"Yes. I just didn't want to disappoint you by telling you about his death."

"What was he like?" Lucy chewed on a fingernail.

"He was...crazy. Not insane, just crazy. Always in trouble, always on the wrong side of everything."

"Did he get into any trouble for it?"

Grace paused, not knowing how much further to go. "Yes, he did."

"So maybe it's a good thing I didn't know him. I don't like bad men, and it would be just awful if my dad was one." Lucy crawled over to sit in her mother's lap.

"Yes, it would have been. I didn't know I was pregnant with you when I called it quits with him. When I did find out, I decided not to tell him, to make sure he was out of my life for good."

"That must've been tough."

"It was. I wasn't just making a decision for me alone. I had a little baby on the way who would be the hardest hit by all of it."

They sat there together, staring at nothing, each lost in their own thoughts.

"I like Kelly. I think she's cool."

"Oh? What brings this subject up?"

"I was just thinking that if I had to have two parents, having her as one wouldn't be too bad. It would be weird, though, having two moms."

"Do you think your friends at school would tease you about it?"

"Maybe. But Kelly says the best way to show someone who you are is to be yourself. So if I'm myself, they'll see that I'm no different just because I got two moms."

THE NEXT DAY, Lucy was in charge of the clipboard as Kelly re-checked the two stands of walnut trees. "And people pay lots of money for these trees?"

"Yep. Their wood is great. Plus, I sell the walnuts each fall. I can't eat them myself, so I don't want them to go to waste." They headed back to the shop.

"What are we going to do next?" Lucy walked along, balancing the clipboard on her head.

"We go into town to talk to a man about the trees. And we get lunch."

As they drove into town, Lucy hummed a song to herself. "Kelly? I like you and think you're cool, but..."

"But what?"

"But I don't like your truck. It may be good for your work, but it's not good for hauling a kid around."

"I can tie you to the roof."

"You could, but you won't, 'cause then Mom won't kiss you again."

"Hmm, you're right about that. It's the only vehicle I've got, so get over it."

"I'll try. Just warn me if you see any of my friends, so I can duck down."

"You better duck 'cause I'm gonna reach over there and smack you!"

THEY WENT TO see the man about the trees and were sitting down for a lunch at a fast-food place. "You know, you're right about the truck. It's good for the job, but it's kinda big to drive for everyday-type things."

"Save up your quarters and get another one."

"Funny. I'd sell you, but then I'd owe them."

"Now who's being funny?" Lucy stole a french fry. "Your face looks weird. What are you thinking?"

"I'm doing math in my head. Finish eating, so I can go by the bank."

"MOM WOULD FREAK if she knew you had that much money."

"Really? Why?" Kelly backed the truck out of the parking space.

"She's weird about that. Lynn had a lot of money, but Mom didn't, and they fought all the time about it."

"So don't tell her. Let me do it later. Someday. Maybe."

"What are you going to do with all this?" Lucy folded up the bank statement.

"A couple of things. I'm thinking of getting a new truck. Want to go with me to look?"

"Yeah!"

KELLY AND LUCY wandered several car lots the rest of the afternoon not really deciding on anything. Kelly looked for the practical things, while Lucy was in charge of the cool factor. They even made up a mathematical equation.

They were sitting in the truck, waiting at a red light, when Kelly made a phone call. "Hey, Mom, whatcha doin'...Yeah? Sounds delicious. Makes me drool...Tell Dad to not eat it all in one sitting. Listen, do you think Mr. Goings is still interested in the Mercedes?...Fine, fine, let me talk with Dad, then." She started driving again but pulled over into a parking lot. "Hey, Dad, do you think he's still interested? Will you sell it for me? Get the most you can out of the tightwad, okay? I am doing gooder by the minute, actually. I was thinking of coming over in June or so, once school lets out...I miss you, too. You have this number? Good, call me when it's sold...Yes, we'll discuss your salesman percentage. Later, Dad!"

"Whose car are you selling?"

"One of mine. It's over at my parents' place. It's an old car, but well maintained. Mr. Goings has been after me for several years to sell it to him. Maybe he's still interested and will offer me a good price. Dad's a good dealer. He'll take care of it for me."

"What do you need with more money?"

"I got a lot going on right now, a lot of money going out. I like to keep a buffer in the bank for things like, oh, busted arms."

Chapter
Thirty-seven

HEFTING THE LARGE ledger board into place, Kelly hammered the nail through it with a single swing and did the same on the other end. With it supported by the nails, she could drive in the huge screws that would be its permanent support. Once the board and the five posts were in place, the rest would go along quickly. She needed to put the cement in around the posts, and then let it sit for a few days before putting up the frame and the decking.

Kelly used a bungee cord to hold the level in place and two blocks to hold the post in a relatively level position. She put in a few scoops of dry cement and pounded it down with her homemade tamper. By the time she got to the fifth post, her arms felt like they weighed two hundred pounds each.

Rain came home just as she was finishing up the last post. "Hey, Kelly, it's looking good. I didn't expect you to get this far so soon." She got her chair out of the back seat and let Jake out.

"Luckily, you don't have any close trees, so digging the holes wasn't as bad as I thought it would be." Kelly continued tamping in the cement.

"You're using dry cement?" Rain was surprised.

"Yes, it's easier and holds just as good. It absorbs water from the ground and it hardens up in much less time." Kelly petted the big German shepherd and tossed the Frisbee.

"Never heard of it. But you're the master of this, not me."

WHEN SHE FINISHED, Kelly stood and looked over her work. They'd decided to build a deck out over the ground that tended to hold moisture and then put in the ramp. Kelly would build the deck just so far, then take the old ramp down in order to finish. Rain would have to spend a night away from home, since it would take another day to finish.

"So we're still looking at Thursday as the day you'll take the ramp down?"

"Yeah, I'm right on schedule for that. I'll pre-build some of the ramp sections, but there's still no way to get it all done in one day."

"It's all right. You're doing this at a great price and in less time than the others said they could. Listen, you need a drink or anything?"

"Nope, I'm doing just fine. I got a cooler full of stuff to keep me going." She stretched and flexed her arms. "I'm getting old, I think."

"You look mighty good for an old geezer." Rain laughed at Kelly's blush. "Oh, Annette said you've done work at The Pride Center. Is it a safe location?"

"Safe enough. It's right on a busy corner downtown. You thinking of volunteering during the Pride Week?"

"I'm thinking about it, but I haven't decided yet."

"I built a box for Masco, to keep her hidden and out of the way. It's big enough for two."

"Masco?"

"A service dog. There's a lady who volunteers there full time. She has a Rottweiler service dog."

"I didn't know about the dog or the lady. It might make volunteering there more interesting, huh?"

Kelly grinned back. "It just might."

KELLY DROVE UP to Grace's house but stayed in the truck a moment. This would be their first test of reality, and Kelly stunk. She had dirt and mud all over her pants, her shirt was stuck to her, and her hair was a mess under the cap. Anna had never liked it when Kelly came home this way. Would Grace survive it? Maybe they should have decided to wait until Friday night.

"Mom, Kelly's here!" Lucy opened the door to let her in. "Hi, Kelly! Ew! You played in the dirt today!"

"Yes, I did. Scoot that chair over here, will you? I need to sit down and take off my boots."

"Sure thing, oh stinky one."

"Hush, kid, or I'll hug you tight and close." Kelly growled, but it only made Lucy giggle harder.

"Hey, hon, I got dinner started. And I put clothes out for you in the bathroom. I figured you'd want to shower."

"Yep. I stinketh to high heaveneth."

"No problemeth. Lucy, take the boots outside, so they can dry." Grace laughed as Lucy picked them up as if they were toxic waste.

"I'm gonna kill that kid. All right, I'm in the shower."

"I'll stay away from the water. But give me a kiss first."

Kelly paused before giving Grace a big kiss on the lips.

"You don't smell that bad. I don't know what you're so worried about. You got more dirt on you than smell. But take a shower, so you feel better." Grace swatted her butt as she passed by.

Kelly closed the bathroom door. For the first time, she noticed how girly the room was. She'd been in there before, of course, but this was a different day with a different set of circumstances. A spare roll of toilet paper was in a cute flowery box on the back of the toilet. The liquid soap on the sink was in a matching dispenser.

She laughed when she saw the brand-new-still-in-its-package towel rack leaning behind the door. A big thick towel lay on the toilet seat and a pair of sweats and a t-shirt hung from a hook on the wall. Kelly stripped and dropped the clothes on the floor while she waited for the water to get hot.

Once in the shower, she picked up the soap, expecting it to be perfumy. Instead, it smelled like oatmeal cookies. It foamed easily and was great for the layers of dirt on her hands and the back of her neck.

She jumped when a hand touched her bare bottom.

"I thought maybe you needed a hand in here." Grace grinned through the steam.

"It depends on what you plan on doing with the hand."

"I can think of a few things. But with dinner on the stove, I was thinking of holding a cloth with it and scrubbing your back."

"Really? You don't have to, you know."

"I know. But I know that when I work up a sweat, it trickles down my back, and I hate that."

"Here, feel free to scrub away." Kelly handed her the soapy washcloth and turned, putting her hands on the shower wall.

Grace started at her neck, going side-to-side, dipping down her shoulders on each side. She then scrubbed up and down in short strokes, working from right to left then right again. She rubbed both of Kelly's buttocks, going around and around, slowly dipping the cloth further and further down. Without thinking, Kelly parted her legs more, giving Grace access to her vagina. As Grace washed it from behind, Kelly moaned.

"God, woman, if you don't hush, I'll burn dinner." Grace's voice was deep, revealing she was also aroused.

"Then you'd better stop, or you'll get your clothes all wet when I pull you in here." Kelly turned, taking the cloth before putting Grace's hand between her legs, to feel the slick labia and clitoris.

"Stop that! Geez!" Grace laughed and stepped back as Kelly reached for her again. "No way! You need to turn the hot water off and cool down!" She laughed again as she opened the door to leave. "But not too cold. Save some of it for me later."

THEY SAT AT the table together and ate the wonderful dinner Grace had made. "What's this called again?" Lucy put a forkful of meat in her mouth.

"Pot roast. You like it?"

"Yeah, not bad. What do you think, Kelly?"

"I think it's a great bucket roast."

"Not bucket roast, pot roast." Lucy stared at Kelly and tipped her head from side to side.

"Pan roast?" Kelly sounded genuinely confused.

"No! Pot, pot, pot roast."

"Wonder what kind of plant?"

"I give up, Mom. She's all yours." Lucy shook her head.

"Gee, thanks. I appreciate it. After dinner, have Kelly look over the math homework I helped you with. We may have done some of it wrong."

"Nope, I checked over your work, Mom."

Kelly almost choked on her drink. "Ahem, Lucy, you better be careful. She'll poison your food one of these days."

"I keep forgetting that."

When they were done eating, Lucy and Kelly loaded the dishwasher while Grace put away the leftovers. "Do you want any of this for work tomorrow?"

"Nah, no way to heat it up."

"A sandwich again?"

"Yep. Me like PB and J. Me like cookies."

"Lucy? You, too?"

"Yep. Me like PB and J. Me like cookies."

"Great, two Neanderthals in the same house." Grace put some of the dinner in a plastic container for herself and the rest into larger ones.

"But I'd like to have two sandwiches. One just isn't enough most days." Kelly closed the dishwasher door and dried her hands.

"Even with the carrots?"

"Carrots? Is that what those things were? Long orange-ish sticks?"

"Yes, Kelly, carrots. What did you do with them?" Grace put her hands on her hips.

"I ate 'em, but there's nothing to them to fill me up."

"Mom, Kelly needs a lunch box. That way you can look in it and see what she ate or not."

"Hush, kid."

"That's a very good idea, Lucy. We'll go get one tomorrow."

"Thanks, Lucy. Now I gotta find some way to dump the orange sticks."

"Don't bother. She'll know. I don't know how she does, but she will." Lucy shook her head.

GRACE CAME INTO the bedroom where Kelly stood by the bed. She was emptying the pockets of her muddy jeans.

"I keep meaning to ask you why you have so much crap in your pockets." She stood on tiptoe to look over Kelly's shoulder.

"Can you see me carrying a purse?"

"No, no, I can't." Grace put her heels down and wrapped her arms around Kelly.

"God, that feels good." Kelly leaned back into Grace.

"I have to have you tonight, Kelly. Make love to me?"

Kelly turned in Grace's arms, looking down into her eyes. "Yes, oh, yes." She kissed her, until they both were leaning against the dresser trying to breathe.

Kelly took Grace's hand and led her to the bed. She sat down on the edge, with Grace standing between her knees. She lifted the shirt and kissed her belly, licking under each breast as it was exposed. With the shirt off, she pulled Grace to her, hands on the small of her back, lips on her hot skin. Grace's hands stayed on Kelly's shoulders, as she tried to remain standing as Kelly devoured her.

Kelly felt Grace pulling on her shirt at the shoulders. She shrugged to help it off, not bothering to unbutton it, just letting Grace pull it up over her head. Her jeans felt rough to Kelly's hard nipples, but they didn't stay there long. Grace pushed her back, chewing on her through her jeans.

Kelly pulled her up, so she was on top of her, grabbing Grace's buttocks and grinding their two crotches together. She heard Grace start to moan, so she clamped her mouth over hers, kissing her, absorbing the cries as Grace came.

The rest of their clothing was off quickly, and they lay naked, side by side. As much as Kelly wanted to enter Grace, she wanted to take it slow, to better prepare her. Instead she toyed with her clitoris, watching Grace arch and gasp. To her delight, Grace just got wetter. Finally, she couldn't wait any longer. Kelly sank her first two fingers into Grace, feeling them surrounded by hot moist flesh. Grace pushed back, and Kelly complied, pushing harder against her. She began stroking, in, out, in, out, feeling Grace's hips move in rhythm with her hand. She slipped a third finger in, filling Grace further. She paused as Grace did, pressing against her. She began stroking again, and this time, Grace lay still, accepting the feelings as they happened. It wasn't long until she could feel her tighten around her. She again kissed her, muffling Grace's moans as the second orgasm hit her.

Kelly ground herself against her lover's hip, bringing her own orgasm. Exhausted from the day's work and from the wonderful lovemaking, she was soon fast asleep, her hand lying against Grace's still wet groin.

Hours later, just as the morning birds began singing, Kelly slowly woke up, feeling something happening to her. She gasped, realizing that Grace was sucking on her clitoris, pausing, licking from the entrance back up the clit, then sucking it again. Kelly reached down and stroked Grace's hair, feeling her arousal grow. It was taking a while, though, so Grace scooted up and used her hand to bring Kelly to a quicker climax. Kelly, being a larger woman, was able to take three fingers immediately. Grace had put her fingers in, all the way to the knuckles, pressed, and then came out to stroke her clitoris before diving back inside.

Kelly felt it—a strong orgasm threatening to explode as she got closer to the peak. Somehow she managed to be silent, arching her back and gasping for air as Grace continued to plunge in and out in a steady rhythm.

KELLY WAS AT Harri's, digging the trench for the gutter drain. At noon, she sat on the tailgate of her truck to eat lunch. In the paper bag, she found two peanut butter and jelly sandwiches wrapped in wax paper, three carrot sticks in plastic wrap, two cookies, and a handful of corn chips in a little plastic bag.

She also found a single button taped to a note. "This came off your shirt last night as I pulled it over your head. Think about that."

Kelly moaned, feeling herself get wet. They'd only made love three nights total, and each time it was different and better. *How does she do this to me?* She wasn't within ten miles of her, and she could feel her touching her, stroking her like she had that morning.

"LEAVE ME ALONE."
"C'mon, Anna, open up." Kelly nibbled on Anna's bare thigh.
"Leave me alone, I said. I'm not interested in morning sex. Don't you have work to do today?"

THE RAIN IN the afternoon meant Kelly had to stop work for the day. She packed up her tools and headed to the house on Oak Street. Since she'd be home first, she wondered what she should make for dinner. She was a lousy cook, but it only seemed fair.

She left her muddy boots on the porch and went to the kitchen. She was surprised to find two frozen lasagnas in the freezer. She saw on one box that it was served on a plate alone, but had a bowl of salad in the background.

She put the lasagna in the oven, and set the timer. She took a quick shower before starting the salad, finding everything she needed in the refrigerator. She also buttered some bread and put it on a cookie sheet to put in the oven just before the lasagna was due to be done.

When Lucy and Grace came home just after 5:30, both were surprised to find dinner cooked and ready to eat. Grace kept staring at Kelly and grinning.

"What? Even butch girls can cook a frozen lasagna."

Chapter
Thirty-eight

THEY CAME TO cut down the first stand of trees and haul them off to the mill. The supervisor handed Kelly an estimate once he had seen the trees and before he ordered the cutting. He walked with her to the second stand and decided they would wait to see how much they harvested from the first one.

While they were walking back, Clarence drove up in his truck. "I see you're taking the trees down. Hope you got a good price on 'em. I'll be expecting payment."

"Here you go. That should be the first half. I'm financing the rest." Kelly handed him a cashier's check from her coat pocket.

"Are you serious?" He unfolded the check and whistled. "You are serious. This will make the accountant happy. Y'all want a ride back to the wood cutting?"

"Sure, we'll just ride in the back." The supervisor and Kelly hopped up onto the tailgate of the truck.

"WALKER, I NEED to speak with you a moment." Clarence waited by the truck as Kelly made her way through the mud.

"What's up?"

"Now, we ain't never talked about it, and I'm hesitant to talk about it now, but it's got to be done. Have you told her yet?"

Kelly looked at him for a moment, realizing what he was saying. "No, I haven't. Why?"

"It's getting difficult to keep it quiet at the warehouse without the boys knowing anything they don't need to know."

"I see. I'll take care of that next weekend. I can have a big bonfire here and invite everyone. No one knows about this but you."

"That'll do just fine. Now, you better, 'cause like I said, it's getting kinda difficult." He looked down at his boots a moment. "You like her a whole lot, don't you?"

"Yes, sir, I do."

"Me and my wife have gotten rather fond of her, and the kid,

too. And I'd hate to have to beat the shit out of you for doing something stupid."

Kelly didn't dare laugh. "I understand. Don't worry. This is
not a passing thing."

"I figured not. You ain't never, you know, brought anyone
around before." He coughed and readjusted his cap. "I gotta get
back to work. And you got a cookout to plan."

As Kelly walked through the mud toward her truck, she
decided Nikki was just the person to help her plan this.

KELLY WAITED AT her house as everyone started arriving.
Most headed straight for the lake, anticipating the escape possibili-
ties from the summer heat in a couple of months. Finally, Grace and
Lucy arrived, and Kelly led them to the lake, too.

Nikki approached her and signaled she needed to talk with her
alone. "I brought some kerosene, just in case we need it to get the
fire going right."

"Cool. When we're ready, we'll heft Annette and Rain up in
the back, and you'll drive everyone over there." Kelly looked
around, seeing Grace over with Spam. "Just make sure Grace and I
get there first, and give us a minute or so."

"No problem. I'll swing wide." Nikki grinned. "It's looking
good. I'm jealous."

"Ha. I'll send you the unpaid bills."

"No thanks. You can keep those."

They all gathered around and goofed off until Annette and
Kaye arrived, and Pat came soon after. Four people surrounded
Annette's chair while two others stood behind it. They lifted her
straight up and into the back of the truck. She laughed the whole
time, which gave the lifters the giggles, and they almost dropped
her once. Once she and Rain were inside the back of the truck,
Nikki attached the trailer so everyone else would have a ride over.

"No, Grace. Walk with me?"

"Sure. Lucy, you listen to Kaye, and do what she says, okay?"

"Yes, Mother."

While everyone else fought for seating in the hay, Kelly and
Grace walked on. Kelly was nervous, afraid something would go
wrong, or that Grace would say no.

"Grace, I know I've told you this before, but I love you."

"I love you, too, Kelly." Grace knew something was on Kelly's
mind.

"I also love your daughter. She's a great kid." Kelly paused,
waiting until her heart got out of her throat. They were walking
through some woods; the leaves overhead were still small, still

growing in the fresh spring air. The two held hands, swinging their arms as Kelly spoke. "I'm not rich, although I'm very comfortable financially. I have my own business that's stable and unlikely to fail. I'm not perfect. My hands are calloused, and my work gets me dirty and smelly."

Going up hill, Grace could see the sun through the trees ahead, indicating a clearing. Behind them, she could hear the others laughing and singing silly songs as the truck made a wide swing through the hilly area around the lake.

"I've told you before, I don't mind that your work often gets you dirty and smelly."

Kelly had timed it right. "But, if you and Lucy will have me, I'd love to love you both in a new home."

They topped the hill. Grace realized they were above the old homestead. But now, in the middle of the depression, was the skeleton of a house.

"What?" Grace continued walking forward to stand on the edge of the rise.

"I designed it, and Clarence's company is making it. There's a lot of work still to be done to it, stuff we'll have to do ourselves to save money."

"What?" It was obvious the house was going to be large. The chimney that had been all that was left of the older house was now a pile of stones stacked neatly to the side. The ground had been raised, so it was out of the flood range. A row of trees, hilled in until ready for planting, lay near the lake. Stacks of lumber, stone, and other materials were near a small building bearing the Thompson Construction logo Grace knew so well.

Near the lake, just off from the nearly finished dock, was a big pile of wood, ready for the bonfire.

"We managed to keep it a secret among just me, Clarence, and Nikki. No one else knows. So now, before anyone else sees it or sees us, what do you say?" Kelly turned Grace around to face her. "Will you and Lucy live with me? Will you sleep in our new bed? Will you let me help raise your child?"

"Oh, Kelly. I..." Grace could no longer see, her tears blurring her vision. "Kelly, of course, I will. Of course, we will. Shit, woman, I love you so much, how could I not?"

"Oh, good! Wowzers!" They laughed and came together in a kiss. Kelly would have laid her down and made love right then and there, but she could hear the truck coming over the hill.

NEARBY, THE NOISY people on the wagon got quiet as they came over the ridge. Only Nikki spoke, getting out of the truck, so they could all hear her.

"Kelly wanted to build a new house and decided to put it where the old homestead used to be." When she saw Kelly and Grace kissing, she got Lucy down from the truck.

"There's your mom and Kelly. Why don't you run over there and see what's up?"

"Ew, they're kissing again. That's what's up."

Everyone broke into laughter.

"Yes, Lucy, but you need to go over there anyway."

"Oh, all right." Lucy walked at first, but was soon skipping.

"Now that she's out of hearing, I'll tell you the rest." Nikki told them, and just as she was finishing, they heard a loud "Wowzers!" from across the way as Lucy was told the same thing.

THE BONFIRE WAS huge. Logs had been set up all around it to act as seating. Nearby, a smaller fire was being used for cooking. Kelly had given everyone a tour of the new house while the sun was up enough to provide light.

"Nice place, Kelly." Annette was pleased that wheelchair access was an integral part of the design.

"I thought you might like it. You'll have to come in the back door, but that's where friends come in anyway."

"No problem there." Annette leaned forward and kissed her on the cheek.

"Hey! No kissing unless it's me!" Kaye came over with Annette's drink.

"Jealous, dear?"

"Hell, yeah! Her house is going to be new and organized, not our rambling thing."

"I like your house." Grace had come up behind Kaye. "It's huge!"

"It is at that. The original house is just the kitchen and living room. We've been adding to it for years now." Kaye slipped the drink cup into the holder on the side of the wheelchair.

"We've considered starting from scratch and putting a house just above the studio." Annette leaned back against Kaye's belly. "But then we'd have to move everything, and that is just NOT a fun idea."

Pat came up to join them. "I bet! How long you two lived there now? Ten years?"

"Fifteen. Can you believe it's been that long?? Fifteen years of accumulated crap would not be easy to pack and move, even if it were just farther up the driveway."

Chapter
Thirty-nine

"LUCY, KELLY IS going to be my partner, which means she'll be a parent to you." Grace sat on the top step with Kelly at Kaye and Annette's house. In the background, a group of goats chased each other around a rock. It had been a week since the bonfire.

"Okay."

"That also means, kiddo, that I'll have the same rights that your mom has. I can tell you what you can and can't do. I can also send you to your room or ground you or whatever." Kelly was nervous, not wanting to say the wrong thing.

"Ah, now I remember. I still don't think it's fair." Lucy stomped a foot, her mouth a deep frown.

"It may not seem like it, but I've been thinking about this. You'll have two parents, something you've never had. That means two people to love you, two people to hug you, two people to get you stuff, all that." Kelly clasped her hands in front of her, holding on in hopes that Lucy would like the idea.

"Does that mean you can sign the notes from school and all that?"

"Yep."

"And that you can come to parent-teacher conferences?"

"Yep."

"This may work out after all." Now the girl wore a big smile.

"I was wondering, Lucy, if you would want to help finish the house."

"Like paint and stuff?"

"Yeah, paint and use tools, and other things Kelly will think of for you to do." Grace shifted so Lucy could sit between them.

"Sounds like fun! I get to use tools?"

"Yep."

"Great! Can I go play with Marley now?"

Grace sighed and hung her head. "Yes, Lucy, go play with Marley."

They watched as she raced off to play with the huge Rottweiler. "The two dogs that are Spam and Marley's parents are going to have another litter soon."

"Really? I bet the puppies are adorable."

"They are. I saw Marley and Spam when they were just five days old." Kelly stood, helping Grace up from the step. "I was wondering if maybe Lucy would want her own dog."

"I don't know, Kelly. She's awful young."

"Not really. She's been helping to feed Marley as well as the goats. She's taken on a lot of responsibility. Nikki heard they have one pup that's not spoken for."

"But they aren't even born yet, are they?"

"No, another couple of weeks or so, I think. But they know from x-rays about how many are in there. They won't know for sure until they're all born. They thought they'd seen all of them, but the latest x-rays showed another one."

"I'll think about it." They walked to the fence to watch the baby goats. "I'm still kind of numb from this house and moving in together and all that. A dog might be too much right now."

"I still think about it and think it's just a big, crazy dream."

"Are you ready, I mean really ready, for the two of us to invade your life?"

"I think so — as ready as I can be. How about we three go camping when she's out of school? We can take a week or two and just go somewhere."

"I guess. I'll have to ask Clarence, but I'm sure he won't mind. I guess we need to pick a date soon, so you can schedule your work."

"Yeah, I need to do some catch-up work this week, plus get ahead, so I can use some time to start working on the house."

"If there's anything we can do to help, we will."

"Make me dinner?"

"Sure! I can do that. Want Lucy to bring you the paper and your slippers?"

"And a pipe. Don't forget the pipe."

"HEY, KID." KELLY put the camera to her eye.

"What?" Lucy turned around, showing her paint-speckled face and clothing. She made a face after Kelly clicked the camera. "Kelly, stop it."

"But you're so cute!" Kelly laughed and put the camera down. "You're getting more paint on you than on the wall!"

"Hey, I'm doing this for free. What do you expect?"

"You do have a point. Here, let me show you how to do this."

"Do you have to? I mean, can't I just have fun?"

Kelly laughed and raised her hands in defeat. "Fine, go right ahead. Oh, and I came here to tell you lunch is ready."

"Why didn't you just say so?"

GRACE WATCHED LUCY and Kelly use a handsaw to trim boards that would be shelving in Lucy's bedroom. Kelly took a ruler and gave it to Lucy, letting her measure and mark the next piece. Kelly nodded and put the saw in Lucy's hand, showing her how to hold it. When the first two pulls of the saw skipped, instead of taking the saw from her and getting it started, Kelly stood behind her, holding her hands as she taught Lucy how to do it on her own.

Grace had to hold her chest, afraid her heart would leap out. *How could I have gotten so lucky? What did I do to deserve this woman?* As if she could sense it, Kelly looked up the hill to where Grace stood. She smiled and waved; Grace waved back.

LUCY TOOK HER new telescope out to the front yard, as far from the house and its lights as she could get. It was still hot outside, but the breeze off the lake was cool. She set up the tripod and took the cap off the lens.

Looking up at the stars, she thought about how far away they were, how far out of reach they seemed. Not that long ago, seeing her mother happy seemed to be just as far away. She smiled when she heard the laughter come from the house behind her. They'd not moved in yet but had come to camp here for the weekend of her birthday. Her parents—she considered Kelly to be a parent already—were on the front porch kicking back with some beer.

Lucy looked back at them, taking her eye away from her birthday present, to see if they were going to join her. They were, walking slowly, holding hands and swinging them.

"Come on, you two old geezers. I can see Jupiter."

"Cannot."

"Can, too."

"Cannot."

"All right, you two, cut it out. Lucy, can you really see Jupiter?"

"No way. It's not even in the sky tonight."

"Told you so."

"Kelly, stop it." Grace elbowed her partner.

"Here, let me look, Galileo." Kelly looked through the lens. "I don't see no Jupiter. But I do see the man on the moon."

If someone had been within hearing, they would have heard the squeals of laughter as Kelly was jumped by the two females she loved the most.

FORTHCOMING TITLES
from Yellow Rose Books

Solace: Book V of the Moon Island Series

by Jennifer Fulton

Rebel Monroe is a Californian yachtswoman sailing solo around the world. When her yacht—Solace—capsizes in a perfect storm near the Cook Islands group, she puts to sea in a lifeboat expecting she is not going to make it. Eventually she washes up half-dead on the shores of Moon Island, where she is found by ex-nun Althea Kennedy.

Althea, who entered a Poor Clare order at 20, has recently turned her back on religious life after a traumatic experience in Africa. Questioning both her faith and the church, she is on Moon Island recuperating from malaria and pondering her options.

Rebel, considered a hero by the island's owners, is invited to stay a while and she forms an unlikely friendship with Althea. When this blossoms into something more each woman must rethink her identity, her demons, and her life choices before she can find real happiness.

Coming May 2007

Family Values

by Vicki Stevenson

Devastated by the collapse of her long-term relationship, Alice Cruz decides to begin life anew. She moves to a small town, rents an apartment, and establishes a career in real estate. But when she tries to liquidate some of her investments for a down payment on a house, she discovers that she has been victimized by a con artist.

Local resident Tyler Sorensen has a track record of countless affairs without any emotional involvement. Known for her sexy good looks, easygoing kindness, and unique approach to problems, Tyler is asked by a mutual friend to figure out how Alice can recover her money.

While Tyler's elaborate plan progresses and members of her LGBT family work toward the solution, they discover that the con game involves more people and far higher stakes than they had imagined. As the family encounters unexpected obstacles, Tyler and Alice struggle with a growing emotional connection deeper than either woman has ever experienced.

Coming July 2007

Lavender Secrets

by Sandra Barret

Emma LeVanteur has written off any chance of true love and is focused on her graduate thesis, when Nicole Davis, a beautiful British instructor, turns Emma's world upside down. Emma thinks she can finally break out of a comatose love-life, but when Nicole convinces Emma to help with her upcoming wedding, Emma's brief hope for romance seems lost. But is it?

Nicole Davis is marrying into a socialite family. But Emma's friendship pulls her in another direction, sending her tumbling into a world of undeniable longing. When Nicole can no longer silence her feelings for Emma, will she give up her picture-perfect future to gamble on a love she can barely comprehend, or will she stick with the life she's always known?

Set in New England, "Lavender Secrets" explores the boundaries that define love, lust, and friendship for Emma, Nicole, and the world they live in.

ISBN 978-1-932300-73-4

And Playing the Role of Herself

by K. E. Lane

Actress Caidance Harris is living her dreams after landing a leading role among the star-studded, veteran cast of *9th Precinct*, a hot new police drama shot on location in glitzy LA. Her sometimes-costar Robyn Ward is magnetic, glamorous, and devastatingly beautiful, the quintessential A-List celebrity on the fast-track to super-stardom. When the two meet on the set of *9th Precinct*, Caid is instantly infatuated but settles for friendship, positive that Robyn is both unavailable and uninterested. Soon Caid sees that all is not as it appears, but can she take a chance and risk her heart when the outcome is so uncertain?

The leading ladies and supporting cast of this debut novel by newcomer K. E. Lane will charm you, entertain you, and leave you with a smile on your face, eager for Ms. Lane's next offering.

ISBN 978-1-932300-72-7

OTHER YELLOW ROSE PUBLICATIONS

Sandra Barret	Lavender Secrets	978-1-932300-73-4
Georgia Beers	Thy Neighbor's Wife	1-932300-15-5
Carrie Brennan	Curve	1-932300-41-4
Carrie Carr	Destiny's Bridge	1-932300-11-2
Carrie Carr	Faith's Crossing	1-932300-12-0
Carrie Carr	Hope's Path	1-932300-40-6
Carrie Carr	Love's Journey	978-1-932300-65-9
Carrie Carr	Something to Be Thankful For	1-932300-04-X
Carrie Carr	Diving Into the Turn	978-1-932300-54-3
Linda Crist	Galveston 1900: Swept Away	1-932300-44-9
Linda Crist	The Bluest Eyes in Texas	978-1-932300-48-2
Jennifer Fulton	Passion Bay	1-932300-25-2
Jennifer Fulton	Saving Grace	1-932300-26-0
Jennifer Fulton	The Sacred Shore	1-932300-35-X
Jennifer Fulton	A Guarded Heart	1-932300-37-6
Jennifer Fulton	Dark Dreamer	1-932300-46-5
Anna Furtado	The Heart's Desire	1-932300-32-5
Lois Glenn	Scarlet E	978-1-932300-75-8
Gabrielle Goldsby	The Caretaker's Daughter	1-932300-18-X
Melissa Good	Eye of the Storm	1-932300-13-9
Melissa Good	Thicker Than Water	1-932300-24-4
Melissa Good	Terrors of the High Seas	1-932300-45-7
Melissa Good	Tropical Storm	978-1-932300-60-4
Maya Indigal	Until Soon	1-932300-31-7
Lori L. Lake	Different Dress	1-932300-08-2
Lori L. Lake	Ricochet In Time	1-932300-17-1
K. E. Lane	And, Playing the Role of Herself	978-1-932300-72-7
J. Y Morgan	Learning To Trust	978-1-932300-59-8
A. K. Naten	Turning Tides	978-1-932300-47-5
Meghan O'Brien	Infinite Loop	1-932300-42-2
Paula Offutt	Butch Girls Can Fix Anything	978-1-932300-74-1
Sharon Smith	Into The Dark	1-932300-38-4
Surtees and Dunne	True Colours	978-1-932300-52-9
Surtees and Dunne	Many Roads to Travel	978-1-932300-55-0
Cate Swannell	Heart's Passage	1-932300-09-0
Cate Swannell	No Ocean Deep	1-932300-36-8
L. A. Tucker	The Light Fantastic	1-932300-14-7

About the Author:

In a nutshell, Paula is a disabled, educated, Southern lesbian living in North Carolina with her partner, a bunch of dogs, and a few cats, in a one-hundred-year-old house with a leaky roof. Open the nut, and Paula loves dogs, tolerates cats, uses buckets in the kitchen, and believes love can happen anywhere (even at 8th and Market in Philadelphia, June 23rd, 1990.) Her writing comes from within, where she runs on the gerbil wheel that is her mind.

Printed in the United Kingdom
by Lightning Source UK Ltd.
119315UK00001B/290